DEREK CRESSMAN

REALITY™ 2048
WATCHING BIG MOTHER

DEREK CRESSMAN

Poplar Leaf Press
3104 O St #327
Sacramento CA 95816
www.DerekCressman.com

This is a work of fiction.
Any resemblance to real people, real products, or reality™ itself, is serendipitous
Edited by Mary Rakow
Cover design by M Rainey Creative ArtBook
Layout © 2017 BookDesignTemplates.com

Reality™ 2048 Derek Cressman. -- 1st ed.
ISBN 978-1-7339567-0-3 (paperback)

For Rachel

*Every gal has a right to risk her life if that's
what it takes to save it.*

—Jacqueline Russo

CHAPTER 1

The elevator screen flashed something unexpected as Vera took her daily ride up to the 23rd floor of Magnificent Estates.

Now's my chance.

After the routine weather forecast and the gladiator sports highlights, the screen had announced that tonight's big reality TV episode would be canceled due to a sudden medical emergency of a key participant.

She detested the canceled program, *Big Mother Gets Real*, but viewed it regularly so she would be able to talk about it with colleagues at work. Further, she worried that if she ignored the program, the datatrackers would notice and possibly recommend a MyndScreen upgrade. A recent incident at work had convinced her that too much deviation from normal viewing habits could be dangerous.

Members of the Establishment, such as Vera, primarily watched episodes through MyndScreen chips implanted directly into the cerebral cortex, which received signals sent through upgraded 11G cellular towers. Most members of the lower consumer class, known as Vues, hadn't yet received an implant. They still relied upon the older technology of MyScreen virtual reality helmets, which fit over the head, not inside it. Dome-shaped individual screens covered each eye, surround sound speakers encased the ears, and touch simulators in the helmet stimulated the scalp and forehead.

After eating a dinner of Italiozagna™ Pepsoilent, Vera opened her single kitchen cabinet to find a stash of green tea she procured months ago, at considerable expense. This was not green-tea-flavored Pepsoilent, but actual tea leaves smuggled in to avoid the high tariffs put in place during Chinasia's trade war with Globalia. She brewed the tea in an old ceramic mug she purchased on a whim from a thrift shop that carried turn-of-the-century items. It was her sole piece of dinnerware.

As the tea steeped, Vera glanced at the two wall screen windows in the living room of her LuxureLife™ suite. One showed a live video feed from the exterior cameras of Magnificent Estates, along with a continuous scroll of temperature, wind, humidity, and weather forecast information for her precise GPS location. The other screen depicted a live shot from the African savannah, where a few antelope wandered in the distance. The only outside view from the apartment came from the sliding glass doors that opened to the small delivery balcony.

While sitting down on the hard faux-wood floor next to the couch where she normally viewed programs, she deliberately allowed the re-broadcast of last week's episode of *Big Mother Gets Real* to pop up on her MyndScreen. The show's jingle, "Watch *Big Mother* — reality like no uuh-ther!" cried out an irresistible earworm that looped endlessly in Vera's head all day long. It was followed by the usual promotional tagline, "brought to you by Timeless Warning –Amusement is Peace."

Vera knew what would happen, not only because she had seen this episode just last week but also because the plot formula of *Big Mother Gets Real* was dreadfully predictable. She could anticipate how each show would play out after watching the first five minutes.

As the rerun began, she waited for the scene where a lead character called for mediation of a dispute over who would get to remain on the program for next week's episode.

As the celebrity guest mediator began questioning the participants, Vera opened a second MyndScreen window and searched for the term "meditation." She opted against running it as a confidential search, fearing the mere fact she was engaged in that behavior during an episode of *Big Mother* would create a metadata point. Vera convinced herself that the SpeidrWeb™ metadata engines would conclude that her search for "meditation" would be dismissed as a typo for "mediation" and therefore not tracked as anything of significant marketing value.

She had grown curious about the practice of mindfulness ever since accidently stumbling upon a decades-old medical journal article. She'd found the dense text while searching for a verified fact about overstimulation of the lab-grown food economy for her job at the Department of Information. The medical experts quoted in the article suggested that overstimulation of the brain could cause mental illness and anxiety. The symptoms described in the article were familiar: loss of appetite, fatigue, fidgeting, nervous scratching, insomnia, panic, and nausea. She thought it would be good to learn techniques that calm the mind, but she also feared what might happen if she pursued the interest too far.

After she lost track of her husband in 2045, Vera had found herself increasingly bored with her life. She'd found solace in travel shows where quirky hosts explored exotic places far beyond MyndScreen transmissions, but the programs now exacerbated her desire to get away, to find something new. There was certainly no lack of entertainment in Los Angeles, the city at the heart of the Globalian infotainment firm economy. But, the daily bombardment of new programs, hot celebrity sightings, and never-ending anime conventions no longer stirred her soul as they once had.

She intentionally skipped the first five screens that came up in her Noodle™ search, including the "featured" search item at the top of each page with the "breaking" news headline: "Legal expert Aneeka Randall discusses the pros and cons of today's ruling by the Tribunal of Experts on Attention Withdrawal Syndrome." Vera was certain these results would lead to highly viewed episodes and articles, which meant they had been heavily promoted by one of the major infotain firms. The corporate ownership of these studios had a direct interest in obscuring the information Vera was searching for. So much of the world's prosperity depended upon infotainment "views" that any effort to escape the firms' programming threatened not only shareholder profits but also global stability and safety.

Yet escape was precisely what Vera sought.

On the ninth screen, Vera found an old link titled, "ten-minute meditation guide," which had a mere 174 views. It looked amateurish and almost certainly had not been produced by an infotain studio.

Doubts wriggled into Vera's mind as she kept the Big Mother episode running in a multitask window. Can I really concentrate on anything for ten minutes straight? Will my inattention to 'Big Mother' trigger a metadata point? Is meditation any fun? Annoyed by a boisterous laugh track exploding on the Big Mother episode as a contestant ripped her bikini bottom on a wild boar's tusk in an obviously staged jungle encounter, Vera steeled her resolve.

I'll do it. She knew in the end it would ruin her, that nobody ever really escaped. But nothing felt worse than the inanity of ads, chatterfeeds, emojicons, facts and entertainment that bombarded her incessantly and made it impossible to think on her own for even a moment.

Calling up the link, she was at first confused as her MyndScreen displayed an image of a glowing orange ball — nothing more. Five seconds later, the sound of waves crashing into a beach entered her mind — it reminded her of a documentary she'd seen recently about sea stars and life in tidal pools that had been narrated by a stunningly gorgeous Hollywood actor with a nice set of six-pack abs and flowing blonde surfer-style hair.

After what felt like an hour, a deep soothing voice said languidly, "Sit with your spine straight, and take a deep breath, down into your belly." A woman in a gray leotard with highlighted brown hair pulled up in a ponytail assumed a cross-legged, sitting position on the floor. Vera thought that her own hair might look similar if she grew her bangs out and added some blonde streaks.

Vera's heart pounded like a bass drum, thumping against her rib cage at a faster rate than normal. The eczema on her left elbow suddenly itched sharply. How could she breathe deeply while on the edge of panic?

The voice said, "There, good," before Vera had managed to inhale.

The *Big Mother* jingle blared back into Vera's consciousness as the program cut to a commercial for

Pepsoilent's new LemonMeringue™ dessert. "Watch *Big Mother*, reality like no uuh-ther. Brought to you by Timeless Warning — Amusement is Peace."

Vera almost gave up.

Fidgeting on the floor and crossing her legs in the other direction, she felt blood rushing into her calves that had begun to tingle from lack of circulation. She scratched her elbow and managed to regain her calm composure by concentrating on the sound of the waves.

"Take another deep breath and draw your attention to the center of your body."

Vera thought about her pasty white belly, with a soft roll of skin bulging only slightly beneath her pink polyfiber T-shirt. She thought again about the nature show narrator with his six-pack abs and the sea stars. She tried another inhalation, and this time was able to draw fresh feeling air deeply into her lungs, smelling its crispness as it passed through her nostrils. Holding her breath for a moment, she was dumbfounded when a thump in her head beat a rhythm corresponding to the pulsation of her heart. She exhaled and noticed that the cadence of her heartbeat slowed.

"Now," said the voice, "let go of the thoughts, worries, and curiosities that are running through your brain. Don't force them out, just let them pass through undisturbed."

Taking several more breaths, she concentrated on the sound of her heartbeat. She failed to notice that the episode of *Big Mother* had ended.

For a moment, Vera was absorbed in silence.

Her mind began wondering what she could have for breakfast the next day. There were 14,447 options loaded onto her Pepsoilent home extruder but a new flavor of danish, PerkyPersimmon™, was scheduled to be released tomorrow. She'd been seeing pop-up ads for it every day for the past week whenever she sent her order in. It might not be that good, but it was something to look forward to.

The voice interrupted, "Now, draw your attention down to the soles of your feet."

Vera tried, but had a hard time using her mind to locate her feet without simply grabbing them physically in her hands. While failing to focus below her knees, Vera basked in the tranquility of being lost within her body. No sound from the outside world or image from her MyndScreen broke the spell.

She sighed.

The shrill ring of her doorbell startled her out of the trance.

Had her search been too careless? Was the tech doctor squad already here to upgrade her MyndScreen? After a split-second of panic, Vera concluded that wasn't likely. She wasn't really sure how they performed upgrades, but it seemed doubtful they could do it on-site.

Besides, even if her Noodle search had triggered a SpeidrWeb report, it was nearly impossible to think the tech squad could have reacted so quickly.

Maybe it's the paramedics, she thought, remembering an aunt whose life was saved when her MyndScreen sent a distress signal after registering inactivity during normal daytime usage hours. The emergency response team had been quick, rushing to the scene with lifesaving drones in time to save her from the stroke. While the portion of her brain responsible for long-term memory had been damaged, the brain technicians had expanded the deep recall functions of her MyndScreen with back-up files of her previous Noodle searches and the corresponding results. Many of her past thoughts and queries had been, in effect, restored.

Almost by reflex, Vera hastened to the door. If she didn't respond, the paramedics would break in and she'd have to explain why she was not lying unconscious on the floor despite her recent brain inactivity.

Her heart quickening, Vera pressed her thumb on the print reader to unlock the door. As it swung open, she saw Mrs. Manquin, her neighbor across the hall, looking slightly peeved.

Vera unleashed an audible breath and invited Mrs. Manquin inside.

CHAPTER 2

*Creativity is piercing the mundane to find
the marvelous.*

— *Bill Moyers*

"It's my sink," complained Mrs. Manquin, as she stomped into Vera's entryway wearing a 1950s revival floral print dress. The prefix of "Mrs." suited her well, having recently come back in vogue among a small group of nostalgic women as a bit of a rebellion against the politically correct notion that a wife's identity should be separate from that of her spouse.

A stout woman with loosely curled short auburn hair atop a wide face adorned with too much makeup, Mrs. Manquin had never been a favorite acquaintance of Vera's. They exchanged the usual pleasantries when they met in the parking garage below Magnificent Estates, but Vera was usually quick to look for an escape from the conversation.

"It's clogged up, and I can't get the replacement drain pipe to fit. Can you take a look?"

Vera walked across the hall to the Manquin apartment and winced at the acrid smell of molten PlastiCABS™ used in home 3D protruders. "Say hello to Vera," Mrs.

Manquin instructed her children, Marsha and Reginald, who were both engrossed with virtual games inside their MyScreen helmets. At age 5, Reginald looked a bit like an insect, with the outside of the MyScreen virtual cinema retinas forming two shiny green convex protrusions on the front of the helmet that mimicked the bulging eyes of a fly.

Marsha, nearly 13 years old, looked uncomfortable as she had outgrown her helmet. It pressed tightly against both ears. Her blonde hair extended beyond the bottom of the helmet near her neckline, giving the appearance of a golden mane draping around her shoulders.

"Hello?" Marsha said in a muffled voice, without removing her helmet. Reginald didn't respond.

"Kids these days," exclaimed Mrs. Manquin. "You try to teach them manners, but they can't pull themselves out of virtual reality into real reality. All I hear is constant complaining about what new app or game their Chatterfriends are playing and how we need to make more money so they can download them too. I'm not even sure if those Chatterfriends are real people, but I guess it doesn't matter so long as they're having good, clean fun."

Mrs. Manquin walked Vera into the bathroom, which was spotless and freshly sterilized. "I was able to remove the old drain," she said, pointing to the dangling plastic pipe in the cabinet under her bathroom sink. "But I can't get the replacement back on. It just won't fit."

Vera looked at the U-shaped gray plastic pipe that Mrs. Manquin held in her stubby-fingered hand and asked her if she had just fabricated it on the 3-D protrusion printer.

"Yes, I did a Noodle search for the design and sent that to the protruder," said Mrs. Manquin. "If my husband were here, I'm sure he'd know how to properly attach it," she added, somewhat lamely. "He's one of the few men who still know how to use a wrench," she added, even though tools really weren't required for the quick release latches employed in most plumbing repairs.

Vera knew Andy Manquin well from her office, where he worked down the hall in a different cluster of the Department of Information. She often saw his tall, lanky figure hunched over the latest limited-time sandwich special at lunch or chomping brownies on the 4:20 p.m. afternoon break. She had grown to dread their conversations.

Andy Manquin took the *Big Mother* episodes to a depth of immersion that surpassed even the most up-to-speed viewers. He not only diligently watched every episode but also subscribed to multiple Chatterfeeds that gave him extra updates and gossip on the characters throughout the day. He could tell you biographical details about each contestant and why their scheme to outwit Big Mother was sure to fail (as it always did).

Big Mother was the only steady character on the program with the others rotating out every few months. The character of Big Mother herself also appeared on numerous spin-off programs, like *Laughing with Big Mother*, *Travel with Big Mother*, or *Big Mother on the Beat* (a show where she accompanied anti-Fear Monger patrols on their daily investigations). Andy Manquin watched them all, but was particularly engrossed with the original reality program, *Big Mother Gets Real*.

The problem was obvious. "I think you pulled up the wrong model," Vera noted. "See how the width of the curve is too big?"

"That's odd," Mrs. Manquin responded, a bit defensively. "I used the top-rated search result for drain-trap replacement."

"Sometimes you have to dig a bit deeper," explained Vera. "This sink is outdated. It's probably 15 years old, like the building. You need to find the model number," Vera explained, as she strained her neck under the sink.

Vera brushed off some cobwebs that concealed the 16-digit number etched into the underside of the sink. While still beneath it, she ran a search and pulled up the proper design.

"What's the password for your protruder?" Vera asked. "I'll send the pipe design over."

"Nooooo!" screamed Reginald, from the couch.

"Why not dear?"

"They just downed my V-drone!" exclaimed Reggie. He threw his helmet on the floor. Looking dazed with the helmet off, his face so pale it looked almost blue, he raced around the sofa five times before throwing himself on the floor and pounding it with his fists and feet.

Seeing the boy's face, Vera's jaw locked firm in an instinctual defense against an event deep in her past. She felt a cord tighten within her, compressing the disks between each vertebra and contracting the muscles of her abdomen. The tension kept the memory at bay as if by forming a pressurized field around her that deflected both thoughts and feelings.

"You'll hurt yourself," scolded Mrs. Manquin. "Come take a breath," she instructed as she pressed an inhaler into Reggie's nostrils and dispensed a BrainSooth™ pharmaceutical spray designed to reduce video-stimulated hyperactivity. "Now, please come over here to say hello to Vera and thank her for fixing our sink."

"Hi, Vera," sobbed Reggie, struggling to catch his breath. "What is it you know that my mom doesn't? Hey, can I get one of those friendship bracelets?" he asked, seeing the strand of pink and green plastic fibers woven into an intricate pattern around Vera's wrist. "All the kids at school have one."

"Now run along Reggie," scolded his mother. "Why don't you watch a nice StoryBits program on the wall screen instead of playing that horrid game all the time?" Turning to Vera, Mrs. Manquin chuckled, "V-Drone. What clever use of Effispeech to shorten 'virtual' to 'V.' And he's only 5!"

"I'm so sick of those helmets hiding their pretty little faces," Mrs. Manquin confided in Vera after Reggie had returned to the couch. "Marsha can't wait to get her MyndScreen installed next month when she turns 13. I know she'll still watch the same silly episodes and play the same violent games, but at least I won't have to look at her face covered by that helmet all the time."

Like most pre-teens, Marsha was eagerly anticipating the rite-of-passage that would allow her to undergo a MyndScreen implantation surgery. It was all done robotically now, with an astounding 96 percent success rate. Despite that track record, the Tribunal of Educates had ruled the procedure could not be performed on anyone under the age of 13 in order to allow the parietal lobes to develop adequately. Thirteen was also considered a competent age to give proper consent.

"I know what you mean," said Vera. "Now, what's that protruder password again?"

Within minutes, Vera had the correct pipe manufactured on the home protruder. Now that the fit was right, even Mrs. Manquin could easily install the new pipe.

"I can't thank you enough," Mrs. Manquin exclaimed as she tossed the old pipe in the recycling chute along with the dirty dishes from that evening's dinner.

Vera's shoulders dropped more than an inch as she returned to her apartment. Only after she had said goodbye to Mrs. Manquin did she realize the anxiety she'd experienced after being startled out of her trance. Her first instinct had been to never again take a chance on meditation, but as she walked into her living room she reconsidered. Nothing bad had come of it. In fact, maybe due only to the satisfaction of being helpful to a neighbor, Vera felt more content than she had in a long time.

Walking out onto her balcony, Vera smelled the damp air blowing in from the ocean. She retrieved a box with tomorrow's outfit, which had been dropped off earlier that day by drone, and headed into the bathroom.

She selected Cinnamint™ to flavor her instant toothbrush and methodically began scrubbing her teeth. She noticed, as if for the first time, the slight tickle that the toothbrush gave her gums as she stroked it up and down her teeth.

As Vera looked in the mirror while brushing, she saw faint crowfeet creases at the sides of her hazel eyes and wondered if they were due to the way she often squinted to obscure her normal vision while reading her Chatterfeed so as to make it easier to concentrate on the images displayed on her MyndScreen.

After she finished rinsing, she tossed the brush into the recycling chute, relaxed her face and took a slow, close look in the mirror to see tiny wrinkles in the skin where the crowfeet creases had been.

If I'm ever going to meet someone new, I should do it before my skin starts to sag.

At thirty-four years of age, Vera had never felt old before. But as she peered into the mirror, pop-up ads for skin cream and tightening agents appeared on her MyndScreen.

"🕐 4 a new MyMakeover™?" asked one ad that grabbed her attention. It had been at least a month since she'd updated her makeup and blunt bangs hairstyle. Surely people would notice if she didn't make a change soon.

"Maybe next week," Vera told herself. "Right now, I'm too overwhelmed to think about anything."

As she looked into the mirror, Vera noticed that the brand name and logo on her pink T-shirt was reversed in the image, making it unreadable. Taking off the shirt, she lay it out on the bed before tossing it down the recycling chute. Its letters were clear and going the proper direction.

Obviously, the mirror is real and the shirt is real. But the mirror image isn't accurate. In fact, it's the exact opposite of reality.

"🕐 4 a relaxing MyMassage™ 2 EZ UR stress?" asked another pop-up.

Vera ignored it and crawled onto the bed. She noticed that sitting cross-legged on the mattress was more comfortable than sitting on the floor, and she still could attain the same position recommended in the meditation video without cutting off circulation to her feet.

She didn't dare try another MyndScreen search to retrieve the meditation guide, but she saw no harm in simply sitting in the middle of the bed, her legs crossed underneath her.

Taking a deep breath, she held it in as her MyndScreen began playing her normal late-night talk show. She rarely found the program hilarious, but it was often at least mildly amusing. Tonight, the host interviewed a comedian who played a news anchor on another program produced by the same infotain firm. He was talking about how he never watched the actual news at home, but his daughter had him hooked on *Big Mother Matchmaker*, a dating show where Big Mother eliminates a would-be bride for her son during each week's episode by means of poison, strangulation, or other treachery. Vera tried to remember what she had looked like on her own wedding day, but the details escaped her.

Vera normally enjoyed the routine of falling asleep while listening to the banter of the host conversing with various celebrities, but tonight she wasn't interested. *What do I care about the fake news anchor's daughter or what programs she likes to watch? It's not like I'll ever meet her.* There was something ingenuine about a talk show host who was obviously reading off cue cards interviewing an actor who was ostensibly out of character. Both simultaneously strove to entertain the audience with pre-planned jokes about other people's viewing habits, but it seemed just one step too contrived. Letting the episode run, she concentrated on her breathing instead of the show. After a while, the sound of her heartbeat was stronger than the outbursts of laughter on the program. She opened a multi-tasking window in her MyndScreen and began playing the latest Torryd™ romance episode. A woman walked alone through a desert landscape at sunrise. The clouds in front of her lit up like embers from a campfire, spreading orange and amber streaks across the morning sky. Tall saguaro cactuses soared up from the ground to meet the clouds, their spines glowing a golden yellow in the sunbeams and creating an aura around the cactus trunks. A man with flowing blonde hair and a chiseled jaw strode confidently down a hillside in blue jeans and a white silk shirt. He ran to meet her, unfastening a button on his shirt with every step.

The late-night program ended in her other Myndscreen window, and the silence jolted her out of the romance scene as well. The steady thump-thump of her own heart was the last thing Vera heard before falling asleep.

CHAPTER 3

Information is understanding.
— Ngo Quan Niver

Vera's MyndScreen woke her at 6:30 a.m. with the monotone voice of a Globalia Public Media announcer reciting the daily statistics for economic prosperity and security. Consumption of cosmetics and clothing (known as C&C in Effispeech) was at an all-time high, leading experts to predict a rise in the worldwide stock indexes. She took her daily regimen of pharmaceuticals to prevent diabetes, high blood pressure, and Alzheimer's disease.

After breakfast, she put on exercise clothes from her delivery box and followed her MyndScreen prompts for the daily *Physical Jerks.* She stretched and jumped to the latest workout episode, struggling as usual to keep up with the attractive and cheerful host who bounced effortlessly in her tight-fitting aqua and orange spandex outfit.

"OK, Globalians," exulted the host, her blonde hair up in two pig tails as she lifted each knee up to her waist and kicked her legs up above her shoulders. "I want you to focus on your breathing as we do another round of leg lifts."

Vera complied, as usual, but for the first time noticed a slight tickling sensation as her inhalation swept air through her nostrils and a faint vibration on her lips as she forced air out her mouth with each lowering of her leg.

After the workout, she followed the host's routine invitation to recline in her MyMassage vibration chaise lounge, straddling her legs around the oval-shaped padded post in the middle. Cool air came out of thousands of tiny jets as the lounge eased back into a reclining position that tilted her body nearly horizontal. Vera's nose wrinkled at the scent of her own perspiration evaporating in the chair's breeze.

Like a clamshell hinged along the entire length of Vera's left side, the top half of the lounge folded over automatically and slowly lowered until it pressed gently against the front of her torso. With Vera sandwiched between the top and bottom halves of the lounge, the massage began with slow compressions along the length of her legs and arms, squeezing blood toward her center. Pressure rollers and ballooning airbags kneaded her muscles and stretched her joints, followed by warm and gentle vibrations.

As the vibrations became more rhythmic and moved from the extremities to her core, the exercise host's voice faded in her MyndScreen and a scene from her favorite Torryd episode appeared as a visualization. The vibrations evolved into undulations, focused around Vera's chest and groin. Her vocal chords involuntarily released an undulating moan.

Within three minutes, it was over. Vera sat up slowly, her body in a complete state of bliss and relaxation. And yet, something deep within her didn't feel quite right. She took an antacid.

* * *

Vera's car, a cute MiOtto™ coupe, met her at the elevator doors. Its pink racing stripe down the right side of the white hood still brought a smile to her face, but she felt the interior fabric was looking a little dated. It had been nearly six weeks since she'd redecorated.

The luxury of owning your own car was one hallmark that distinguished Establishment members from the Vues, who relied mostly on driverless cabs for transportation. Vera pitied the teeming masses, who couldn't express their individuality through their auto-décor and had to rely solely upon clothing and cosmetics to fashion an identity. Many Establishment members didn't need cars because they telecommuted to work on their MyScreens, but Vera had one of the few jobs where an "in-person" presence was deemed important.

As her MiOtto travelled the clotted freeway to work, she watched the Globalia Public Media (GPM) announcer describe a trial of thirty radicals who had been arrested for protesting the war against Fear Mongers outside of City Hall. "Rads busted 4 🗣 " ran an Effispeech message scrolling in a chyron across the bottom of the screen in yellow letters.

Protests were a daily affair, but they were usually ignored entirely not only by passersby but also the news media. This demonstration had become an ongoing encampment, where several dozen radicals had continuously occupied the space at City Hall Plaza for a period of weeks. People hadn't noticed much until one day when the area's MyScreen transmissions had been interrupted. Experts on the GPM program expressed no doubt that the interruption was due to a hack by the Luddyte Sisterhood, a subversive organization attacked in the press for being unpatriotic and dangerously anti-prosperity.

Moreover, a larger than normal group of Vues had been at City Hall Plaza that day, waiting in line to pay fines for loitering. It was a hot day, and most Vues had removed their MyScreen helmets, which lacked sufficient battery strength to run their cranial air-conditioning systems for more than an hour. With their helmets off, the Vues could observe the protesters — provoking immediate agitation. Fistfights broke out as the Vues hurled insults of "traitor" and "freedom hater" at the radicals who in turn derided the Vues as "dupes" and "simpletons."

Listening to the story, Vera learned that the police had, for the first time in decades, arrested and charged the protesters, who they suspected of collaborating with the hackers. *Maybe the police were just embarrassed they couldn't catch the hackers that jammed the transmissions, so they arrested whoever they could find,* she conjectured.

The GPM announcer interviewed a legal expert who blandly explained that the protesters were relying on a pre-Globalian principle known as "free speech."

Footage of the morning's trial depicted the nodding heads of the nine members of the Tribunal of Educates bobbing above their black robes as the prosecution explained that free speech applies to advertising, of course. "However," the lawyer went on, "since these protesters had not paid any fee to transmit their speech, it was not covered under the free speech doctrine. The protesters are allowed, as everyone is, to purchase bandwidth prioritization on MyScreen broadcasts and Chatterfeed streams. But they cannot be permitted to physically interrupt the tranquil viewscapes and quiet public spaces that

Globalian citizens have a right to enjoy undisturbed. After the Great Saturation in the 2020s, Tribunal doctrine unequivocally ruled that physically audible and visual speech, which does not play by the same rules and regulations as advertising, does not enjoy the same free speech protection."

To Vera, the case seemed routine and uninteresting. But what sent the Chatterfeed on high tilt was the blissful look on the face of one of the protesters. He smiled calmly in his red-and-black checkered flannel shirt as the prosecutor arrogantly droned on and on with his arguments. There was a noticeable gleam in his eyes even as his scruffy, unshaven visage gave him an unkempt appearance. It looked like he wanted to be there; was eager to be on trial.

Rather than getting out of the car in front of The Department of Information and having the MiOtto park itself using autovalet, Vera decided to ride along to the parking lot and walk back to the office. The fresh air would do her good.

The Chatterfeed couldn't let go of the protesters uncanny glance toward the camera. Was it some new contact lens? Some pharmaceutical that rendered him tranquil yet caused the cornea of his eyes to shine? A new cosmetic Lasik surgery? Something about the lighting in the courtroom or the camera angle? He certainly is handsome for a ruffian, isn't he?

Vera realized she had been sitting in her parked car for at least five minutes transfixed on the live trial coverage and accompanying Chatterfeed. Looking up, she saw an athletically built man wearing blue jeans and a white T-shirt sitting on a motorcycle that was parked directly in front of her. She hadn't heard the whoosh of an electric motorcycle, which typically were equipped with exaggerated jet-engine sound effects, so she figured he must have been sitting on his cycle even longer than she had been parked in the car — she hadn't looked away from her screen as she pulled into the parking space, so it was hard to be certain. He was facing away from her, but as she opened her car door he stepped off the bike and spun around while giving her a sheepish smile indicating that he too had been engrossed in the trial coverage.

"I say we deport those radicals if they don't appreciate our freedoms," the stranger said to Vera as she closed her car door. There was something half-mocking in his tone of voice, nearing a strained southern drawl, and his wry smile caught her attention. Her mouth watered with a strange metallic saliva.

The man wore black wayfarer sunglasses over a tan face. He had a well-defined jaw and prominent cheekbones — an unusual and somewhat dated look that reminded her of the man in her romance episodes. He was looking straight at her and she wished she could see his eyes, as if that would reveal if he was serious or not. He rode his cycle without a helmet, giving a windswept appearance to his dirty blonde hair, which fell a few inches above his shoulders. His biceps and forearms had more definition than any she'd seen recently on an actual person.

Vera noticed a tattoo with the logo of the Virtual Sex Liberation League on his tanned left forearm and turned away in disgust. She had no romantic notions that physical intercourse was superior to virtual liaisons — in fact she knew of its disappointments from her past marriage. But she was not attracted to the idea of interacting romantically with another person only by means of

MyndScreen transmissions, and she was outright repulsed by the commercial product placements and pop-up ads that the League depended upon.

Her co-workers were still talking about the trial as Vera sat down in her cubicle. But the discussion soon drifted to the relative merits of the Patriaders gladiator team compared to the SeaChargers. It was a running conversation in the office, with each team's partisans well known not only for their water cooler banter but also for their food and beverage branding preferences. Patriader fans only consumed Pepsoilent drinks and flavored soy-algent meals. SeaCharger fans, on the other hand, were fiercely loyal to Cokaid products. There was even a fringe group of Broncboy fans who liked something called OrangeSmash, but nobody in Vera's office admitted to drinking the stuff or even acknowledged the existence of this team.

As she listened to her office mates argue, Vera began to wonder if people had always been so passionate about the Cokaid–Pepsoilent rivalry. Some of her research had suggested that race, religion, national origin, and sexual orientation had once been more central to people's self-image than brand loyalty. *Why would that have changed?*

The office conversation changed abruptly as news broke of a Fear Monger incident at an animal shelter in the Greenland region. A team of masked men in dark uniforms wearing gold chains had stormed into an unsecured facility that provided intensive care to puppies that had been born prematurely. The men savagely beheaded seventeen beagle pups with hedge clippers while reciting religious extremist stanzas. The shocking event was broadcast live on the Chatterfeeds of two of the shelter's staff members, who were bound, gagged, and sprayed with blood from the decapitated puppies. The Fear Mongers drew out the horror by executing one puppy every sixty seconds, making the entire event last nearly twenty minutes as view numbers climbed exponentially. A mound of bloody heads piled up on a desktop as dogs barked and whined hysterically in the surrounding cages.

Vera did her best to concoct several outraged posts for her Chatterfeed and promote similar denunciations both from official sources and her virtual friends. Her first two were, "♥2Beagles!" and "17🐕☹!"

She found the voyeurism distasteful, yet addicting. Moreover, being the first one out of the box with a quip in response to a global tragedy was essential to keeping your social capital up, which in turn kept the metadata crawlers classifying your brain activity as "normally engaged."

Vera noted that her "✂☛👽s with 🐕clprs" post (meaning "chop the Monger's heads off with dog clippers) received the greatest reaction in the Chatter, even though she wasn't sure that dog clippers would actually be large or sharp enough to shear off a person's head. She then casually made the same jibe to her colleague, who exclaimed agreement. Vera noted the popularity in the Chatterfeed of the rant "Deport the rads if they don't ♥ our freedoms," and knew that must be where the stranger with the motorcycle came up with the phrase. It annoyed her that her thoughts kept returning to him.

After fifteen minutes of horrified international Chatter, an announcement popped up on Vera's MyndScreen that she was late in beginning her first work assignment of the day. With last week's most popular songs and advertising jingles playing in the background, Vera turned her attention in earnest to her job.

The Department of Information was the Globalian agency responsible for Perception Management, known in Effispeech as PM. For both the war against Fear Mongers and achieving global prosperity targets, the Globalian administration had found it important to provide factual data to counter the misinformation put out by those who would undermine the foundation of society. While the government had run the Department itself when Vera began working there, a few years ago it had been outsourced to DeVritas, a well-regarded Establishment infotainment firm. She had appreciated the boost in pay she got at the time and felt that things were run more efficiently than before. Upon taking over, DeVritas had carved the phrase "Information is Power" into the sparling black granite archway above the entrance to the downtown skyscraper where Vera worked as a researcher in the historical information cluster.

Her cluster's motto scrolled on electronic screens placed on the lintel above every doorframe: "She or he who forgets the past has no future. She or he who uncovers information creates the past."

A screen on the wall of her cubicle flashed her first assignment, which simultaneously popped up on her MyndScreen. "Research the pre-2030 success of antibiotics in combating gonorrhea and antibiotics' more recent role in curing disease overall." In the past month, ever since her former colleague Smithers had been upgraded, Vera's assignments had become more interesting and perhaps, she conjectured, more important.

Smithers had simply failed to come into work one day. Nobody bothered to ask why. It had become an almost monthly occurrence for a colleague to suddenly vanish. It was universally accepted that those who disappeared had been retired to an entertainment home where they would spend the rest of their days enjoying comedy, news, drama, and other programs full time. Shortly before his disappearance, Smithers had mentioned to Vera that he had stopped watching his MyndScreen programs, preferring instead to visit art museums. He'd even begun dabbling in painting himself. Perhaps these activities had provided a relief from his stressful work.

Had they also led to his upgrade?

As was her habit, Vera first did some MyndScreen searches looking for clues as to why this assignment would be pressing for the Department.

Gonorrhea wasn't normally a concern of the Establishment, primarily because the physical intercourse by which it spread had become increasingly rare among Establishment members. The experience of the vibration massage lounges, augmented with Effiporn MyndScreen imagery, had so greatly surpassed the sensations of physical intercourse that sex had simply become obsolete. Those in the Virtual Sex Liberation League had even less interest in, or need for, physical contact as they enjoyed the thrill of sexual pursuit with other humans (or computer-generated avatars) online without any of the messy entanglements of human relationships. Establishment reproduction was accomplished reliably by in vitro fertilization (IVF). But among the Vues, who couldn't afford vibration lounges or IVF procedures, human intercourse still prevailed — albeit often enhanced through both parties wearing MyScreen helmets in order to provide visual and audible embellishment.

Vera soon found that gonorrhea outbreaks had become widespread in the South American region of Globalia and that the leading antibiotic regimen, produced by LingerLife™ Pharmaceuticals, was failing to treat the disease or prevent its spread.

Vera remembered that her husband most likely still lived somewhere in South America, but she guessed he faced little exposure to venereal disease. When they got engaged, marriage had felt like the thing to do, the next step in life so to speak. He was attractive enough and went to some effort — with spray tans and tailored suits — to keep his appearance up. He was clever in the Chattersphere, where he had a massive following. She enjoyed sharing his posts with her friends, although eventually she found that many others were saying essentially the same things he was. He had a habit of rapidly sharing and reposting her messages, often without even reading them himself.

Vera began to think that establishing her own individuality was more important than tethering herself to another's. She wanted to be seen as her own person, not just a reflection of him. Or, maybe the trouble was that his persona wasn't his own either, but rather a composite of the identities paraded around in episodes, the Chattersphere, and ads.

About four years after they had married, he received a job offer with an advertising firm in the southern provinces of Globalia — somewhere in Brazil. He hadn't expressed much interest in the region or shown either concern or curiosity about where he was going, or even wondered why he received the opportunity.

She had meant to visit with him on a MyndScreen chat, but always seemed to be too busy. That had been three years ago, more or less. She wished that she missed him.

There were several news articles on the outbreak in the past twenty-four hours that particularly focused on the rapid decline of the antibiotic's efficacy, including a few business section stories conjecturing what that might mean for LingerLife's profits.

Vera surmised that the Department needed some facts to wage a perception management campaign that would reassure both those affected by the disease and shareholders that antibiotics were still generally effective.

With this context in mind, Vera began her research. She found data indicating expert projections on the success rate of various antibiotics in clinical trials.

Vera could make a statistically reasonable estimate about the number of antibiotic doses produced each year in Globalia and then make some educated assumptions about the number of people who actually took those doses as opposed to the number of doses that were destroyed or unused after reaching their expiration date. From there, Vera could take the data from peer-reviewed clinical trials to determine the rate at which the drug was effective and thus establish the overall number of lives saved by the drug.

Accuracy was imperative at the Department of Information even if truthfulness was not. By qualifying her "fact" on the verifiable data of what highly educated and acclaimed experts had extrapolated, Vera could arrive at an impressively large projected number of 37 million lives saved annually due to all antibiotics in production.

Further, Vera found some information on how the current LingerLife antibiotic had been discovered in the 2020s, at great expense. The scientific triumph allowed for the replacement of the previous antibiotic azithromycin, which gonorrhea had also grown resistant to. Reminding people of this long-forgotten history would reassure them that LingerLife's scientists would surely prevail yet again and that ongoing profits for the manufacturer were justified not only to repay the previous expense but also to justify another round of investment by leery shareholders.

Vera compiled her research into three succinct, but accurate, paragraphs and sent it along to her supervisor through a private Chatterfeed message. She knew that from there it would undergo "fact checking" by another department and then be compared with the research of several other colleagues who were no doubt given the identical assignment.

Next, an editing department would pick the one or two most compelling "facts" and ship those off to the distilling cluster to simplify them into headlines, newsreader soundbites, and emojigraphs — simple Effispeech graphics that communicated ideas far more efficiently than words. Message distillation was necessary to give the Department of Information a chance of penetrating the glut of text, sound, and imagery that bombarded both the Vues and the Establishment every waking moment.

Vera had once been quite proud that the Department of Information had developed such expertise in simplification. She felt gratified knowing her research would reach a large audience and help debunk rumors and conspiracy theories that could spread like wildfire if left unchecked. Dispassionate facts were the best response, but they had to be weaponized in order to get the message out amid all the tabloid garbage. The Department had the communications firepower to promote its information in every possible venue. In this instance, it would likely disseminate the antibiotic research Vera had helped compile through an official news bulletin to the *Two Minute Spate*, a segment that every MyndScreen channel was required to carry as part of its 90-minute news programs. The Department also promoted its research through a network of pundits and opinion leaders in academia, business, entertainment, and the nonprofit sector.

While it remained fulfilling to know that her work would reach such a large audience, Vera had developed a nagging feeling about it. *Maybe message distillation is leaving out details that were truly important.* For a headline, Vera imagined her research might be simplified into "Experts Stunned at Projected Success of Antibiotics Saving 37 Million Lives" and an emojigraph of a child leaving a hospital.

If anyone doubted the veracity of the "fact" anywhere along the distribution chain, the caveats of "experts project" and careful citations would be dragged out in support. But Vera couldn't remember a time where that had happened.

Vera had come to believe that people were too gullible in swallowing "facts," which she knew from her job were often manufactured to run counter to an underlying truth. She recalled a time Smithers had told her of his research finding that three percent of geologists trained at a particular prestigious private university had cast doubt on the theory that the Earth was round, based upon surveying data gathered in Nebraska. He'd passed that research up the Department's chain of command and was stunned a few days later to hear a sound bite on the evening news that "Experts are divided on whether or not the Earth was in fact round." She was disappointed that none of the pundits or broadcasters along the distribution chain had ever bothered asking to see the research that provided the foundation for the headlines they delivered.

But today Vera thought of a more troubling explanation than credulity for people's uncritical acceptance of the Department's "facts." *What if people know they are misleading, but simply don't care?*

What if they expect every "fact" they encountered to be both deceptive and unnecessary? Maybe people aren't dumb, but sanely focusing on the few things they could have some control over. If they cannot control the veracity of the information they consume, why bother themselves with it?

This was the first time since she could remember that Vera dwelled on the consequences of her work. She noticed a slight pinch in her abdomen, as if a sharp object had lodged itself in her bowels.

A news flash burst onto her MyndScreen. "Hackers reveal actor James McGuilicutty waxes his bikini line with duct tape!" The celebrity news channels were suddenly aburst with commentary on how such a handsome and highly respected movie star, who had won several Oscars, would stoop to such a low-tech grooming technique when most of the Establishment used laser hair removal. There was a photographic image hacked from a former girlfriend that offered undisputed proof.

Vera decided it was time to head to the extruder food court. As she strolled two blocks toward her lunch destination, Vera took in the blank stares or squinted eyes on people's faces as they walked by. Almost everyone was

focused on their MyndScreens rather than their surroundings, managing to avoid bumping into one another
only through use of the AutoPed™ app in a multitasking
window. As she crossed Spring Street, Vera suppressed a
small gasp as she saw another pedestrian similarly scan-
ning the faces in the crowd.

For a moment, their eyes met.

Vera saw a glimmer of light reflecting off the woman's
dark brown irises, setting off butterflies in her stomach.
In that instant of mutual recognition, a shiver went down
her spine that caused her shoulders to visibly quake.

Both Vera and the stranger averted their gaze after
what couldn't have been more than two seconds. As they
walked past one another, Vera studied her counterpart in
her peripheral vision. She was certain it was Aneeka
Randall, the expert on Tribunal of Educates doctrine who
frequently appeared on news programs.

Aneeka held her head erect. Her black hair, layered in
a pixie cut, flowed up to reveal a flawlessly smooth forehead and eyebrows that blended softly into the warm
honey tones of her face. Unlike the black power suit and
low-cut white silk blouse she normally wore in TV appearances, Aneeka was wearing a white lab coat over a
light blue button-down shirt and navy pants. Vera became self-conscious about her own boring brown bangs,
pale arms, and dated orange tunic. She vowed to act on
that MyMakeover option as soon as she got home.

Randall's authoritative stride matched the confidence
she normally projected when she explained Tribunal doctrine in pithy sound bites. But the sparkle in her eye
today and the warm smile on her face suggested she was
not simply a cog in the higher Establishment machine. In
that moment, Vera was sure that Aneeka Randall was

someone who produced her own ideas instead of vapidly consuming others'.

Could it be, thought Vera from out of the blue, that Aneeka Randall is part of the Luddyte Sisterhood?

The Sisterhood was a fabled network of radicals working to overthrow the Establishment regime of Globalia. Their ranks were said to come originally, but not exclusively, from the four percent of people who had experienced an unsuccessful MyndScreen implant. With the parietal lobes of their cerebral cortex damaged, they could not receive MyndScreen transmissions. Many also had trouble processing information from their own eyes and ears due to scar tissue in the brain left by the botched operation. In some cases, the procedure rendered recipients entirely blind or deaf. The misplants, as they were known medically, couldn't even use the less sophisticated MyScreen helmets, because those relied upon the nerve passages between the eyes, ears, and brain, which were damaged when insertions went awry. Worse off than the Vues, their boredom left them resentful of the Establishment members with successful MyndScreen implants. Misplant "sisters" had begun taking out their revenge by sabotaging the MyndScreen 11G network, creating occasional shutdowns.

The Sisterhood was comprised of both men and women but garnered its name from a radical nun known as sister Bernice Wohrn, who voluntarily chose an antiquated life of silent prayer as a teenager instead of receiving a MyndScreen. There had been numerous, but unsubstantiated, reports of Sister Wohrn's sexual liaisons with other nuns, priests, and animals. People said the gold chains that held the cross around her neck were made from melted down crowns in teeth she had pilfered from

20th century gravesites. It wasn't certain she was still alive, but for good measure the Globalian Church had excommunicated her for heresy. There was an unofficial news blackout of any mention of Wohrn by the major infotain firms, but rumors popped up periodically on the Chatterfeed about her whereabouts and lack of fashion.

One of the telltale signs of a Sisterhood member was reportedly a mischievous look in the eyes. Aneeka Randall's curious gaze suggested to Vera that she was actively observing the world around her instead of concentrating on her MyndScreen infotainment. Vera's heart froze momentarily as she realized, *perhaps she is thinking the same thing about me.*

As she reached the food court, Vera sent an order through the Chatterfeed for a GrandeJalapenoCheez-Whiz™ burrito to the Pepsoilent vending extruder. After producing its creation, the extruder wrapped it in foil and dropped it into a plastic bin. Vera grabbed the burrito and sat down at an empty table. Minutes later she was joined by Andy Manquin.

"I hear you're quite a whiz at plumbing," said Manquin as he unwrapped a Pepsoilent MonsterBurg™. "Thanks for helping my wife out yesterday." As he looked down at his food, Vera examined the shine on the top of his pinkish head, surrounded by a semi-circle of short, mousy brown hair. She wondered, half seriously, if his premature baldness was due to wearing a MyScreen helmet too long as a teenager while he waited for his family to afford an implant. His stupendous frame hunched over the burger and ketchup oozed out the sides as he took a bite, dripping down his chubby forearm, almost spilling onto his orange and blue madras shorts.

"No problem," replied Vera, grateful that he hadn't started in about the latest goings on with the *Big Mother* episodes. "Your kids are quite, ah, … vivacious," she added.

"Sorry about that," said Manquin. "Normally they are pretty well behaved when they are using their helmets, but I guess sometimes their creativity kicks in. I try to tell them that imagination just isn't everything it's cracked up to be, especially compared to the virtual games you can get these days," explained Manquin. "But sometimes they just can't seem to listen to a word I say.

"It reminds me of that episode on *Big Mother Gets Real* where that guy Joey was so distracted by the way a coconut fell from the palm tree that he didn't hear the instructions on the double-perilous challenge round of elimination and wound up getting his foot chopped off …"

It had begun. Vera nodded her head and pretended to listen while Manquin babbled on and on about poor Joey, who had returned to the next season of the show on crutches. She glanced at her MyndScreen's Chatterfeed and saw that the thirty radical protesters had indeed been sentenced to deportation rather than offered the choice of rehabilitation or an upgrade. A well-regarded scholar in psychosociology had released a statement in the official dialect of Expertalk saying, "mental health epidemiological research indicates that remedial procedures have a weak probability of reintegrating such deviants into the folds of civilized society due to the circumstances of their sub-normal behavior that fomented an ideasphere that is disproportionately and unequivocally unconducive to global security and prosperity." While Globalia had long ago abolished the death penalty, deportation served as its equivalent because exiles were unlikely to survive more than a few days under either the hostile societies of Chinasia or in the regimeless territories where Fear Mongers thrived. Besides, none of the protesters had MyndScreens in the first place, meaning there was no way to opt for an upgrade even if one had been offered.

*　*　*

Before eating dinner, Vera sat down to meditate. It was no longer a question of whether it was too risky, nor even a conscious decision that she weighed the pros and cons to resolve as she had that first evening when the *Big Mother* rerun provided an opportunity. Rather, a gut instinct simply drew her toward the process, as if it were the most natural and inconsequential of acts.

Vera cleared her mind with only minimal effort while her MyndScreen played so faintly as to be hardly noticeable. After about seven minutes, Vera's thoughts began to meander.

What will happen to people with gonorrhea if a new antibiotic is not found? Does my research today make it more, or less, likely that the pharmaceutical companies will actually find a new antibiotic? Wouldn't it be better to sound the alarm about its failure so that people could at least take preventative measures?

The Establishment wasn't threatened, as virtual sex provided no exposure to the disease, but what would this mean for the Vues? If there were any hope of helping them, it would have to come from the Vues themselves. They would need to circulate the truth about the failure of antibiotics among themselves at a rate faster than the disease itself could spread.

A rumble in her stomach reminded her it was time to eat. She picked a dish of ChickenCacciatory™ from the extensive Pepsoilent menu and a fruit salad dessert. As the meal was produced, Vera noticed that both dishes smelled essentially the same — like chalk dust. Their texture, too, was similar — like gelatinous candy infused with celery fibers. It was only in color, shape, temperature, and flavor that the two dishes varied.

While she was eating, she watched an episode of *Whaddya See?*, a mockumentary involving hidden camera videos taken of unsuspecting people caught in embarrassing situations. The episode was filmed at a boutique grocery store that still carried soilborne food. The show's producers had found people who had never eaten real fruit before — it had not been hard. They showed one person an orange, allowing them to feel its texture, remove its peel, and smell it. Behind a screen, they gave another person a banana. They then asked the two to decide together what they should make from the fruit.

"Let's make a cream pie," says the middle-aged makeup artist from Ohio.

"That's crazy," says the teenager from the Bronx. "Juice is about the only thing these are good for. They smell funny, and there's something wrong with the packaging." They argued about it with increasing fervor, each accusing the other of being totally out of touch with reality even though neither had ever seen a real piece of fruit before.

When the host suggested they make a fruit salad, both participants looked at him and called him a "phony sellout poser" who obviously didn't know what he was talking about. Vera chuckled.

* * *

As she was falling asleep, Vera reminisced about her encounter with Aneeka Randall. If it was even remotely conceivable that a notable expert like Randall could be part of the Sisterhood, maybe the group wasn't as sinister as Vera had been led to believe. *What if the radicals are on to something? It must take great conviction to risk deportation and exile.* The calm demeanor on the protester's face suggested a deep confidence that he was acting righteously, not out of malice or vanity. Aneeka had the same self-assertive look simply walking across the street.

How does someone become so certain of anything?

* * *

On her way home from work the next day, Vera saw a post from her Chatterfriend, Phoebe: "Just had the world's best MochaTangeloDulceCappacino at LuckyStar's café on Wilshire," along with a selfie posing with a drink the size of her head. "But stay away from the smoothies at JambalaDrink," she added. "I was on the toilet four times with the runs after having one yesterday."

"Ew. TMI," Vera responded. Too much information indeed — maybe I do need a break, she thought to herself.

Vera had her MiOtto stop at the coffee shop, located in a Vue neighborhood. She rarely drank coffee in the afternoon and the coffee-flavored Pepsoilent they served at the office was hardly worth drinking. It tasted like coffee and had a caffeine boost, but it had no smell and it somehow felt slippery instead of smooth when it went down. But beyond the desire for refreshment, Vera was happy for an excuse to get out of the car and into the world in a way that wouldn't seem out of the ordinary to the metadata trackers. There was no parking lot, as Vues rarely owned cars, so she had the MiOtto circle in a holding pattern around several blocks as she went in to the dingy café. As the door slid open, she noticed the powder coating peeling off the aluminum frame.

After ordering a double cappuccino and a Pepsoilent brownie topped with real hashish frosting, Vera noticed an old woman sipping tea from a plastic cup in the corner — a Vue. Amid the dull roar of video screens on the wall, the woman was softly singing to herself:

We'll meet again
Not sure where
Not sure when
But I know we'll meet again some sunny day.

Inexplicably, Vera felt an urge to ask the woman a question.

She worried it would draw too much attention for a member of the Establishment to share a cup of coffee with a Vue, and there were at least a dozen Establishment members sitting at tables staring blankly at their MyndScreens. She could tell who was and wasn't Establishment because of the helmets on the tables, which the Vues had taken off in order to drink. Vera hoped nobody would raise an eyebrow and edged her way toward the woman, "That's a pretty song. Would you like to share a bite of my hash brownie?"

The woman sighed and said, "I suppose so dear, it's been a long time since I could afford the stuff."

Vera guessed the woman must be at least fifty, meaning she was born in the late 1900s, before the Secret War and before the advent of MyScreens, let alone implanted MyndScreens.

As she sat down, an antiquated wall screen began playing the *Two Minute Spate* segment of the evening news. "Experts Document Huge Success of Life-saving Antibiotics," flashed the headline. Vera scratched her elbow nervously as she wasn't sure that "document" was quite the same thing as the more factually accurate word "project" that she had researched.

Rather abruptly, Vera asked the woman, "Where did you learn that song?"

"Oh, honey," replied the woman. "I remember my dad singing it. He was a big fan of that Rod Stewart fella, who used to sing it at the end of his concerts." Vera had never heard of Rod Stewart, but the idea of going to a live musical performance intrigued her.

"What was it like back then?"

"Oh, times were good," she replied flatly. "The coffee had an aroma that was out of this world, not like today's stuff."

A large video screen on the wall interrupted their conversation with the familiar jingle "Watch *Big Mother*, reality like no uhhh-ther! Brought to you by Timeless Warning — Amusement is Peace." Vera's stomach pinched.

"Tell me about your father," she prodded, pulling herself back into the conversation.

"He was a nice enough man. His eyes, I think, were blue."

"Anything else you remember?"

The hash brownie was evidently kicking in, and the women seemed to open up a bit. "He really loved watching pro-wrestling tournaments on the TV and then later on his smart phone. There were contestants in these fabulous costumes and such banter and bluster in between the matches. I remember watching with him for hours. It was all staged, of course."

Vera pivoted to the real question she had been leading up to while pointing at the screen on the wall. "What about the news? Could you tell if the information you saw on news programs was true, or was it staged too?"

"I always kind of figured they made up a lot of that, just like they did with the wrestling matches."

"But now," Vera asked, "You know the Department of Information makes sure that only verified facts appear on the *Two Minute Spate*, right? What if you learned some additional facts that made the information you'd heard on the *Two Minute Spate* seem misleading or irrelevant?"

"A fact is a fact," replied the woman dryly. "They have nothing to do with reality. Getting more of them only makes things worse."

CHAPTER 4

If there be time to expose through discussion the falsehood and fallacies, to avert the evil by the process of education, the remedy to be applied is more speech, not enforced silence.

— Louis Brandeis

Vera thanked the woman, excused herself, and stood up. She tossed her cup in the recycling chute and walked out the door. Rather than heading straight home, she thought she'd take a walk through the surrounding Vue neighborhood. She had never done such a thing and wasn't sure why a purposeless stroll now seemed appealing — perhaps it was just that every other way to spend her time seemed even less attractive.

She kept her MiOtto in its holding pattern circling the coffee shop and headed down the street. Vera became self-conscious of how unusual it looked for her to be walking outside. Even the Vues rarely walked. The cement squares of the sidewalk were broken and tilted after decades of rain, alternating with drought, had washed out the dirt beneath them and sprouted weeds growing up through the cracks.

After meandering a few blocks, Vera was relieved to find the parking lot of a rundown strip mall where she was no longer the sole pedestrian. There weren't many people out shopping, but it felt less awkward to be walking about with even a few people entering storefronts. With Pepsoilent machines to extrude their food, and 3-D protruders to manufacture most products on demand either in-home or for instant delivery by drone, most Establishment members had no reason to visit stores. But the older generation of Vues still ran errands to acquire their necessities. Many got around on electric scooter chairs, which provided mobility to those who were disabled, obese, or motivationally challenged. A fleet of on-call self-driving taxi vans was equipped with motorized wheelchair ramps that allowed those who relied on electric scooters to travel distances that were beyond their range.

Vera studied the blank stares on people's faces as they rolled from the shops back into the driverless cabs. A few people walked through a door beneath an illuminated sign that read "Sportsbarometer." Never having been to a bar before, she nervously followed them inside. Once through the door, Vera watched as a man who must have weighed 350 pounds approached the AutoBar and waited for a red plastic cup to print out and fill with IPA-flavored Cokaid.

Two Vues sat down at a table, removed their helmets, and plugged them into a charging port on the tabletop. Rather than watching their MyScreens, the crowd talked and laughed while taking in sports highlights on more than a dozen wall screens that covered most vertical surfaces in the room. It was a dizzying, boisterous scene full of boasts, jeers, and laughter. The place felt alive, buzzing with human noise and energy. Vera bought a plastic glass of chardonnay Pepsoilent from an extruder and took a seat near the two Vues, who were now arguing over bets they had placed on the past weekend's gladiator sports games.

"It's rigged I tell you," one middle-aged, pockmarked man with short sandy hair was telling a brown-skinned delivery truck courier. "There's no way the guy who won had assembled a better team than mine."

"Stats don't lie," said the deliveryman. "The numbers are the numbers. That guy's numbers were better than yours, there's no two ways about it. Just like my drone-loading stats are better than any delivery mule in LA."

Vera was familiar with the gambling app that allowed people to assemble their own gladiator teams, choosing from among all the players in the league. Each Monday, the algorithm would run simulated games using statistics from the weekend's actual competitions and display animated avatars for each player's team based upon 3-D holographic images. The view ratings for the virtual events where routinely higher than for the gladiator sports games themselves.

An older Vue at the next table chimed in, "Give me an old-fashioned NFL game anytime. You kids with your fantasy apps have ruined sports. The damn league may go bankrupt thanks to all the competition your avatars are giving them."

"I saw it with my own two eyes," said the pockmarked man, ignoring the interjection and returning to his previous contention. "My line chucker had a clean shot at his charioteer, and he didn't even release the rod. Even a simple throw would have knocked the guy on his ass."

Intrigued by the energy of their conversation but not wanting to appear nosy, Vera stared at her palm, pretending to be concentrating on her MyndScreen. While she let the screen run, she trained her ears on the two men's dispute.

"That's probably because your line chucker developed bursitis in his throwing shoulder this weekend. The simulation was just reflecting the fact that your guy couldn't throw in real life."

"I still say it's rigged. If you were seeing what I saw, you'd know. His shoulder looked perfectly good. In fact, he made several other throws during the game." The pockmarked man was dug in.

Vera shared the opinion of most Establishment members that the simulation games were, in fact, rigged. Sure, they paraded a winner each week on the evening news accepting a huge payout, but rumors were it was an actor accepting fake winnings. The games did pay numerous small cash prizes, but the virtual gaming company kept far more in profits then it paid out. The Tribunal of Educates had ruled that normal casino gambling regulations did not apply because the virtual games were a form of entertainment and had no physical location within Globalia.

Many Vues lived for the virtual games. They spent hours poring over statistics, assembling their teams, and uploading strategies and pre-programmed plays for each Monday's virtual match. While Establishment members frequently bet on the outcome of the physical games themselves, the Vues far preferred gambling on the virtual simulations.

Vera was impressed at how seriously the pock-faced man took his game. She couldn't recall meeting anyone in the Establishment who cared so much about anything, let alone a completely fabricated event. *The simulations give people a chance to participate, not just spectate,* she realized. *They give the illusion that gamers can control their own fate.*

"What you were watching was just for show," sneered the deliveryman. "I saw the actual competition over the weekend, broadcast live, my hombre. The team pulled him from the game during the third quarter. He didn't make that throw in the simulation because he wasn't actually in the game at that point. Your simulation just put his avatar in there because he's the only line chucker on your roster. It's just a programming glitch, nothing more."

"Yeah, but you were watching a show just as much as I was. You weren't at the actual arena, were you? How do you know that the game you saw on your screen is any more real than the game I saw on mine?"

Vera was now growing bored with the conversation, which didn't seem to have any real point or hope of reaching a conclusion.

"Oh, come on amigo. What I saw was live footage of actual people competing in a real gladiator sports arena. What you saw was avatars playing out a simulated competition based on real-life statistics compiled from the day before."

"Yeah, but you weren't there. You don't know the guy's shoulder was really hurt. He could've just been faking it so he could still draw a fat paycheck but not risk getting his head knocked in. The guy in my simulation was definitely capable of making the throw, and if he had done it I would've beaten that imposter on the news. The whole damn thing is rigged."

A jumbotron screen on the wall blared to life. It was so loud that it drowned out the other screens in the bar and Vera could no longer hear the conversation. A Globalia Public Media announcer appeared on the screen and said, "There is a breaking news development in the war against the Fear Mongers. Globalian drones have infiltrated an underground city in the regimeless Cappadocia region near the border with Chinasia. They found nearly a thousand Mongers living far under the surface of the Earth and eradicated them all with an explosive device known as the GrandMuther of All Bombs that consumed all the oxygen in the complex. General Perlmutter is declaring it the most successful eradication mission in the past five years."

The news segment wrapped up and the jumbotron cut to Vera's least favorite promotional, "Watch *Big Mother*, reality like no uhhhh-ther — coming up tonight at 7 p.m. Brought to you by Timeless Warning — Amusement is Peace." As the screen went quiet, Vera resumed her eavesdropping.

"You know, don't you, that what you saw on your screen didn't really happen," said the deliveryman. "It's just a simulation of what might have happened had those players actually been in the arena together. But they weren't."

Vera's face flushed. "Don't you guys realize that what you are arguing over doesn't matter? The whole thing is just for fun, for entertainment. Gladiator events are games. You watch them, or you watch a computer animation of characters playing a game based upon input data from a game. Either way, it's not real life. Don't you realize there are real problems out there? Don't you know that as we sit here there's a gonorrhea outbreak in

South America and the antibiotics aren't working anymore? They're just distracting you with infotainment so they can keep making money and prevent you from even realizing what they're doing. It's thought control!"

The two men paused their conversation and stared blankly at Vera. The pockmarked man took a drink of his pilsner-flavored Cokaid and set it down. "Whatever," he said at last. "Whadya expect me to do about it?"

"Anyhow, what happened on your screen wasn't real either," he shot back, returning to his debate. "Like she said, the whole thing is just one big show. I just wish they'd do it honestly. If you're going to make a game out of it, your goddamn virtual player should be able to throw through the pain of his virtual bursitis. I had real money riding on this weekend's game. Now I'm going to have to work another two months just to save up enough to finish the season."

Vera had heard enough — too much in fact. She tried to slam the door behind her, but the automatic closer resisted her push and shut the door gradually.

A deliveryman walked out of the adjacent storefront carrying a stunning bouquet of white lilies wrapped in cellophane. Their scent was strong enough that Vera could smell the sickly-sweet perfume even through the plastic, but the deliveryman seemed hardly to notice either the beauty or the fragrance of what he carried. Flowers were one of the few items that did not lend themselves easily to drone delivery, so they were still hand delivered right to the door of the recipient. Flower deliverymen therefore earned less money in a day than a drone mule, who could deliver hundreds of packages from the platform of a self-driving truck simply by loading them onto drones for neighborhood distribution. The flower courier was in a hurry to make one more delivery for the day.

As she walked into the flower shop, a woman in her mid-50s with pale skin and her hair tied up in in a bright blue scarf greeted Vera at the door. "Hi hon. What can I get you?"

The shop was rather dismal. It was far too large for the number of flowers it held. A near empty rack held a few greeting cards covered with dust in the corner.

"I'm not really sure what I'm looking for. Can I just walk around?" Vera replied absentmindedly. She knew she could print out any flower arrangement she wanted on her home protruder, but they wouldn't have the same smell of the real thing. While the protruded flowers last forever, she felt there was just something better about the real ones. "I just wish the scent of real flowers would fill my house like they do your shop even if just for a little while."

The shopkeeper studied Vera for a full minute before inviting her toward the back section of the store. She took down a large glass jar with the words "Ball" and "Mason" written on the side in raised glass letters. Vera had never seen such a container.

The woman slowly unscrewed the sturdy metal lid and held the jar underneath Vera's face.

"Smell," she instructed.

Vera inhaled scents of orange peel, cinnamon, rosehips, and cedar.

"It's called potpourri," said the shopkeeper proudly. "The scent will last a lifetime."

Vera's mind leapt back to her Grandma Selah, who had kept collections of flower petals, pine needles, dried lemon peels, and orris root in little satin bags inside her dresser drawers. Whenever she would give Vera a hug, her clothes smelled of those satin bags. When Vera was a little girl, her grandmother would take them out and let Vera smell them while she told her stories of her own childhood in Ireland. She had many a happy tale, but also spoke of bombs, soldiers, and neighborhoods pitted against one another in what sounded like a civil war.

It had been years since Vera thought of her grandmother, maybe even a decade.

She smiled as she recalled taking trips to visit her. They would go to an amazing zoo filled with elephants, koala bears, and a monkey house that smelled of pungent, sour urine.

But Vera's smile vanished as the reminiscence of her grandmother suddenly surfaced the memory she had steadfastly shut from her mind for more than twenty-five years.

She had been sitting on the couch next to her baby brother who was fidgeting as though he might need a diaper change. Vera was engrossed in a virtual reality video game that she played on virtual goggles, an early predecessor to the MyScreen helmet. The game involved either attacking or protecting insects as they came at you with increasing speed and random patterns. It was a newly released full-immersion game that she had begged her parents to get for months.

As her brother snacked on Vienna sausages that their grandmother had left with them on a recent visit, Vera was approaching her all-time high score. While she maneuvered her flyswatter into position before the final attempt to eradicate the horseflies, she felt a tug on her elbow. She ignored it, seizing the opportunity to finally surpass her previous record, which had stood for weeks.

She did it!

After the excitement, she took off her goggles and screamed as she saw her brother's blue lips and bulging eyes. Frightened by his face — contorted from choking on the sausage — she immediately put her gaming helmet back on and pulled up a cartoon. She didn't remove the helmet for ten weeks, even when she slept, but still she couldn't erase the image in her brain of her brother's frozen face.

As the memory emerged in the flower shop, Vera's insides wretched, her breath quickened and her mind seemed unable to function. She gasped for air as her throat swelled until she could hardly breath.

Nobody ever suggested that it was Vera's fault, but within a matter of weeks she was taken to a foster home for safekeeping. She was old enough to understand that the authorities had concluded her parents had been negligent. Vera knew the truth.

Vera grew accustomed to characters dying in the video games and felt no attachment to them when they did. She'd play a game over and over again, not really striving for a high score but just watching things unfold as she explored every scenario for the character's demise. She kept playing until the deaths weren't real, weren't painful.

A grief counselor encouraged her gaming. "Play is literally the opposite of depression," he'd advised. "It's OK to lose yourself in a game if the real world is getting you down." It took about two years, but Vera eventually blocked off all thoughts of her brother. She never wept or saw her parents again. Their grief had been so severe that she guessed they would have consented to a MyndScreen upgrade soon after the technology became available, as a way to distract themselves from the aching loss. Vera had a hard time thinking about her grandmother without also thinking of the Vienna sausages she had brought. And now, the potpourri uncorked the memories she'd worked so hard to confine.

"I'll take it," Vera told the shopkeeper in a hoarse voice that approached a whisper.

"OK. It's two dollars. If you want the jar, that's another two dollars. That's a collector's item. They don't make them anymore."

She rather liked the way the heavy jar felt in her hands and the texture of its raised letters against her fingers. "Yes, fine."

The store still used a register pad for processing payments, up at the front counter. The woman tapped the screen a few times and kindly said to Vera, "that'll be three dollars, plus tax."

"I think you mean four," Vera replied. "Two plus two is four."

"It says here on my screen three dollars, so that's what you owe."

"No, really, I can show you." Vera took two daisies from a vase and two roses from another. "See, I have four flowers here. Two of these and two of these makes a total of four."

"I don't care how many flowers you have dear. You're buying potpourri and a jar, and the screen here says it's three dollars total. I can show you the screen for yourself if you don't believe me." She pivoted the white screen around and pointed at it.

"I'm not doubting what the screen says, but sometimes machines get it wrong. Maybe it's running on outdated firmware or has somehow been hacked. Just think for a moment, surely you know that two plus two is really four."

"I know what I see with my own two eyes," replied the woman. "Anything else will mess up my accounting software. Now, you can pay me three dollars, or you can walk away empty-handed. The choice is yours, dear, but that's the price you have to pay."

Tired of arguing, Vera paid the three dollars with a scan of her thumb and walked out the door with her treasure. Although she had gotten the better end of the deal, the experience had been unsettling.

After instructing the MiOtto to drive her home, Vera pulled up the evening news on her MyndScreen. The coverage was about a presidential debate held earlier in the day.

The leading candidate had been asked a question about how to deal with the war on Fear Mongers. "I have stood next to some of the bravest men and women in Globalia facing down some of the most horrific situations," began Susan Downley, who had served as a general in the army. "I know a coward when I see one. My opponent is so scared of the Mongers that he wears yellow socks. Our enemies can sense fear from thousands of miles away and we just can't afford to project weakness in today's dangerous world."

Jack Danforth, her opponent, stood astounded with his mouth gaping open. The Globalia Public Media announcers feigned shock and dismay that a leading presidential candidate would answer a foreign-policy question with an attack against an opponent's socks. One commentator affiliated with the Downley campaign claimed it was fair game since Danforth had been making a transparent attempt to appeal to the fans of the gladiator sports teams in each region by wearing ties and base-ball caps that matched the team's uniform colors.

The Globalia Public Radio hosts tried to pivot the coverage toward a response from a third candidate, who had pointed out that the war against Fear Mongers killed fewer people each year than dozens of other threats in Globalia such as disease, pharmaceutical drug overdose, obesity, food extruder contamination, and suicide. Vera remembered researching that information for her job. His claim was correct. However, Vera felt it was a bit misleading to bring those issues up in a presidential debate because they were entirely out of the purview of the President. The Tribunal of Educates had jurisdiction over all economic and social policy, so even if he won the President couldn't do anything about those problems.

It didn't matter. The conversation in both Globalia Public Media and the Chatterfeed ignored the third candidate's response entirely.

Right before the *Two Minute Spate*, the hosts cut to a commercial. The ad was paid for by the Downley campaign and it featured a photograph of Jack Danforth wearing out-of-fashion plaid Bermuda shorts while wildly swinging a golf club. The camera shot followed his stroke down toward the ground, where it missed the ball entirely and took a divot out of the grass. The video then froze the screen, with the chunk of sod in midair and Danforth's ankles in clear view. He was wearing black and yellow argyle socks that resembled a well-bred bumblebee in a bad sweater and clearly were a more gentile fashion than anything a true gladiator fan would wear. "Jack Danforth," said a baritone voice that sounded like a disapproving school vice-principal, "Not a straight shooter. Can't hit the ball. When Mongers attack, he'll go yellow."

After the *Two Minute Spate*, the program switched to a panel of experts, including Lester Lassen, a law professor at the University of California. The Globalia Public Media host asked Lassen if advertisements such as the recent attack on Danforth really advanced the public discourse about who should become president.

"Those advertisements are free speech," explained Lassen, in a scholarly tone as he adjusted his wire rim glasses. "Whether you like them or not, the Tribunal of Educates has declined to identify a compelling state interest that would withstand strict scrutiny to justify a content-based regulation that could have the unintended consequences of chilling their expression, however vapid it might or might not be to some listeners." Lassen spoke in Expertalk, a dialect used by Establishment members to convey their superior knowledge and intellect. "Compelling state interest" meant "important." "Strict scrutiny" was a throw-away line that empowered a majority of the Tribunal of Educates to reject any law that they felt wasn't justified.

"I see," said the host. "Well, regardless of what the Tribunal says, do you, as a person, really think that this is a useful way for voters to evaluate presidential candidates?"

"The remedy to bad speech is more good speech — a lot more," continued Lassen. "Just as the solution to antibiotic resistant bacteria is stronger antibiotics, the solution to coarsened political debate is more potent doses of smarter political discourse. Just as a farmer cannot cut off water without destroying his or her crops, you cannot silence anyone's speech without destroying liberty." He adjusted his glasses again and continued on, "Lack of food starves a body the way lack of information starves the body politic. When it comes to nourishment, freedom, or speech, more is always better. More, more, and yet still more."

The hair on Vera's neck stood on end. Doesn't this so-called expert know that stronger antibiotics only breed stronger bacteria? Is he so entrenched in his own silo of knowledge that he has lost all semblance of common sense?

An ad popped up on Vera's MyndScreen underneath the discussion. "Feeling triggered? Ask your doctor if AngerEase™ is right for you. It's the little blue pill that soothes your blue moods away." A standard disclaimer in fine print, "Advertising Frees Speech," followed the ad. She closed the ad window and returned to the program.

"Ok," said the host, somewhat hesitantly. "So, in the debate, Danforth had a chance to immediately rebut Downley's attack by actually showing us the color of the socks he's wearing today. In the advertisement, which just ran, he couldn't. How does campaign law address that?"

"Well, the Tribunal of Educates has ruled that campaign ads are free speech and it would violate Tribunal doctrine to require any infotainment broadcaster to air a free response after any political ad," explained the professor. "And then there's the issue that not all candidates attract enough campaign donors to pay for an equal number of ads. I think the best solution would be for the Tribunal to give all candidates public funds for their own full-scale barrage of advertisements. That way Danforth could respond to the attacks against him with his own ads showing him in whatever socks he likes, and we could have a robust public debate about what the color of his socks says about his fitness to lead. We could have even more candidates, more, more, more! Some with green socks, some blue, some striped! All speaking prolifically with their own ads."

Vera turned off the program feeling grateful she was able to. She knew that inattention to programming could trigger a data-point that might eventually lead to an upgraded MyndScreen that was constantly on, but she was willing to take the risk. She rode the remainder of her commute home in silence, mesmerized by the blurred glow of taillights on the cars in front of her as they lit up the gentle mist produced by tires rolling over the rain-soaked road.

CHAPTER 5

Vera skipped her morning exercise routine, opting to savor a cup of green tea instead. While waiting for the leaves to steep, she watched the steam rise from the ceramic mug. She admired the turquoise sheen of its glaze and how sturdy, warm, and heavy it felt in her hand when she picked it up in comparison to the plastic protruded cups she normally used. As she took her first sip, she noticed a chip on the rim, directly across from the handle. A reminder, she realized, that even non-disposable items do not last forever. She swallowed her weekly diabetes-prevention pill with the cooling tea as well as a daily dose of anti-inflammation capsules.

After meditating, Vera got ready for her day. As she put on makeup to cover the freckles on her nose, her mind wandered back to her previous day's encounters with the Vues. She reached out and touched her reflection in the cold bathroom mirror. Her hand then moved to her warm cheek, stroking downward to the chin.

"The truth is neither statistical nor empirical," Vera said aloud. The truth is what you believe, but is that the same thing as reality?"

Her MyndScreen window popped up an advertisement for a "true to life" thriller documentary about a religious cult in Eastern Europe, followed by the standard tagline "Advertising Frees Speech." Vera resisted the temptation to click the link.

The truth is what you believe and what others choose to believe. Belief sets us free. Freedom is one person believing you when you prove that two plus two really is four. Until that reality is granted, nothing else can follow.

After riding downtown, Vera noticed the wispy clouds high up in the deep blue sky as she walked to the office from the parking lot. She watched them rush past the rustling leaves in the trees directly above her, giving the sensation that it was she who was moving instead of the clouds. It was a welcome break from the gray overcast weather of the past several weeks. She felt a gentle breeze against her cheek and breathed in the smell of eucalyptus leaves that had released their essence after the recent rains. For a full minute, she stood there listening, breathing, feeling alive.

* * *

Upon arriving at the office, Vera noticed the cubicle next to hers was empty. Her colleague Randolph must have received an upgrade. *How did they get him to consent?* she wondered, trying to guess if there was some personal weakness or character flaw that the Establishment had used against him.

It doesn't matter. Everyone always consents in the end.

"Coworker upgraded. I wonder how long it will take to replace him," Vera mused in a Chatter post to Phoebe, not really expected an answer.

"Who knows, in the meantime it'll be more work for you. Be sure to treat yourself to something special." Vera had been chatting with Phoebe for the past two years after having liked one of her comments in response to a post about wildflowers. She had become a good friend, offering constant encouragement and support.

The presidential campaign meant there was greater demand for the Department's facts than normal. The campaigns themselves would be pumping out information, primarily through advertisements, but also through attempts to insert themselves into the news and information coverage — through press releases, speeches, Chatterfeed posts, and hacking or fabricating contraband information to leak at strategic moments. Infotainment firms would be producing their own research, analysis, and opinion content but they would also rely heavily upon verified facts from the Department of Information. A new segment of the *Two Minute Spate* would be aired every hour, rather than repeating the same segment for blocks of six hours.

Ugh. Is more information always better? Vera pondered, as she pulled up her first assignment. "What is the historical correlation between CEO compensation and the firm's economic growth?" Vera recalled that one of the lesser-known candidates in the presidential race had been arguing that corporate executives were overpaid. Vera imagined that the Department was looking for a verifiable fact to debunk this argument. Or, she wondered, *could there actually be someone high up in the Department who wants to know if the candidate is correct?*

As she pulled up studies in Noodle searches by experts at think tanks, universities, and chamber of commerce organizations, she stumbled upon an article reminding her of a previous assignment. "Pharma CEO doubles down on his firm's shaky success," blared the headline. The article had not been widely read, but Vera justified delving further into it by telling herself it could be relevant to her current assignment:

John Robertson, CEO of LingerLife Pharmaceuticals, announced yesterday that he had purchased three million shares of his company's stock, which has taken a beating in the past two months since its merger with Globalia's leading mental health conglomerate, Mercernary General Healthcare. Both firms are now owned by Renaissance Mercernary Investments, a hedge fund holding company that compensates CEOs well but holds them to high standards of shareholder return. Robertson has retained a derivative option to sell his stock at triple his purchase price if the company's share price rose even modestly in the next 30 days. Otherwise, if the share price falls, his personal fortune will be at risk as his stock option would lose all value. Business experts noted this was a good example of how current executive compensation practices encourage risk-taking and leadership in commerce, leading to an overall rise in Globalian prosperity.

Vera continued researching, looking for other examples and expert analysis on the correlation between CEO compensation and profitability. She found a video archive of a presentation done by a professor at Billerton College in rural Massachusetts. She'd never heard of him, but it seemed on point for her assignment:

"Professor Morton Piro conducted an exhaustive study that analyzed the total compensation packages of the CEOs of the top 500 firms in Globalia. It found that top-level executive pay goes up dramatically in years of strong economic growth, but does not reduce in years of economic collapse. Further, firms that paid their CEOs in the top ten percent saw their stocks produce abnormally low returns in following years. Business experts disagreed about whether the study showed anything useful about executive compensation. Some experts suggested that stock prices become artificially high when investors chase celebrity CEOs — who command higher than normal compensation packages. Other experts said that Professor Piro's work was shoddy and that further research would be needed before any conclusions could be drawn. They noted that Piro had once read a political article that had been linked to the Luddyte Sisterhood and that he was rumored to suffer from severe halitosis."

Vera didn't know what halitosis was, but she wondered if it was relevant to the actual findings in Piro's report. As far as she could tell, nobody was disputing the actual data that Piro had compiled or his method of calculating results. But something still bothered her. She dug deep in her desk drawer and found a pen and a piece of paper, neither of which she had used for at least five years. "Is this the information the Department is looking for?" she wrote.

Staring at the piece of paper for at least ten minutes, she was unable to decide or move forward on the task. She thought she'd take a walk before lunch and return to the assignment later.

As she strolled through a park near City Hall, it seemed surprisingly deserted. A gray squirrel scolded her as she approached a tree he was jealously protecting. A large fountain splashed nearby, sounding like an alpine waterfall and sending droplets of water dancing in the sunlight. Other than a policeman sitting lazily on a pink plastic park bench, she saw just one other person, stooping down to admire the red and white variegated tulips in a circular flowerbed surrounding the fountain. As she drew close, the man quickly turned his head and looked straight at Vera, a warm smile spreading across his face.

Her blood froze as she saw the Virtual Sex Liberation League tattoo on his arm. Realizing this was the stranger she'd encountered at the parking garage, Vera was desperate to avoid him. She thought it would be too obvious if she suddenly changed course, so she just averted her gaze. She wished she could look at his eyes to see if he was watching her, but his dark sunglasses concealed them.

A sign stuck out from the flowerbed warning, "Do not pick the flowers. Violators will be prosecuted." Suddenly, the blonde-haired man bent down and plucked a tulip. The white streaks on the variegated blossom looked like feathers of a dove against the red background of his T-shirt, which matched the red in the flowers perfectly.

There's no way he missed that sign, thought Vera.

Before she could react, he walked straight up to her. He strolled slowly, deliberately, with the legs of his blue jeans softly brushing against each other in between each stride. Vera guessed the jeans were made of real cotton, not protruder fibers. They appeared to have been worn over and over again, washed in between wearings instead of discarded after each use. With his head held high and his smile still beaming, he handed her the flower without saying a word. She felt the outside of his hand brush up against her fingers, which had inexplicably reached out to accept the tulip, and she could hear her accelerated heartbeat pounding inside her skull. As she took a step back, Vera smelled something. Not the tulip, but perhaps his hair had a scent of citrus.

"I'm not really like this," she stammered. "I mean, I wouldn't normally do this." Vera looked nervously at the policeman, who appeared to be transfixed on his MyndScreen. She then looked down, again avoiding the stranger's gaze.

"I believe you," was all he said.

After an uncomfortable moment of silence, Vera asked, "What's your name?"

"Chase. Like the bank."

Vera's MyndScreen immediately pulled up her bank account balance and a notification that her monthly credit payment would post in two days. Her shoulders dropped and she looked up to see him lifting his sunglasses, propping them on top of his head. From this angle, she could see a small camera mounted on the backs of each earpiece, pointed away from the lenses toward the back of the head. She recognized them as the newly released 180°™ glasses, allowing their wearer to see behind himself by beaming images from rear-facing cameras directly into his MyndScreen. That must have been how he saw her coming even as he was looking toward the flowerbed. *He was waiting there for me.*

"You can call me V," she said truthfully, if not entirely accurately.

"OK," said Chase holding up two fingers of his right hand into a V-shape. "I'll see you around, V."

And just like that, he walked off. She waved to him as he went, and in response he held his hand above his shoulder with two fingers extended in a V. He then moved them to his lips in the way one takes a drag off a cigarette, presumably kissing his fingertips although Vera couldn't tell for sure as his head was turned away from her as he strode away.

Vera tucked the flower into her purse.

* * *

When she returned to the office, the piece of paper was still sitting on her desk, staring at her.

"Is this the information the Department is looking for?"

Vera grabbed the pen and scribbled "WHO CARES!" — answering her own question.

She returned to her assigned research question: "What is the historical correlation between CEO compensation and the firm's economic growth?"

Vera thought through the most truthful response she could muster.

"The correlation between CEO compensation and company economic growth varies from firm to firm and industry to industry. But that is not the right question. CEOs are vastly overcompensated."

Rather than researching expert analysis to document the accuracy of her statement, Vera found several public opinion polls indicating that more than 80 percent of respondents believed that CEOs were overpaid. That belief was not empirically verifiable or based upon any statistical analysis. It was a judgment, not fact. But to Vera, the assertion rung true.

She hit "send" to submit her work to her supervisor. Looking about for a trash can to throw out her note, she noticed there was none. Nothing tangible had been created, or discarded, in that cubicle for years. Tucking the note in her handbag, Vera left the building.

* * *

The sky was azure blue as Vera headed out the door — so clear she could see all the way to the snow-capped mountains far beyond Los Angeles. With the sun sinking low on the western horizon, the mountains lit up — appearing almost to glow into the skyline.

The gentle whir of delivery drones sounded like a hive of bees buzzing about an almond orchard. Their pleasant hum was interrupted by the growl of a leaf blower as Vera walked back to her car. She'd made a habit of walking to and from the parking lot ever since the day she'd first tried it. It was only after her car door closed with a "thunk" that Vera sat in silence.

On the drive home, her MyndScreen asked if she'd like to stop again at the café where she'd met the older Vue woman the week before. She wasn't ready to head back to her empty apartment, so she clicked yes, and her car pulled off the freeway.

The smell of baking brownies and real coffee rose in the air as Vera waited in line. The café was advertising a drink special for the week, brewed from actual beans, available at the same price as coffee-flavored Pepsoilent. Because real coffee brewers were slower than Pepsoilent extruders, the wait was longer than normal. A light flickered above the baked goods display, presumably due to a short in the wiring. Vera could feel her toes pressing against the front of her shoes as she stood in line. She let out a sigh and waited patiently, unlike the man in front of her who was nervously tapping his foot against the wall. The back of his T-shirt had the name and logo of a local mayoral candidate on it.

As she waited, an ad popped up on her MyndScreen. "Follow politics? Then we've got just the simulation game for you. Enroll now in this year's Silver538FantasyCampaign™ game. Pick your own personal roster of consultants, pollsters, ad creators, political donors and, of course, candidates! Each week, our state-of-the-art computer modelling program will calculate the odds of your team prevailing in the upcoming selections based on public opinion polling, historical trend-lines, stock indexes, economic forecasts, and anti–Fear Monger security updates. Win big if competing teams get rocked by scandal, leaks, or debate slipups! See if you can beat the pundits! Weekly awards paid to top performers followed by a grand prize of ten million dollars to the player with the ultimate political team. Join now, enrollment ends in 37 seconds — Advertising Frees Speech."

Ugh. They must know I'm following the presidential selections coverage.

Vera ordered a real iced coffee with a hash brownie. As she sat down, a video screen on the wall was playing the evening news hour. Right in the middle of the *Two Minute Spate,* there was a ten-second story about antibiotics:

"A top scientist has leaked an internal document from LingerLife Pharmaceuticals indicating that the company has known for at least a decade that its antibiotics no longer effectively treat gonorrhea. The company's scientists are skeptical that any new antibiotic will work."

Vera smiled. Accurate information, which she had helped research at the Department, was getting out. Maybe things weren't so bad after all. She took a bite of brownie, marveling at the chewy texture and deep chocolate flavor.

"Hey there," Phoebe poked her in the Chattersphere. "How are you doing today?"

Vera replied with a simple emojicon,"☺." She rubbed her thumb and forefinger around the pink and green woven friendship bracelet that Phoebe had sent to her home protruder. It was nice to have a physical reminder of their relationship, something she could feel instead of just see on her MyndScreen.

"Wanna join me for some coffee at LuckyStars?" Vera shot out the request, realizing that she'd never actually met Phoebe in person. It felt old fashioned to meet face to face, but it suddenly seemed worth the hassle of making the logistics of LA traffic work. *I wonder what her voice sounds like?*

"Luv 2, but no 🕐. I'll ping you later."

After the *Two Minute Spate*, the entertainment segment of the news hour came on. It was time for the Celebrity Watch report. Delilah Fish, the number two rated movie star, was on the show talking about her efforts to raise funds to treat disease in South America. Delilah had recently given birth to a baby conceived via IVF and had promptly turned the infant over to a boutique childrearing center, Renaissance Cultivation.

"So, tell us what you're doing to ensure the baby's well-being," asked a charming host wearing a purple cashmere sweater over his yellow button-down silk shirt. He bounced his head ever so slightly as he spoke with practiced voice inflections that seemed to draw Vera into the conversation. He looked at the camera when he spoke, not at Delilah, but she seemed to think nothing of it.

"Well," said Delilah, perkily. The camera zoomed in on her long, thick eyelashes flitting up and down as she daintily raised her hand and lightly touched her neckline, revealing a quarter-pound manufactured diamond set in a gold bracelet. "Renaissance is doing a far better job than I ever could to ensure that my baby will grow into a unique individual. I diligently pumped breast milk for the first six weeks, before the baby could transfer over to

Pepsoilent formula. Now I go to visit each week to snap some photos that I can share over the Chatterfeed." The screen flashed several shots of Delilah holding an adorable infant swaddled in Turkysh™ cotton blankets. In each image, she was looking straight at the camera, almost failing to notice what she held in her arms. Her cheeks glowed with the perfect amount of blush makeup, and her hair had a dazzling new style in each photo.

"And how has this magical experience of childbirth inspired your charitable work?"

Delilah tucked her auburn brown hair behind her ears and spoke in a more somber tone. "You see, I learned that some women have trouble giving birth after contracting gonorrhea. After having a baby myself, I just wanted everyone to feel that joy. There's such a stigma to the disease that I knew we had to find a way to bring it out of the shadows. So, I'm auctioning off my used breast milk pumps to raise funds that will provide free antibiotics to anyone in South America who needs them to treat gonorrhea. I used a freshly protruded pump every day, so I've got forty-two different ones to auction!"

Vera sprayed iced coffee out of her mouth along with some smallish chunks of hash brownie, making a mess on the table in front of her.

Sudden links flashed brightly on Vera's MyndScreen:

"Watch these 4 simple videos 2 control UR anger — Advertising Frees Speech."

"Get ProTheraphy™ 2 manage outbursts."

"6 simple steps 2 reduce UR blood pressure."

"How HOT celebrities keep their tempers cool."

"Hot damn, I'm putting in a bid!" exalted a middle-aged Vue across the café to his buddy. "Just think about what that thing's been squeezing! And besides, it's a chance to do something good for the world." Even a few Establishment members perked up and appeared to be searching for the bidding site on their MyndScreens.

Vera printed a napkin from a fiber fabricator on the wall and wiped up her spewed iced coffee from the table.

"OMG, I can't believe they're at two thousand dollars already!" complained the man who had wanted to bid on Delilah's breast pump. A lively conversation ensued around his table.

Vera threw the rest of her brownie and iced coffee into the recycling chute and walked out the door.

* * *

When she got home, Vera immediately took the variegated tulip out of her handbag. Rather than putting the already wilting flower in a vase, she laid it gently on a side table next to her balcony where soft rays of sunlight lit up the petals.

She stared at her Pepsoilent food extruder and thought about what she wanted to eat. After three minutes of MyndScreen browsing on the extruder app, nothing seemed appealing. She opened her only cabinet and saw a white cloth bag filled with wild rice. A purple ribbon was tied in a bow across the top. Vera had received it as a party favor when she attended a wedding nearly ten years ago.

"How do you suppose you cook rice?" Vera wondered aloud. Several recipes popped up on her MyndScreen, all of which seemed to involve heating the rice in a pot on top of a stove — neither of which Vera had in her luxury suite.

Looking around the kitchen, the only appliance Vera owned, other than her Pepsoilent extruder, was an old cappuccino maker. She filled her ceramic mug half way with the wild rice and placed it under the steam spout normally used for foaming milk. As the rice steamed, Vera began poking around for something to eat with the rice.

On a display shelf in the living room sat a tin can with a red label. White letters identified it as "WOLF brand chili, authentic Texas recipe." Her roommate had given it to her when she was in college — hoping to share a little of her local culture. Vera hadn't been keen to eat something out of a can, but she kept it at the time just to be polite. She had been reluctant to throw it out ever since, as it was the only physical remembrance she had of her time in college.

But how to open it?

Vera searched the can for a pull tab or twisting lid.

Nothing.

She went to her front door and slid it open by pressing her thumb against the print reader. Placing the can in the door crack, she then closed it. "Thunk."

The can dented, but didn't break open. She ran a search for "how to open a tin can" and found lots of devices that had been manufactured to do that. But when she clicked on a few to see if they would be available for instant delivery, she found they had all been out of stock for more than a decade.

About ten links down, she found an ad for a hardware store in Westmont that claimed to have can openers in stock. She went down to the parking garage, hopped in her car and was soon on her way. As her MiOtto pulled off the freeway and turned into the streets of Westmont, Vera was surprised to see small groups of people hanging out on front porches and street corners. Westmont was known as a rough neighborhood, and dirt poor. There was reportedly a lot of gang activity — Vera stared at the people on the street and wondered if they were criminals. Only a few teenagers here were wearing My-Screen helmets; she guessed it wasn't because the rest had MyndScreen chips installed. Vera remembered reading reports of helmet jacking, where thugs stole MyScreens right off the heads of unsuspecting victims by cutting the chin straps with utility knifes — often injuring the person in the process.

In empty parking lots and cracked asphalt school yards, she saw teenagers doing strange dance moves on large cardboard boxes that had been flattened and spread out on concrete. Some did back flips while others literally spun upside down on their heads, looking a bit like a human drone. Loud, rhythmic music boomed out of black plastic devices twice the size of shoeboxes that were placed on the sidewalk.

Old men with coffee-colored leathery skin sat on bedraggled sofas under a fiberglass carport, sipping glass bottles of beer. Two small girls were sitting in the dirt, shooting small round glass balls with their thumbs into a circle filled with a dozen more of the colorful beads. A toddler who could not have been even two years old sat on the ground to watch, breaking into bubbling peals of laughter whenever two marbles collided with one another and reaching out to grab one and put it in her mouth. *That's real,* Vera smiled to herself. *No infotain firm, no avatar creator, not a single living person has yet created a sound as authentic as the laugh of a child.*

Most of the buildings were painted with murals, or fading graffiti, which looked to be decades old. Lawns were overgrown with weeds, but some had rose bushes sporting gorgeous blooms that stood out in their beauty amid the trash that littered the yards and sidewalks. The neighborhood didn't look dangerous, but its disorder was unsettling to Vera. She had never seen people mingle so freely, so aimlessly. The place was bustling with life, although it moved at a tediously slow pace. Pedestrians walked right in the middle of the street, forcing her car to slow to a halt several times, drawing unwelcome attention from passersby.

Aren't these people used to seeing cars?

As soon as her MiOtto pulled into the parking lot of a rundown-looking store, an antique neon sign by the door illuminated, stabbing Vera's eyes with a flash of pinkish-red letters reading "OPEN." Vera quickly got out of her car and headed inside. She looked around the aisles, amazed at the abundance. There were tools and building supplies, lawn chairs, flowerpots, garden hoses, buckets of paint, and an endless row of nails, screws, and bolts.

"Can I help you find something?" asked a small, friendly man with ash-white curly hair wearing a red cotton vest over a disposable light blue button-down shirt. She felt his warm, almond colored eyes look right through her and was embarrassed to have come in at all. She almost turned and fled, but instead gathered a deep breath and mustered the courage to ask if he had any can openers.

"I sold my last one a week ago," he replied. "I've tried to re-order, but I guess they've stopped making them. If you want, I can sell you a hammer and a screwdriver. Between the two of them you could probably punch a couple of slits through the top of a can and pry it open somehow."

"No thanks. It was just a crazy idea I had. Anyhow, take care."

"Why thank you, I will," he said, surprising her with a reply. "You come back anytime, you hear?" It seemed like a genuine request, not just the normal exchange of pleasantries at a place of commerce.

What is it with this place?

On the drive home, Vera mused aloud to herself, "How am I ever going to get that can open? It's like I need claws or something,"

Her MyndScreen pulled up an image of what looked like a medieval torture device.

Vera studied the image. A caption below said it was a "Claw shaped vintage can opener."

Vera sent the image to her 3-D home protruder as she rode back to *Magnificent Estates*.

After Noodling around for some videos demonstrating how antique can openers were used, Vera was ready to give it a try. She plunged the blade straight down into the edge of the can top and then carefully pulled down, levering the cutter around the edge of the can.

While trying to remove the lid, Vera slit the side of her finger on its sharp edge and a narrow stream of blood streamed down to her wrist. A sharp pain, unlike anything she had ever felt, shot up her finger like a hot needle.

As she looked down to see blood dripping into her palm, Vera's MyndScreen blasted up solutions:

"Got a cut? Get KlotCream™ — Advertising Frees Speech."

"How 2 remove blood stains in 3 simple steps."

"The secret to a great Bloody Mary."

With drops of blood now hitting the floor, Vera began to panic.

What do I do?

After taking a deep breath, Vera walked into the bathroom. She washed the cut off in cool water, soothing the stinging pain. The bleeding slowed, but the diluted blood still spread all over her thumb.

Using her other hand, Vera pressed a fiber fabricator button and printed a piece of tissue paper. She wrapped her cut finger in it and then returned to the 3-D protruder printer to produce a piece of tape. Vera smiled as she admired the makeshift bandage, swallowed a PainZapper™ pill from her medicine cabinet, and returned to her meal preparations.

With no obvious way to heat the now opened can of chili, Vera waited until the rice looked sufficiently cooked and then stuck the steam nozzle straight into the can. The chili bubbled with air and steam, splattering red sauce all over the counter. *Now I know why people gave this up for disposable dishes and extruded food,* thought Vera as she fabricated an instant towel to wipe up the mess.

At last, Vera assembled her dinner and took a bite. The rice had a bit of crunch on the inside, unlike the perfectly prepared extruded rice she was used to. It had a mild nutty flavor, rather pleasing she thought. The chili stung her tongue like a fierce sunburn. Worried she had cut it, she raced to the bathroom mirror to inspect. *No bleeding.* Slowly the burn passed, and she took another bite, which was less painful this time, especially when she had some rice with it. Perhaps this is what the label meant when it said "SPICY."

By her fifth bite, a smile of satisfaction spread across her face.

* * *

Vera awoke at three a.m. the following morning, puzzled by images she had seen that were not from her MyndScreen. In the visions, she had been running through a thick forest of trees with leaves brushing against her face. She looked down, hoping to find a footpath through the undergrowth, but saw only a blanket of fallen pine needles. Sounds of twigs snapping came both from in front of and behind her. She kept going, deeper and deeper into the forest — the brisk fragrance of evergreen trees growing stronger with every step. She wasn't scared, but didn't feel entirely safe either.

Was she trying to catch something, or being pursued? And, more puzzling, how could images and sounds appear in her head at night if they weren't coming from the MyndScreen, which was only now powering up with two ads appearing:

"Nightvisions — a new Timeless Warning movie explores the ancient world of dreams."

"Are dreams disturbing your slumber? Find a sleep therapist today."

"A dream," said Vera aloud.

It was a dream.

CHAPTER 6

Once awake, falling back into sleep was hard.

Vera felt alert and alive. The dream hadn't been frightening so much as anxiety filling. She was more familiar with dreams from the romance episodes that she watched, where characters often spoke of dreaming about each other, than she was from her own personal experience.

Her thoughts kept returning to unsettling events from the past few days: the deception of LingerLife Pharmaceuticals, the irrelevant critiques of the college professor's study of executive salaries, the shockingly forward move by the man in the park. She wished she could stop thinking about him and go back to sleep.

Maybe I shouldn't have had that coffee in the afternoon, she thought, sparking another memory of the ridiculous pretense of charity by Delilah Fish. Vera was certain Delilah was getting paid by Renaissance Childrearing to plug their centers in the media, all while raising funds for antibiotics that were not going to work.

It's a sham! The whole thing is as phony as a fake treasure chest buried at Venice Beach, and I'm one of the few people who knows it. I feel like there's something I should do, but what?

Her MyndScreen popped up a slew of ads, "🕐 to do something about those sagging breasts? Consider augmentation today!" "Tulip print nightgowns snuggle you in floral beauty," "Tired of fake hair cleansers? Our shampoo is clinically proven to make a difference — Advertising Frees Speech."

Maybe Chatter is the answer. Billions of people get Chatter posts each day.

After obsessing over the perfect wording for five minutes, Vera drafted a post: "Warning: Gonorrhea kills. Antibiotics Don't Cure It. Be Careful People!"

With some trepidation, Vera selected the "📣" icon on her MyndScreen and sent it off.

She watched her screen attentively as one, two, then three people reposted it. Two were from the East Coast, one from somewhere in Vladivostok. She could tell from the ChatterMetrics that her post had been viewed by 47 people. Somebody, apparently from the medical profession, posted a comment, "Actually, in most occasions, gonorrhea is not lethal — don't be so alarmist."

Vera sighed.

She rolled over and stared at the wall.

* * *

During lunch that day at the food court, Vera sat next to her friend Symeon, a colleague who worked in the Message Distillation Department. Unlike most Establishment types who stared at their palms to indicate they wanted to be left alone with their MyndScreens, Symeon usually welcomed conversation. And unlike Manquin, they could talk about things other than *Big Mother*.

"How are things in emojiland?" Vera asked, somewhat jokingly.

"We're working on a new partnership with Timeless Warning that could give us access to thousands of their privately trade-marked emojigraphs. They are super intuitive and already widely in use, so we'll be able to use them to convey ideas with spectacular efficiently. A picture is worth a thousand words, you know, and millions of dollars too."

"That's great, I guess. I've been wishing I could convey some ideas, but somehow I don't think an emojigraph would do the trick."

"Something you've researched for the Department?"

"Sort of. I had this assignment to document the general effectiveness of antibiotics over the past forty years. While I was looking into that, I found that one disease has become resistant to antibiotics — they just don't work anymore. I've seen some of this information make it onto the *Two Minute Spate*, so I know the Department must be using my research. But the company that produces the drug, LingerLife, is running a perception management campaign aimed at bolstering its share price. They've got this stupid celebrity auctioning off breast pumps to pay for antibiotic treatments that they know damn well won't work. It's driving me crazy. I feel like I should tell people, not only about the antibiotic, but about how our whole news industry is doing us a disservice."

"So, you need to find a way to get your message out. That *is* going to take more than a simple emojigraph. It's gonna take money. What industry stands to make money by LingerLife's failure? Is there a competitor with a new, better antibiotic that would fund a perception management campaign to expose them?"

"That's just it," complained Vera. "I haven't found one — maybe because we've created a disease so resistant to antibiotics that no new drug will combat it. I think the solution lies more in prevention, which is far less profitable than treatment."

"Well, maybe there's a charitable organization that would help. They care about people and have gobs of money to give out. Try contacting the OrangeVine Foundation, they have offices around here. The only way to fight off LingerLife's bad information is with an overpowering stream of good information — they should understand that."

"Hey guys," exalted Manquin, sitting down to join them. "Did you see last night's *Big Mother*? It was the best yet. I just couldn't believe it when Stella lied about stealing the GameChanger token from Esmerelda — even while she was blatantly wearing it around her neck. It's like nobody even bothered to look at her, they were so busy trying to analyze her voiceprint for bluffing tells with their gambling apps."

"Yeah," responded Symeon, without a hint of irony. "It just goes to show you that if you're too obsessed with your MyndScreen apps you can miss what's right in front of your face. Sometimes I think there are game changers in our midst every day, and yet we can't see them through all of our own troubles and distractions." He winked at Vera.

"I know just what you mean," chuckled Manquin, cluelessly. "It's like that time last year, when the triplet cheerleaders were trying to fool everyone into thinking

that they really didn't like those sensual oil massages...."
He was off again, spouting out a fifteen-minute mono-
logue about last season's *Big Mother* highlights.

Symeon is going to get himself into trouble, thought Vera.
*He understands things a little too well for his own good. I
wonder why he hasn't been upgraded.*

That afternoon, in between research projects for the
Department, Vera ran a Noodle search on the Orange-
Vine Foundation. The charity had been founded by a
construction mogul who bought out the patent for self-
erecting high-rise plastic protruders that can build a skyscraper underneath themselves by printing and
assembling plastic girders, walls, floors, ceilings; all with
integrated circuit boards, LED lighting, HVAC, and
plumbing features. Once they finish a building, the construction protruders are helicoptered off by drones and
placed in a new site to start another project. The firm was
so profitable that its owner had started the foundation
after the effort of staffing and maintaining the fifty-seven
private estates he owned across Globalia became overwhelming. He downsized to a more manageable thirty-
two family compounds, keeping the best islands and
mountaintops intact, and used the proceeds from the liq-
uidated properties to fund good deeds and avoid paying
taxes.

In reading up on the foundation, Vera ran across a
name she recognized, Caspian Blaine, one of the foundation officers. She had seen Chatter posts from him
occasionally, talking about how brand loyalty had surpassed cultural identity as a trending topic in the
Chattersphere. He had even run some numbers on it to
prove the point, and these had been picked up in the *Two
Minute Spate* one evening.

She looked him up on her MyndScreen and was heartened that he was one of the few people who still used what appeared to be a real photo as his profile picture. His orange-tinted plastic glasses framed his round, brown face in a manner that appeared both friendly and knowledgeable. She found a timeline chock-full of witty yet wise posts.

"Is Cokaid actually the real thing?"

"Pepsoilent — the choice of a zombie generation."

"Have a Cokaid and a smile and then shut the f**k up!" That one made her laugh out loud.

But Vera's mouth hung open when she saw a post from two weeks back. "Are pharma bros addicting us to flavored soyalgent?" with a link to a news article about how LingerLife Pharmaceuticals was partnering with Pepsoilent to create additives that would ensure consumers physically craved their products.

Vera sent off a private Chatter message to Caspian, linking to his post. "Hey, saw your Chatter and couldn't agree more. Would you have time to meet? I have a project I think you'd be interested in."

Days passed and there was no response. Vera went through her normal ritual of morning exercise following the *Physical Jerks* program, mindless banter with work colleagues during lunch and breaks, and routine research for the Department. She used evenings to explore new meal options on her extruder, check out the latest fashions, and binge watch nature documentaries. She had subscribed to a quick Chatterfeed summary of each night's *Big Mother* happenings to get by in her interminable conversations with Manquin, so no longer felt like she needed to watch each show.

But each day brought Vera a growing sense of unease. Her daily activities no longer held the same satisfaction they once did. She continued to dabble in meditation, unassisted by the online meditation guides for fear of triggering a SpeidrWeb data point. But somehow, mindful contemplation only made things worse. She became increasingly aware of how hollow her life was, yet nothing emerged to fill the void. It was as if there had been a helium balloon deep inside her abdomen keeping her buoyant and full for years and suddenly it leaked out all its gas.

One afternoon her insides reinflated.

"I have an opening from 3:27 to 3:42 p.m. on Thursday. Meet me at my office. — Caspian."

He'd responded! He would meet! For the first time, Vera felt like she was breaking through. A grant from the OrangeVine Foundation could fund a massive public outreach campaign to let people know about gonorrhea.

Vera took the afternoon off on Thursday and jumped in her MiOtto at 2:13 p.m., precisely the time her navigation app told her to begin the trip to ensure she would arrive at the OrangeVine office on time. Vera admired the real polished rose- and charcoal-speckled granite on the walls and floor as she waited for the elevator to take her up to Caspian Blaine's office. She waited nervously in the reception area as a secretary informed Caspian that his appointment had arrived. An arrangement of flowers set in a large crystal vase on a marble pedestal caught her attention –fiery orange sepals on each slender green stem surrounded smaller bluish-purple petals, which looked like the intensely hot interior of a flame. A quick Noodle search informed her they were called bird-of-paradise flowers.

As he emerged from a hallway, Caspian's warm smile immediately released the knots that had tied themselves in Vera's abdomen. She returned the smile, initially puzzled when he extended his hand out toward her. She quickly remembered she'd seen this gesture on older TV reruns and with only a slight hesitation reciprocated the offer and shook his hand. The lighter skin of his palm contrasted with the darker ebony on the back of his hand and arm. His grasp felt warm, soft, and firm. His braided dreadlocks swung back and forth, brushing the tops of his shoulders as his whole body seemed to bobble up and down with the handshake.

As they walked to his office, Caspian put her at ease with some chitchat about the weather and bemoaning how busy he was before setting the stage for Vera to make her pitch; "I've done some due diligence, and I gather that you are a well-respected researcher at the Department of Information. Tell me about your project."

"I've learned that there is a serious health problem with a disease known as gonorrhea, you may not have heard of it but it's reaching epidemic levels in South America."

"That's well documented. And the bacteria have grown resistant to all known forms of antibiotics. I've seen your posts on this and read the articles you've been sharing. What's your plan to solve it, and what specific sort of deliverables to you envision?"

Vera wasn't sure if deliverables was some sort of foundation Expertalk or a reference to the packages brought daily by drones to customers' balconies. She decided to steer clear of the term and give a safe answer.

"I was thinking there should be some sort of perception management campaign to warn people about the disease, with an emphasis on prevention rather than treatment. The pharmaceuticals like LingerLife only make money on treatment, so they have no incentive to inform people about prevention."

Caspian cut her off. "In fact, they're spending money hand over foot to still push their antibiotics. Everything's connected, like a giant web reaching all across the whole wide world. Did you see that ridiculous stunt by Delilah Fish with her breast pumps?"

Oh my god! He gets it. Vera's head almost exploded as she felt she had found a kindred spirit.

"Right, and the Department of Information has only so much time to devote to each issue. It's covered gonorrhea in the *Two Minute Spate*, but people hardly seem to have noticed."

"Not to mention that the Department has outsourced most of its workload to DeVritas, which will probably soon be bought out by Renaissance Mercernary, the investment firm that also happens to own LingerLife."

Vera's jaw dropped. "You don't think that Renaissance would try to influence the Department of Information's priorities, do you?"

"The only real question is what can we do about it? Who is your consultant?"

"Huh?"

"A major foundation like OrangeVine expects accountability from its grantees. One way we ensure that is to fund projects that utilize highly qualified experts who are familiar with our standards of NGO excellence and can make certain that deliverables get fulfilled according to agreed-upon timelines using best practices as identified in results-driven data sets and peer-reviewed metrics."

"Oh, I see. Ah..."

"Are there any other foundations involved? My board generally doesn't like for OrangeVine to be the only funder of a project — we tend to follow the lead of smaller incubator shops that seed startup philanthropic ventures that we can then lift to scale."

More Expertalk. What the hell is he talking about?

Caspian leaned back in his chair and paused, waiting for Vera to collect her thoughts.

"I guess I didn't know this was going to be so complicated."

Smiling warmly, Caspian offered a new path forward. "It seems like you might not be quite ready to present a proposal that would meet our funding criteria. That's OK. Everyone needs to start somewhere. I like you, you've identified a serious issue, and I'd really like to help if I can. We do have one niche program that I don't oversee, but maybe it's worth your consideration. It's aimed at promoting the interests of underprivileged OrangeSmash customers, who our founder feels have been marginalized by societal oppression. Is there any particular threat to OrangeSmash customers posed by gonorrhea? Like, are they somehow more susceptible to the disease or something? If you can find an angle like that, maybe we could squeeze you into that funding stream."

Vera saw that her time was almost up and sighed. "I'll look into it I guess. Thank you for taking the time to meet. I'm just glad I found somebody who understands what's going on."

"One more thought," said Caspian, as he stood and walked Vera toward the reception area. "There's someone who might be able to help you. You can find him most evenings in the Santa Monica community garden, usually around eight o'clock. His name is Aldo. Tell him I sent you. Good luck, Vera."

Looking up through her MiOtto's moonroof on the way home, Vera saw blue rivulets peeking out between wispy white clouds in the crack of sky nestled between the skyscrapers that towered above her. Traffic moved at a crawl, giving her ample time to examine her surroundings. Sunlight intermittently lit up the upper fifth of the high-rise at the end of the block, making its windows glisten like golden fireworks as her car drove through their reflected beams. Vera felt small in comparison. The clouds seemed to move at an incredible speed, leaving her narrow view within a minute of when they entered, each one replaced by a larger, denser version of itself.

* * *

It was hard to discern the man's features in the dim light. As Vera approached, she saw his silhouette cut against the dark, dusk sky — a thin figure of moderate height wearing a straw cowboy hat, which cast a deep shadow over his face. A feather stuck out of the headband, pointing straight backwards and toward the rising moon.

She had come to see him the same night she'd learned of his existence. Her meeting with Caspian left her dejected, but as she'd eaten another Pepsoilent dinner she'd concluded she simply couldn't spend the rest of the evening watching episodes and shopping.

Something had changed inside her, something that could not be undone.

The heavy duck cloth fabric of Aldo's pants had folds and creases, giving his outline a jagged appearance with bulges at the sides of the knees and ankles. As she got closer, the moonlight revealed he wore a black, long-sleeve collarless shirt, which buttoned down the front and with sleeves rolled up to his elbows. His brown leather boots bore scratches and scuffs so realistic that Vera wanted to ask him were he'd ordered them from.

"Hi, Aldo? Caspian Blaine suggested I talk with you."

"Is that so?" The figure didn't move as the words left his mouth, his thumbs were hooked into belt-loops on either side of his waist. Vera wished she could see his eyes or get some sort of a read on his facial expression, but she could only see darkness underneath the rim of his hat.

"I'm trying to warn people about gonorrhea. But, really, it's bigger than that. … I want people to know that most of what we see on the news and from infotain firms isn't real. I mean, it happens, but it's not what really matters. This is just one example." Vera wasn't sure it was wise to share so much, but the declaration just spilled out.

"Come in," he motioned toward a gate along an enclosure of chicken wire surrounding several rows of vegetable beds. "It's nicer to talk in the garden. This keeps the rats and pigeons out."

As she followed him into the fenced-off area, in the dim light Vera could just make out his long black braid sticking out from under his hat and running down between his shoulder blades. They sat down on a wooden bench, next to a rose bush.

Aldo reached into his shirt pocket and pulled out a handful of black-and-white-striped oval objects the size of breath mints. "Want some?"

"To plant, you mean?"

"To eat!"

Gross.

"Um, no thanks. I just ate."

He popped a few into his mouth, chewed, and spit out the splintered shells onto the ground. He pointed toward a row of plants towering seven feet high, with large heavy blossoms bent toward the ground "They come from those. Sunflowers. Even now, we still have the sunflowers."

Aldo paused, turned his head to face Vera and asked, "Are you sure you want to go down this path? The gravity of what you find may bring you down just as the weight of those seeds bend even the strong stem of the flower. Sometimes it's too heavy, and the stem breaks."

"I have nothing to lose. I was so excited when I met Caspian to find someone else who gets what's going on. I was hoping the OrangeVine Foundation would fund a campaign to educate people about gonorrhea. But they have all this criteria and deliverable expectations that ensure it will never happen. Then he wanted me to concoct some sort of reason why gonorrhea is especially bad for OrangeSmash drinkers — as if that has anything to do with it."

"That is the way it is. The OrangeSmash company once killed thousands of people with botulism before it changed its name and became a completely artificial beverage made from flavored soyalgent. They lost most of their market share and now their few remaining customers feel oppressed and discriminated against because their preference is so unpopular — they are in a small minority.

"Some OrangeSmash fans, like the founder of OrangeVine, have drawn conclusions from the struggles against past oppression. People were once deemed inferior based upon the color of their skin and enslaved, raped, tortured, and killed. Others, the first people who lived on this land, were systematically butchered and displaced. Eventually, society recognized the immoral nature of these deeds and took steps to redress centuries of injustice by protecting members of these minorities from continued violence and discrimination."

"I never knew all that."

"I'm certain that you did. It's taught in all the schools. You certainly studied slavery, segregation, and the inhumane treatment of Native Americans.

"But most have forgotten that history, to the extent that it was ever really understood. People can absorb information when it fits comfortably with their identities, but truths of the wrong shape fail to penetrate our consciousness. What you read in schoolbooks went in and out of your mind just as water flows in and out of a river. To really take something in, you need to slow down the flow, like a marsh allows water to gradually seep into the earth instead of running over it. Your schools, your news media, your Department of Information have all added water to the rushing flow of the river, but fossilized your mind's capacity to soak it in."

"OK, but what's that got to do with OrangeVine?"

"OrangeVine's founder can pay attention to information that fits within his identity. He has absorbed one part of our history — that people in a minority deserve respect and equal protection of the law. He is applying that lesson to how he feels due to his ostracized beverage choice."

"Well, he's got a point I guess. Isn't it wrong to discriminate against anyone for anything?"

"Sometimes it is right to discriminate. We single out murderers for their activity, we cast judgment upon their deeds, and we punish them — you could say we oppress them, but it is just. We are intolerant toward those we call Fear Mongers when their actions kill and terrorize people who have done them no harm. We judge their actions, but we should still listen to those who hold views contrary to our own but act in peace."

"Huh. … What's that noise?" Vera interjected as a screech came from a corner of the garden that sounded like a car slamming on its brakes — only much softer.

"A cricket. It rubs its wings together to find a mate. Their sound is unique, but in most of the city crickets cannot be heard over the cars, drones, wall screens, and so on. It is quiet enough here for the crickets' chirp to resonate, which means they can give life to their offspring. Their survival depends upon the silence."

Vera inhaled slowly, taking in the wet, grassy air of the garden as she listened to the crickets.

Aldo waited.

"I still don't see why OrangeVine is so fixated on the plight of soda drinkers that it can't bring itself to care about other things, like gonorrhea."

"OrangeVine's founder does not see the plight of those who suffer from gonorrhea just as you did not see what was done to African Americans and Native Americans when it did not fit within your own experience. For now, this is the way it is."

"But does it have to be that way? What if everyone knew what you just said. What if we found a way to tell them the truth?"

"It is not enough to hear the truth. It is not enough to speak the truth. We must teach others to both absorb and understand the truth. To do that, you must first believe it deep in your heart, not only comprehend it in your head. You must build up your strong core, your stem, which can hold the weight of the truth you seek to lift up. That is not only necessary to provide you with the stamina you will need, but it is safer for you as well."

"What do you mean?"

"That chip in your head can understand what you think with your brain. It can interpret and track the stream of information that is brought in by your eyes and by your ears, for it connects to the mind just where they do. But that is not the entire world. It does not detect what you feel with your hands or with your heart. It cannot detect what you smell. You must build your reality, your core, upon more than your sights and more than your thoughts, for those can betray you."

Aldo took Vera's hand in his. She felt his rough callused skin guide her fingers to the rosebush.

"Feel the soft petals with your skin, breath in their scent with your nose, and remember that sensation in your heart. Feel the barbs of the thorns and know deep inside you the pain they can bring. Do not think about these things — feel them."

He knelt on his hands and knees, beckoning her to follow.

"Feel this stickyweed growing in the garden. Pull it up by its roots. If we want good things to grow, we must first remove the bad. It does not matter that it is too dark to see the leaves, you can discern the weed from the snap pea by its texture."

Aldo taught Vera how to distinguish arugula from dandelions by their smell. He showed her how to grab the dandelions at the base and twist to pull them from the ground. He reached out and felt her face with his fingers and placed her palms on his cheeks. He took in the smell of her breath as she exhaled. His smelled of sunflower shells and salt.

Vera felt intrigued but also slightly creeped out. Aldo was not threatening, yet he was behaving in ways she had never experienced. *Is he trying to make a move on me? Is he trying to tell me something? What was I thinking coming to this place alone at night? Why did Caspian think this would help with anything?*

Aldo stepped back and bowed his head.

"As I said, reality can be disconcerting. It can be a heavier burden than you are able to bear. Think about if this is the path you want to go down. Feel the path with your feet, do not follow it with your eyes." Slowly, he turned and walked out of the garden, leaving Vera to absorb its smells, its sounds, its tranquility.

She stayed for a long time.

CHAPTER 7

Information is more important than knowledge.

— Alfred Eisenstine

The elderly woman moved slowly, almost zombie-like, on the grass by the sidewalk. She wore white cotton shoes and loose-fitting pink silk clothes that looked like pajamas with six horizontal strips of cloth fastening her shirt across the chest. Her motions were graceful and deliberate, sliding her tan arms through the air as her wide face maintained a steady calm. Her black hair brushed the top of her shoulders as she pivoted left, facing Vera directly. Vera felt as though she was watching a 3-D kung fu movie in slow motion, with the woman battling an imaginary opponent.

Vera had taken a slight detour to see what a small crowd had gathered around as she walked from the parking garage to her office. A smiling, demure man offered Vera a flyer, which she accepted: "Clear your mind to free your soul. Tai Chi in the park, daily at 8 a.m."

Nobody else took one.

The crowd dispersed as a news flash popped up on everyone's MyndScreens. Someone had driven a Humvee into a high school football stadium during halftime in Peoria, Illinois. Two men rode in the open back, spraying cheerleaders and the marching band with bullets from Browning .50 caliber machine guns mounted on the roof of the vehicle. A live broadcast captured an aerial helidrone firing a missile directly into the Humvee, sending bits of metal, body parts, and flame into the stands. Dozens were killed, and hundreds injured, in the seventy-eight seconds it took for the entire event to transpire.

Vera's Chatterfeed lit up:

"Double the defense budget!"

"Globalia won't run and hide!"

"We're not afraid of fear! Deport the foreign murderers!"

"Time to ban gold chains, or at least use them to lock up whoever's wearing 'em."

Most commentators assumed that the attack was carried out by Fear Mongers, because the machine gunners were clearly wearing gold chain necklaces in the footage replaying endlessly – a signature look for adherents to one extremist group. Others thought it was the work of clandestine agents of a Russia–Chinasian Evildoer regime posing as Fear Mongers because the gunners had pale skin and blonde hair, while most Mongers were dark-skinned and had black hair. Still others thought they were just three mentally unhinged Neo-WhiteBreits seeking attention. There was little evidence to examine as the drone strike had obliterated the Humvee and its inhabitants.

* * *

The elevator smelled of Windex as Vera stepped inside. She tried to make eye contact with two other people who entered at the same time and asked what floor they were going to, offering to press the button for them.

"Watch *Big Mother*, reality like no uhhh-ther!" sang out the jingle as a screen in the elevator played a clip of the upcoming episode for that night. Nobody said a word.

The people pressed their own buttons.

Vera's work that day was less than interesting. It was ratings week, so the *Two Minute Spate* would be cut to one minute for the entire week. There was half as much need for timely verifiable facts, so the Department was prioritizing research for high school historical texts.

The task was harder than it appeared. There were so many topics that students were expected to learn, and such a copious amount of content to absorb, that each subject needed to be presented extremely efficiently; all while maintaining complete accuracy. Vera was given an entire week's worth of assignments at once:

"Accurately summarize the American Revolution in twenty words."

"Explain Stalinism in twenty words."

"Summarize the Invisible War of the 2020s in twenty words."

"Describe in twenty words how the invasion of Afghanistan in the early 21st century affected the American psyche."

The final assignment intrigued Vera, as she had been born while that war was happening. Indeed, it was still happening.

The war on Afghani Mongers had been a constant fact of life for as long as Vera could remember — probably since about the time the War Unseen ended. She conjectured that the Department would be looking for history texts that would embolden future generations to keep up the fight many decades into the future. They must be looking for an "effect on the American psyche" that was overall positive, or at least lasting.

Beginning her research, she ran across a story of a professional athlete who walked away from a multimillion-dollar contract to join the army — putting his country before himself. After his death on the battlefield, he was posthumously awarded the Silver Star Medal — a high honor granted only to those who demonstrate gallantry in combat with the enemy. Members of Congress and media pundits used him as an example of the heroic character of Americans.

"Perfect," said Vera, aloud. If one needed evidence that the war in Afghanistan was a positive impact on the American psyche, this was it.

But then, there was more.

As Vera read further, she learned that the soldier had not, in fact, died fighting the enemy. He was shot by American troops in his own platoon through a series of tragic mistakes and errors in judgment. Worse yet, high-ranking military officials had known the truth but had deceived the soldier's family and the American public about how he was killed. They had intentionally used his death to feed a false narrative of heroism and the glory of war.

When the facts came out, the incident struck a severe blow to Americans' faith in their own government. Entire books were written, documenting every detail of what happened. The cover-up exploded in the face of top military brass. The very idea that people could trust what they heard on the news programs had been undermined.

Censorship failed in the end, thought Vera. Muckraking journalism had prevailed. The truth had come out. And yet, nobody remembered. The truth that could not be censored had been buried instead, forever lost in a landslide of trivia, data, and images. Worse, while no one could recall the details of the event, the one thing that stuck with them was that nothing was to be believed. Exposing the facts had made it harder for people to believe that any truth existed.

Vera glanced at the motto on her office wall. "She who forgets the past has no future. She who uncovers information creates the past."

It wasn't possible to tell the entire story she had researched in twenty words. Further, she was pretty sure it wasn't the story the Department was looking for. Even if she managed to condense the narrative, it was unlikely the Department would choose these verifiable facts for dissemination into student texts.

While launching a Noodle search on "heroism" to make it appear she was busy working, she went outside for a walk and absentmindedly clicked the links. She found herself in the park, near the fountain where she'd met Chase the previous day. Nobody was there.

A gentle breeze rushed past Vera's ears, sounding like white noise. The air smelled of gunpowder — perhaps from a nearby Monger deportation raid. As she walked back, she heard a yelp — as if somebody were drowning. She looked up and saw a young man, maybe eighteen years old, flopping around on the sidewalk like a fish yanked out of the water. His limbs shook in unison as the back of his MyScreen helmet banged against the sidewalk.

"Help, someone help!" Vera yelled, looking around to see if anyone was nearby. After just a split second of panic, her MyndScreen flashed a response: "Epileptic seizure, need help now." She fired off the thought into the Chatter-feed along with a NoodleMap pin for her geolocation.

She had now reached the man, whose limbs were still rigid. His breathing was erratic, at first rapid but then halting for up to ten seconds before another burst of gasps shook the air. After two minutes, a policeman wheeled up on an electric scooter. "I'll take it from here, ma'am."

He carefully removed the man's virtual reality helmet, revealing a blueish face. Next the policeman inserted a small device with an electronic screen into a port on the side of the helmet. He pulled Vera back as a lifesaving drone descended from the sky and grasped the man's arms in its tentacle-like claws, which dangled below its still whirling rotor, restraining him and somewhat calming the spasms. Other, smaller robotic arms grasped and steadied the man's head while an oxygen mask extended from the center of the levitating drone, covering his nose and mouth. Vera saw a colored puff of vapor fill the clear plastic mask for a few seconds until he inhaled it.

Within seconds, the man calmed down and his limbs relaxed.

"Where am I?" he asked, as the drone released its grip and lifted back up to the sky. He rubbed his temples and winced, either from the pain of a headache or the bright sun reflecting off the white clouds that illuminated his helmetless face.

"You're in downtown Los Angeles," the policeman informed him, not unkindly. "And, judging by your helmet's activity log, you've been playing a lot of video games over the past six hours. Take it easy for the rest of the day and you should be fine."

Vera closed her Noodle search on heroism and slowly returned to the office. She sat down. Using pencil and paper, she drafted a summary about the war in Afghanistan's effect on the American psyche:

"Americans were inspired and emboldened by Pat Tillman's bravery. He sacrificed his fortune, fame, and life in the Afghan war."

It was twenty words.

It was accurate.

It was verifiable.

It concealed an underlying truth.

And yet, Vera was satisfied. It left a trail of breadcrumbs that could lead someone to a profound realization — if they were willing to look for it. A search on Pat Tillman's name would bring up the important details of how his death was falsely portrayed. Placing him as the centerpiece of her research would make it hard for the message distillation team to remove his name or convert it to an emojicon, if the thought even occurred to them.

Hah! They won't even know I'm resisting.

Just for fun, Vera wondered how the condensing department might distill her fact into Effispeech. She came up with this:

* * *

A few days later, as Vera's car pulled into the parking garage near her office, she looked up and saw "I ♥ U V" scrawled with red lipstick across the headlamp of a motorcycle parked directly in front of her usual parking place.

She got out and picked up a folded piece of paper that had been tucked in between the cycle's front fender and tire.

"Meet me in the park at 4:20."

Wow. That's pretty forward. What's with this guy Chase?

Vera's MyndScreen pulled up her bank statement. She smiled as she left the balance on the screen and began walking to her office.

The office was unbearably dull that day. She pinged Phoebe in the Chatter to find out what was new with her, but Phoebe was evidently lot logged in. The Chatterfeed was abuzz about a celebrity who was photographed wearing an outfit that had been worn the previous month by another A-list film star.

"OMG her hairstyle is the SAME as it was six weeks ago," sounded one alarmed commentator.

"That makeup is completely unoriginal," bemoaned another.

"🕒 for a new MyMakeover™?" Vera's MyndScreen reminded her. It had been weeks. *Yes,* she thought and went to schedule it. But then she hesitated.

"Lacks her OwnImage," noted a third comment, using a popular Effispeech term to describe the unique look that everyone was expected to cultivate and update regularly as others followed the same trends.

Appearances do not reveal your true being, Vera thought. To her surprise, her Chatterfeed typed up the comment and asked her whether to submit it. *Why not?* she thought, clicking send.

There was no response.

At 4:15 p.m., she eagerly headed outside for a break. As she was crossing the street, someone grabbed her hand and said, "Don't look, keep walking." She could tell it was Chase by the texture of his fingers and the citrusy smell of his hair.

When they had crossed, he said, "Pull up *My Romance with Big Mother* and let it play while we're talking." Once they both had the program running, Chase stopped and turned to face Vera directly, his eyes boring straight through hers deep down into the squishy insides of her torso.

"Hi."

"Hi," she smiled back. "Like I said, I don't usually do this — and I never do it virtually."

Chase blushed and looked at the tattoo on his arm. "Oh, that," he chuckled. "That helps ensure your Mynd-Screen picks up a normal thought pattern when we meet. It helps protect us both, just like my name."

"What do you mean?" Vera asked.

"It's quite safe to interact emotionally with other people, so long as you don't think too much about it. If the datatrackers keep picking up routine thought signals from your MyndScreen, everything registers as normal. So, the trick is to keep your MyndScreen occupied with ordinary thoughts, freeing up your emotions to experience whatever you want — like how I'm now feeling about you," he said, reaching out to touch her cheek with his fingertips.

"How do you know this? Have you done it before?" Vera was struck by his choice of the phrase "interact emotionally."

"I work for Timeless Warning as an episode writer. My boss knows that I need some level of creative capacity to produce quality content — otherwise I'd just put out drivel like most of my colleagues in the industry. Nobody watches their crap. He also knows that if I got upgraded, he'd have to spend years cultivating and training a replacement. So, he has an interest in keeping me around and cognizant. He's shown me some tricks over the years. The tattoo is one of them."

"And, yes," he said after pausing. "I've done this before. Does that bother you?"

"No," Vera said, truthfully. Fact was, it oddly excited her. She rubbed the tip of her thumb against the palm of his hand, feeling the leathery calluses left by years of gripping motorcycle handlebars. He smiled and said, "Remember how my hand feels."

Her fingertips touched the surface while the muscles of her hand felt the firm pressure of his palm. Deeper inside she sensed something, too, like a lightbulb glowing in her abdomen.

They walked.

"I was married," Vera blurted out. "Still am, technically."

"I know. I Noodled you. … It's OK."

Vera wanted to kiss him. She didn't.

"It's best if we part, for now, V," continued Chase, giving her hand a gentle squeeze. "Keep your Mynd-Screen running."

"When will I be with you again?"

"Soon. You'll see."

And with that, he let loose of her hand and left her standing in the park, by the tulips.

* * *

That evening, the sports segment of the news hour aired a lengthy profile of a gladiator who would be competing in the upcoming weekend's games. These games were the season championship, scheduled at the end of ratings week, so the buildup was intense.

The featured star, Wildey Oddfellow, was fighting to avenge the death of his wife, Jenna, who had died during the half-time segment of a gladiator event exactly one year earlier. In a contest billed as Extreme Hydrathon, the competitors were vying to see who could drink the most cups of water during halftime, without getting up to go to the bathroom.

Jenna had prepared herself by drinking no fluids for twenty-four hours in advance of the event. She had secretly worn adult diapers underneath her clothing. As the challenge progressed, the hosts had marveled at her ability to keep downing glasses of water, joking about how her belly had swelled so much that she looked like she was four months pregnant.

The cheers in the stadium built to a roar as each contestant was eliminated one by one. Soon it was down to just two finalists.

There had been warnings on the Chatterfeed at the time, alerting the tournament hosts about something called water intoxication. One of them had posted a half-joking response saying, "Yeah, we know. We don't think she's got a drinking problem." Other broadcasters built the tension by commenting that there was some actual risk involved in the contest, as with every sport. The

MyndScreen audience built into hundreds of millions worldwide.

Ten minutes later, Jenna collapsed — right on live broadcast. The Chattersphere exploded as a lifesaving drone descended from the sky to swoop her away. She was pronounced dead upon arrival at the hospital.

To atone for her death, in the upcoming weekend's games, the gladiator league had decided to place the host who had sent the insensitive "drinking problem" post atop a fifty-foot marble-colored PLAStick™ column in the middle of the gladiator coliseum. The man would be stark naked, holding only a martini glass filled with water. If Wildey's group, known as a ruffian pod, could reach the column during the competition, he would have the opportunity to knock it down — potentially injuring or killing the host. If the glass didn't break, Wildey and his pod would lose.

During the profile interview, Wildey wore a T-shirt with the words "I'm Your Drinking Problem" on it. A banner on the bottom of the screen said, "If you've got a problem with what you're drinking, Cokaid's got the solution! — Advertising Frees Speech."

Ugh, thought Vera. *There's no escaping it.*

An advertisement for a rectangular blue box, no bigger than a finger, with white wires coming out of the top, popped up on Vera's MyndScreen. The vintage item, called an iPod, was listed on an auction site under the headline of "Escape the hustle and bustle of daily life with meditation." The sales description said that the antique device still worked and was loaded with guided meditation scripts, chimes, and timers.

For weeks, Vera had wanted to pull up the meditation video she had initially found in her MyndScreen search.

She hadn't done it because she was worried that repeated views would be more likely to trigger a metadata point. Maybe guided meditation would give her greater relief than she'd been able to achieve on her own. This antique item was not connected in any way to MyndScreen transmissions.

Vera began playing a *Big Mother Gets Real* episode in another MyndScreen window so that she could safely consider the purchase. Chase had said that the key to avoiding SpeidrWeb tracking was to keep the Mynd-Screen occupied. She imagined that maintaining a regular pattern of purchasing would also keep her data looking normal.

Vera looked at the wilted tulip by her balcony. The petals had fallen off and were beginning to shrivel. She picked up the stem and threw it out but left the petals where they were.

Her MyndScreen still flashed the ad for the meditation iPod. A promotional spot came on for a new investment, IMutual, "In just ten years you could save enough for placement in a top-rated entertainment home, Peaceful Stimulations. Past performance is not indicative of future results."

She bid forty dollars for the iPod.

For dinner, Vera used the Pepsoilent extruder. Her adventure cooking rice and chili had been exciting, but she wasn't up for it again. She chose a Sowl™ menu of macaroni and cheese, barbequed ribs and collard greens and waited for the extruder to produce the meal.

Soul food had been a favorite of Vera's husband. They had married when she was twenty-eight — after a few months of compatibility surveys, dating, credit checks, and genome screening. She supposed that they had first met through the Chatterfeed, but she didn't quite remember. She'd met thousands of people through the Chatter over the years, through more than a million posts. So, statistically speaking, he must have been among them, but it was no longer possible to sort it out.

The few times they had made love had not lived up to her expectations. She was familiar with physical intercourse from a few near random hook-ups in college, but had harbored the idea that, if she met the right partner, it might be more than a purely tactile experience. After graduating, she experimented enough times to debunk that theory.

His breath had smelled of worn socks and his tongue tasted like tepid sashimi-flavored Pepsoilent. He rushed things to a climax and thrust his whole midsection too hard, as they did in the Effiporn segments. She had a desire to give birth to a baby, an irrational urge that she'd been unable to explain to him. He went along with the idea because his parents told him it was the right thing to do. They watched romantic comedy episodes and family sitcoms together but gave it up after two expensive IVF failures. She soon found she preferred her MyMassage vibration lounge, which was fine with him. He immersed himself in a virtual sex app. Vera didn't consider it a form of infidelity, just a convenience that kept him entertained and, quite frankly, less of a hassle.

While she didn't miss him, Vera was beginning to feel like she was missing *someone*. There wasn't any objective explanation for it. She had everything she needed: a tony apartment, cool car, the latest apps on her MyndScreen, thousands of friends on Chatter, endless options for food, and top-rated sexual stimulation from her MyMassage.

She felt that men, generally speaking, weren't reliable or even interesting.

Phoebe poked her in the Chatter, "Hey grlfrnd. How R U?"

"OK, I guess. Wondering if my life would be better if I was with someone."

"A woman needs a man like a fish needs a bicycle! I'll always be your BFF."

Vera laughed, but not too deeply.

* * *

Vera did not see Chase for a week.

One afternoon, when she arrived at her car, she discovered another note stuck underneath the windshield wiper blade:

"Run a MyndScreen search right now on "casinos." On Saturday morning, run the same search and select Las Vegas. Choose "Caesar's Palace, Navigate." When you get to Halloran Springs, take manual control of your car and disengage. Drive 21 miles more and exit on Baily Rd. Turn right (keeping the sun to your right) and drive down a dirt road for 0.8 miles. I ♥ U V."

This guy's pretty cheesy. It's like he thinks life is some sort of romantic comedy.

Still, she couldn't help but smile as she stuffed the note in her purse. There was something almost sincere about his presumptuous missive.

She ran a Noodle search for "Chase," but the first hundred links were all for credit card applications, MyndScreen checking account balancing apps, and career opportunities. The mysterious motorcycle man did not seem to exist online, plus she didn't even know his last name.

When Saturday morning came, Vera didn't bother with either her morning exercise routine or her green tea. She gulped down some Pepsoilent-flavored coffee and an extruded bagel with lox and cream cheese.

Once she was in her car, she ran a Noodle search for Caesar's Palace Casinos. She panicked when her car said it would be a 40-hour drive. She couldn't possibly get there and back during the weekend. Why would Chase send her to such a bizarre location?

Drawing in two deep breaths, Vera retraced her mental steps. Going back a screen from Caesar's Palace she found her Pepsoilent breakfast order for bagels and smoked Atlantic salmon on her MyndScreen browser history. The following screen pulled up Caesar's Palace, but in Atlantic City instead of Las Vegas, no doubt using data recorded by SpeidrWeb from her previous search.

Aha! *Past Pepsoilent is not indicative of future results*, she thought to herself, smirking in recognition that she had created her first bad pun. She was tempted to post it to Chatter, but decided to simply savor the achievement herself.

She re-ran a query for Las Vegas casinos and saw Caesar's Palace pop up as the fourth option. She sent the directions to her car and was on her way.

A gentle rain splashed the windshield as she linked with other cars in an auto-train and slowly slogged through LA traffic. The rhythmic windshield wipers matched Vera's oscillating mood.

The auto-train picked up speed as it left the city, into a barren land she'd never seen. The hills were comprised of reddish mud with washed out crevasses spilling into small gravel alluvial fans. As she sped by a sign saying "Baker" and a small cluster of boarded up buildings,

Vera's car audio speakers and MyndScreen both went silent. The rain had stopped, so even the swishing of the wiper blades no longer kept her company.

The only noise Vera heard was the wind whistling around her car, a faint rush that sounded a bit like the gentle sound she imagined a mountain stream would make.

Immediately after she passed a sign saying Halloran Springs, Vera reached for the red lever to take the MiOtto out of autopilot. Vera pulled back on the joystick in the console and the car slowed, unlatching from the car in front. The auto-train re-engaged itself and sped past as Vera pulled into the adjacent lane.

Resuming her speed, she had to keep her hand on the joystick and was unable to scratch her left elbow, which was itching terribly.

There were numbers scrolling on her dashboard screen that she'd never paid much attention to, gradually increasing as she drove. This must be the mileage gauge, but how far had she already gone? Navigating life without a digital roadmap wasn't easy.

Out of nowhere, a faded green sign appeared on the horizon pointing to Baily Road. She slowed and maneuvered the car off the freeway onto a muddy pathway that looked like it hadn't been driven on in years. With the sky still overcast, Vera could not see the sun, but she felt confident that it would be to her right as she left the highway behind.

Two minutes later, Vera could go no further. Erosion had washed out deep cuts in the road and left small mounds of gravel intruding on the sides.

Wondering what she had gotten herself into, she stepped out of the car. If a wild animal or Fear Monger were to attack, she had no place to hide and nobody to help her. She had no real idea where she was, nor had any way of contacting Chase beyond the MyndScreen range. She was no longer certain she'd gone the right direction when she turned off the freeway.

This isn't rational.

A low, sweet whistle sung through the air to Vera's left. She looked around and saw a reddish rock outcropping rising above the muddy flats. Her eyes followed the rock upwards from the ground. On a ledge one-hundred feet up, a figure dressed in a white T-shirt, yellow rain jacket, and familiar pair of faded blue jeans was waving.

Vera ran up the rocks as Chase scrambled down. They met in an embrace as tight as a wrestler's hold, clasping their hands behind the other's back as Chase arched backward and lifted Vera off her feet. He set her down gently, brushed back her hair, and raised his sunglasses to rest on the top of his head so she could see his eyes. They kissed.

Like an awkward teenager on her first romantic encounter, Vera began unbuttoning her blouse as she'd seen women do in Torryd romances. Chase gently grasped her wrist and whispered, "not yet." He laced his fingers through hers, pulling her around the rock face to a narrow path that headed away from the road.

Vera smiled as they walked quietly through a landscape littered with strange rotting plants as tall and thick as the lampposts on old Olvera Street. The limbs were distorted, with crooked arms flailing upward like an overstuffed inverted octopus. Many had fallen over, but those still standing had tufts of straw-colored fibers extending from the tip of each arm. A pale stench wafted through the air.

"What are those?" Vera asked, breaking the silence.

"This was a desert," he replied. "They were called Joshua trees. They could live on just a few inches of water each winter. The past five years of rain have split them open, killing them off. I came here ten years ago, during a drought, and they were thriving."

"I was wondering why my car's screen said we were driving through a desert," Vera noted. "They should update it. It's more like a mud puddle."

"It's an information desert if nothing else. No Mynd-Screens, no jumbotrons, no entertainment," he replied.

"No *Big Mother*!" Vera laughed.

"And yet, you'd be surprised at what you can find in the emptiness."

They walked uphill for about ten minutes before arriving at a flat area. White clouds surrounded by blue sky reflected in a pool of still water, which stretched eighty feet in front of them. The water was as smooth as glass and crystal clear in the quiet air of the afternoon.

As they approached the water's edge, Vera could see four green circles floating in the middle of the pool. Each was the size of a large pizza, with a lighter green ridge protruding up about a half-inch all around the edge, like a Chicago-style deep-dish crust. Near one of the disks bloomed a single flower with white petals tinged with pink surrounding a bright yellow center. Vera gasped and held her breath a moment as she stared at the lily.

Beneath the plant, a solitary root plunged through two feet of water, sinking into a crack in the sandstone underneath.

"That wasn't here before," Chase said, somewhat astonished.

He moved around to the other side of the narrow pool and sat down, wrapping his arms around his knees. He was directly across from Vera, and she could see his reflection in the water. "Sit," he implored, "and look at me. Really look, without saying a word."

"Oh, come on. For how long?"

"Until something breaks the stillness of the water."

She went along with it, sitting cross-legged and focusing her gaze directly between his eyebrows so that she could see both of his pupils simultaneously. She allowed her breathing to slow until it was barely noticeable. Her eyes began to water and her buttocks ached as they pressed against the hard ground beneath them, yet she did not move. Her thoughts wandered to her meditation sessions back at home, to her former husband, to the thrill and irresponsibility of meeting a relative stranger in the middle of a barren place where anything could happen and help was nowhere to be found. These thoughts came and went. Her attention each time refocused on the dark pupils within Chase's eyes, shining back with a bottomless quality that drew her in.

She sensed his gaze burrowing down inside her, revealing her thoughts, her desires, her fears to him. She felt vulnerable and self-assured at the same instant, knowing within her that it was nothing less or more than the rush of life coursing through her arteries, her heart, her emotions. She was ready for it. She felt his sadness, his mischievousness, his masculinity, his cocky self-confidence. At times, it felt as if her solar plexus would burst open out of serenity, or pain, or excitement.

Could the moment last? The discomfort faded as did the awkwardness of revealing herself to an unknown. For now, she knew him. More than anything she had ever known, or felt, or imagined, she knew the person sitting across from her. Inexplicably, she felt as though she had just begun to know herself.

Dropping out of the sky, a ruddy-headed avocet lighted down in the middle of the pool, a ripple emanating around it. It dipped its head in the water and bathed, refreshing itself from a long migratory flight.

She giggled.

"Now?" she mouthed to Chase, raising her eyebrows and bringing her hands to her blouse.

He nodded, smiled, and stood up.

She took her time undressing, one button at a time, as his eyes soaked up the smoothness of her skin reflecting in the rippling water. She stood naked to the world and to him, at ease with her body and mind and her whetting appetite.

He quickly removed his clothes as she jumped in the water, sending the avocet aflight long before it was ready. The pool was too shallow to swim in, but she pulled herself through with her fingertips gripping the sandstone bottom and emerged right in front him — shiny, wet, and with goosebumps all over her body.

Vera had never felt so present. She could hear his breath releasing out his nostrils as she smothered his mouth with hers. With her MyndScreen out of range and no sounds of civilization, she noticed not only the smell of his hair and the shivers down her back, but also the fullness inside her as Chase gently pressed down. She looked up and saw soft white clouds hanging effortlessly in the sky. She became self-conscious of her own sounds, but then ecstasy blew away all contemplation and the world became empty, and still, and quiet.

They lay silently for a long time. A faint, slightly lemony scent tickled Vera's nose. For a long moment, she heard nothing but the beat of his heart underneath her ear. Eventually, a trickle of water dripped into one end of the pool.

"This is dangerous," Vera whispered, as much to herself as Chase. She could feel hard pebbles underneath her, pressing deeper into her skin. She rolled onto her side, resting her head against his shoulder.

He smiled and looked deep into her eyes. "Living entails risks. Avoid all danger and you are not really alive."

"I'm sorry I was so eager earlier," she said, while putting her blouse back on. "But you have to admit it was pretty weird for you to suddenly declare your love on a motorcycle headlight after barely meeting me."

"Subtlety has become invisible, my love. If you want someone to notice you, you have to go big, go all in. When I saw you having your driveway moment, listening to that story about the protesters, I knew you were someone who pays attention. I was drawn to that. I went all in, and you noticed. Are you sorry for that?"

"No."

Moments later, Chase was less philosophical. "When we leave, you must continue on to Las Vegas and spend the rest of the weekend at the casino. Gamble heavily and do lots of shopping. The datatrackers have no way of knowing we were here or were together anywhere. I will go to Lake Mead. It will be a while before we can meet again."

"How do you know all this?"

"My boss, Ned Bernaise, at Timeless Warning, needs to keep me around. The company has exclusive rights for MyndScreen broadcasts, so I know how to find the coverage map. When you're out of range, like we are here, your mind can wander and nobody will ever know. It's funny how to find something, or someone, you need to get away from everything else."

"Does Timeless Warning also do the SpeidrWeb metadata collection?"

"That has been outsourced to Noodle," he said. "But they're bringing it in-house now that Renaissance Mercenary has bought Timeless Warning. They're really building up the datatracking department and using the information they gather to tell us what sort of content they want."

"Wait, Renaissance owns Timeless Warning too? They just bought LingerLife Pharmaceuticals and their CEO is a total fraud. What sort of content is Timeless telling you they want these days?"

"Lately, believe it or not, it's been poetry. They'd love to claim that Timeless Warning invented poetry. I bet if I could prove that to them, I could retire and move out to the country — where MyndScreens never reach. Trouble is, if I started searching around for poetry I'd probably get engrossed in reading the stuff. My productivity would drop and then Bernaise would have no interest in protecting me. So, I'll just keep cranking out scripts to daytime dramas and skipping out of range when I can — especially if you'll join me."

While she'd been experimenting with mental escape, the idea of physically outrunning MyndScreen transmissions had never occurred to Vera. She knew that there were rural places, beyond MyndScreen broadcasts, and that these regions weren't entirely unpopulated. But the thought of abandoning civilization entirely had been too farfetched to entertain.

"Sounds better than an entertainment home," she replied. "They make it sound like a paradise, to receive your MyndScreen upgrade and spend the rest of your years being pampered twenty-four-hours-a-day. But I think there's something creepy about it."

"What's creepy is that you no longer have any thoughts of your own," he replied. "You spend all your existence consuming entertainment — and it's not just taking up your time but really all your brain's cognitive capacity. The ads sound awesome, but it's a living hell."

That confirmed it. While they had not talked politics, indeed they had hardly spoken much at all since they'd met, Vera had an instinct that Chase also was looking to escape the world of infotainment, the world of *Big Mother*.

"The only reason they market these entertainment homes so much is they're required to get your consent before the upgrade," he continued. "They don't target you until you've saved up enough money to cover an annuity for indefinite care — unless, that is, the datatrackers identify you as an economic security threat. That's why we need to be careful."

Vera stared at the water lily, the edges of its petals lighting up as the sun fell lower in the horizon. As she sat up, Chase admired the silhouette of her body against the sky and pulled a harmonica out of the pocket of his jeans as he put them back on. He played a tune that Vera hadn't heard before, with sad slow notes that built into an upbeat ditty.

"What's with the song?" she asked.

"'Sole Sister.' They play it all the time." Chase said. "Here's a little life hack for you. If you associate a feeling with a song, every time you hear that song it will evoke the feeling. The datatrackers won't know, all they pick up on is the fact that you're listening to a song — not the emotions that go with it. Come here." He wrapped his arms around Vera, spooning her as she faced away from him, soaking in his embrace.

He sung.

"Your lipstick stains
On the left lobe of my
 World-wide brains
I knew I couldn't forget you
And so I had to let you
Own my mind.
Let you own my mind."

Vera grasped his arms and thought a moment. Speaking of sisters, "what do you think about the Sisterhood?" Vera asked, as she stood up and pulled on her pants.

"If they existed, I'd be rooting for them," replied Chase, somewhat lightheartedly as he put the harmonica away.

"But don't you want to believe in something? Even if you can't objectively prove it exists, wouldn't your belief in it make it real for you? If you don't believe in anything, then what's left?

"I believe in you, V." He kissed her neck. "There's no way to bring down the Establishment. The best you can do is outsmart it. Escape it. Like we're doing now. It'll blow your mind."

He pulled Vera on top of him and entangled her in another round.

CHAPTER 8

Is not the truth the truth?

— Sir John Falstaff, Henry IV
by William Shakespeare

Vera had never been more flattered. In fact, up to now, she'd never felt flattered at all.

In response to a post Vera had sent into the Chattersphere, Aneeka Randall had commented — *the* Aneeka Randall — drawing hundreds of responses.

"Truth is more important than accuracy," Vera had said.

"And we all can find our own truth," Aneeka replied, sparking a chorus of agreement:

"Empowering,"

"True dat!"

Even Phoebe had chimed in, "I find my truth at Macys.com! ☺"

Vera had made her original comment out of frustration with the coverage of the presidential selection. A major infotain producer had released a story documenting that, years earlier, leading presidential candidate Susan Downley had received promotions in the army even though she was absent from her base over extended periods of time. The story claimed she had not received the required military leave and alleged that her promotions were due to her family's connections to political donors and powerful CEOs.

Downley's absences had been well documented over time, with dozens of pictures surfacing of her sunning on the beach or drinking at a nightclub while her battalion had been on assignment. Favoritism had long been suspected as the reason Downley was not reprimanded, but it had never been proven. It was old news.

That changed when somebody leaked a series of six documents, known at the time as emails, between Downley's superior and Charlie Coach, a prominent investor and political donor. One email appeared to be a request for the commanding officer to look the other way:

"I understand that military discipline is important and that the army is a demanding place for both soldiers and senior officers. I know that you also understand the world is a complicated place and that the military is stronger when its commanders have friends and allies in high places. I can, in all truth, assure you that should you find means to protect the interests of the country in the matter regarding S. Downley, that your efforts will not go unnoticed or unappreciated."

Property records at the time showed conclusively that, shortly after the email was sent, Downley's commanding officer acquired a home in the Florida Keys valued at one-hundred-and-thirty times his annual salary.

The story took an additional twist when the *Two Minute Spate* reported that three of the six leaked emails had been proven forgeries. This was an undeniable fact, authenticated by the Department of Information.

Many people rejected the entire story as a falsehood. Even though she hadn't worked on the research at the Department, Vera wondered if the underlying charge of favoritism could be correct even if some aspects of the narrative were inaccurate. The email suggesting that the officer's lenience would be appreciated was not among the three emails proven to be forgeries. Vera wasn't authorized to research additional aspects of the story for the Department, nor did she really have time to.

So, Vera just sent out her comment about truth and accuracy into the Chattersphere without reference to anything in particular. It appeared that she had struck a nerve, with none other than Aneeka Randall. Vera blushed at the realization that a nationally recognized expert had publicly acknowledged she viewed the world in the same way Vera did. She scratched her elbow as it dawned on her that if Randall believed this too, could it be evidence that there really was a movement like the Sisterhood? Maybe that meant Vera should be in it too.

*　*　*

That evening, Vera had plans to meet Chase at the opera. It had been at least a week since their trip to the desert, and she had avoided reaching out to him with a Chatterfeed message, which could easily be tracked. She found a note tucked under her car windshield wiper as she left work:

"Meet me at the performance hall at 7:30 for the opera. Find me in section B."

Vera arrived early, dressed in a tight-fitting black dress with a string of pearls around her neck. She had painted her lips crimson red and drawn her hair back into a bun. Before she left, she took a PainZapper pill to ward off any potential headaches, but as she swallowed it, she wondered if was really necessary.

Having time to kill, rather than entering the building, Vera glanced down the street. Next to the opera hall stood an art gallery with a "Going out of Business" sign hanging in the window, and she decided to peek inside. A table near the door held a small bowl of mixed nuts and a note saying, "Back in ten minutes, please have a look around."

On an interior wall facing the entrance, an impressionistic painting of olive trees on rolling hillsides covered with golden grass hung directly adjacent to a color photograph of the identical scene. A black and white photograph appeared on the left, also of the same landscape. Vera examined the images carefully. She thought the color photograph in the center was an accurate rendition of the landscape, with every detail presented true to life.

The painting on the right looked more like a sketch done with paintbrushes. Its colors were exaggerated and its lines blurred together, leaving an image that was imprecise and yet evoking more emotion than the color photograph. While staring at the painting, Vera felt as if she was transported to the landscape it depicted. She could imagine the sounds of the wind blowing through the leaves and of hidden birds singing in the branches. It made her feel cheerful, serene, and almost in awe of the natural setting. The black and white photograph had crisp lines but lacked the details of color presented in the other two images. It felt silent — conjuring no illusions of the sounds of nature. Yet, the texture of the tree bark seemed more apparent and the light bouncing off the clouds appeared more radiant than in the other two. A rounded boulder popped up through the grass underneath one of the olive trees. It had a similar shade gradation as the dried grass, yet a completely different shape and smoothness. When she looked back at the full color photo, she saw it was there too — but she had somehow missed it at first glance. The black and white image made Vera feel alert to study it, as if she was noticing minutiae about the world that she had been overlooking her entire life.

The center image is the most accurate and has the most complete visual information. But the painting feels more authentic and the black and white more detailed. Sometimes less can be more.

Once in the theater, Vera saw six jumbotron screens on either side of the stage, each playing either an infotainment episode, sports highlight reel, or promotional clip for products and refreshments sold in the lobby. The growing crowd bustled with energy, talking boisterously among themselves above the steady din of the jumbotrons.

One screen showed an interview with a middle-aged man whose daughter had reportedly run away to join the Sisterhood. "I don't get it," he said, his words scrolling across the bottom of the screen. "She told me she was attending a pottery-making class, and an hour later I get a police report that her MyndScreen had been disabled and they couldn't locate her. That was a week ago and we haven't seen or heard anything from her."

The opera hall was bustling with activity. Nearly everyone in the crowd was standing, waving to acquaintances who had poked them in the Chattersphere as they found their seats and shouting greetings across the packed performance hall. Vera looked in vain for Chase, or any familiar face, but there was no sign of either.

At 7:28 p.m., Vera heard a voice yelling her name. She turned around to see Manquin, her neighbor at Magnificent Estates, beckoning her to come toward him. Given that she had no seat or companion, she couldn't quickly think of an excuse not to respond. As the show was about to begin, she walked over quickly.

"Hey Vera, don't you look smashing!" gushed Manquin. "Our babysitter canceled at the last minute, so my wife had to stay home with the kids. I say she's the lucky one — it means she'll get to watch *Big Mother Gets Real* undistracted while I'll have to multitask it here while the opera is playing. Say, since she's not here, I've got an extra seat. Why don't you join me?"

Nothing could have been worse. But Vera had no choice. Without finding Chase, she had nowhere to sit. Her eyes stung and her vision blurred as if they were filled with drops of water — something she couldn't recall experiencing before.

"Ladies and gentlemen," said a soothing but firm voice over the loudspeakers. "Please take your seats and finish your conversations. The show is about to begin. Out of respect for your fellow audience members, we must insist that you refrain from all audible conversation until the performance ends. Feel free to share your thoughts and appreciation of the players over Chatter using the hashtag OperaRocks."

Vera hesitated a moment and then sat as the room fell silent. She had worried that Manquin would bend her ear with reality TV gossip, but the warning seemed to have silenced him as well as everyone else — either that or he had already begun streaming the *Big Mother* episode in his MyndScreen.

"I love you V!"

The words rang out like a bell in the dead of night. Vera stood up and, along with dozens of people, turned around to see Chase. He was standing up five rows back, waving both arms with a broad smile across his face. His orange shirt nearly matched the color of the seatbacks. When she had come in, it was simply too crowded and noisy to find him.

The audience heads surrounding Vera turned back to the jumbotron screens up front, fearful that they might be ejected for engaging in conversation during the show — although it had not yet begun. Vera thought she should explain to Manquin what had happened, but he appeared not to have noticed either her standing up or Chase's shout.

The hall went dark and the stage lit up.

Being trapped next to Manquin during an entire opera while Chase was just a few rows back was unbearable. It would be better to get kicked out. Vera stood up and walked calmly back to his row. Saying, "excuse me" multiple times, she maneuvered past six people to reach the open seat next to him.

Nobody said a thing.

"It's OK," Chase whispered, grabbing her hand and sliding it onto his lap. She squeezed.

The show was wonderful, although Vera rather wished they had stopped the jumbotrons during the performance. That would have made it easier to read the subtitles that flashed on small screens on the back of each seat — along with ads for Cokaid.

Why the hell do they still do operas in Italian? thought Vera, a dead language that was no longer spoken anywhere.

As the music built to a crescendo near the end of the show, Vera was filled with joy. The ache she had felt in her stomach when searching for Chase had been replaced by a warm glow. She was only briefly ashamed at herself for doubting for even a moment that he had come.

Vera spontaneously blurted out a post into the Chatter:

"Breaking the silence is easier than breaking through the noise."

Without a second thought, she hit send, just as the tenor reached a high note that seemed to go on forever.

There was no response.

* * *

The next day, Vera received a Chatterfeed notice from the auction company. She'd won the collectable iPod with the guided meditation scripts.

"Please let me know the address to ship the item," said a note from the seller. "Alternatively, you can pick it up from my home. I also offer privacy apps for your MyndScreen that can block meta-datacrawlers. 100% legal. Signed, A. Randall."

Vera's jaw hung agape.

It was her. There could be no doubt that A. Randall was Aneeka Randall.

Further, Vera was now certain that Aneeka Randall was indeed part of the Sisterhood. *A privacy app?*

With her pulse throbbing inside her head, Vera carefully responded. "I can pick it up." There was not an immediate response.

* * *

Vera's first assignments at work felt tedious.

"How much has the Globalian Entertainment Consumption Index increased over the past twenty years?"

"By what percentage has manufactured soyalgent food production exceeded traditional food product outputs over the past ten years?"

She cranked out fairly straightforward facts along with substantiating proof and passed them up the chain of command for fact checking and Effispeech conversion. Her third assignment was more interesting.

"Has growth in poetry ratings led to an increase or decrease in property values?"

How odd, thought Vera. *Why would anyone want to know that?*

For whatever reason, the assignment gave Vera a plausible excuse to research something that might interest Chase. She couldn't stand poetry, so was unlikely to get pulled into reading any poems that she came across. And, her research was part of a work assignment, so any metadata reports would not flag any personal interest or marketing potential in her queries.

Vera found that poetry had experienced somewhat of a renaissance from 2017–2025. In the decade after that, the number of top-rated poets diminished but the sheer sales of poetry skyrocketed.

In an article that would surely thrill Chase, Vera found:

"In 2024, newly formed infotainment conglomerate Timeless Warning signed the top three leading poets to ten-year, multibillion-dollar contracts. Known as the SuperBards, Roberta Willon, Len Coughman, and Wally Jovialson were promoted heavily and for years outsold even the top mystery writers and romance novelists on the best sellers lists. Timeless Warning was credited as 'reinventing' poetry by finding a way to market it to the masses, one line at a time."

If Timeless Warning couldn't claim to have invented poetry, reinventing it was next best. She sent that article to Chase via Chatterfeed, not worried that the communication would be flagged. "Thought this might be useful for your work." She smiled while signing it, "2U from V."

Vera continued researching. There were dozens of pictures of the three poets, who had achieved celebrity status — complete with their names etched into sidewalks along with golden stars. For a period of about ten years, tour buses took rubbernecking sightseers on guided trips through the trendy neighborhood where all three had private residences.

In searching for property values in the chic neighborhood, Vera discovered they had increased during most of the ten-year period that the SuperBard tours were in operation. They had also increased since then, while other neighborhoods had gone down in value. Vera wondered about the larger population of lesser-known poets who had seen sales of their work diminish during the period of the SuperBards' stardom. She had no way to research that, nor could she find any expert analysis of it.

Vera settled on the following fact to send up her chain of command:

"High ratings of top poets during the SuperBard era correlate with an increase of property values in the immediate neighborhoods of the poets."

* * *

That afternoon, A. Randall replied through the online auction form, "OK. The address is 861 West Rustic Road. Drop by anytime this evening."

Vera gripped the arms of her chair so tightly that her hands turned pale.

She had been excited that morning and had nervously checked back all day for a response from A. Randall. Now that it arrived, she felt uncertain.

Maybe A. Randall wasn't Aneeka Randall at all. And even if she was, Vera had no real evidence that she was a member of the Sisterhood. *Am I really going to do this?*

Vera's MyndScreen lit up with a breaking news broadcast. John Robertson, the CEO of LingerLife Pharmaceuticals, was announcing a major philanthropic venture to distribute antibiotics in South America to combat gonorrhea. LingerLife would donate one-million free doses of the drug, and Robertson was personally hiring gladiator Wildey Oddfellow to embark on a goodwill tour to promote the drug in seven countries that were severely stricken with the disease. A smiling Robertson announced that he'd personally donate ten percent of his recent stock-option windfall, a result of the increase in share price following the positive attention from Delilah Fish's breast pump auction. LingerLife's parent company, Renaissance Mercernary, was so excited about the project it was going to reach out to its frequent business partner Noodle to see if they would finance one-million MyndScreen implants for underprivileged South American youth. Both leading presidential candidates were lauding the announcement as the perfect example of how technology, celebrity, and charity can combine to make people's lives better. Timeless Warning had even coined a new Effispeech term for it: CeleTecharity.

Vera fumed. She knew what she had to do.

She left the office early and waited in the parking lot for Chase to find his cycle. It was six-thirty when he arrived.

"Hey there!" he smiled.

"What took you so long?"

"It's ratings week. I was in the office working on a season finale for one of my daytime drama shows. What's up?"

"Start an episode of *Big Mother* and come with me," Vera said, taking him by the hand.

They walked through the park where they had first officially met. When they were by the fountain, she sat down on a pink park bench and looked straight ahead as she talked. "Run a search saying, 'I need a candle.' OK?"

"Uh, OK," said Chase. Moments later, "So, I've got lots of candle options."

"Good. Start browsing them and listen carefully. Don't respond until I'm done. Tonight, I'm going to meet someone named Aneeka Randall. She's a high-ranking Establishment member who is part of the Sisterhood. I need you to come with me. Depending upon what she says, I might never see you again otherwise. They might give me an assignment, and who knows what that could entail or where I'd have to go. Please, Chase, will you come?"

"I'm looking at some nice candles, V. Are you sure yours isn't burning on both ends? Where will this wind up?"

"Listen, Chase. I can't go on living in a world where nothing is real. Where nothing's true. Since I met you, I understand what's been bothering me for years. Everyone knows the Establishment edifice is a fraud, but everyone goes along. It's because they think everything in the whole world is a fraud — that there is no truth anywhere so you might as well enjoy yourself and go along for the ride. But you know that's not right. When you held me in the desert, that was real, wasn't it?"

"Yes."

"You said that living entails risks. I want to feel alive, and I want you there with me."

"OK, V. I believe you," he sighed, not sounding entirely convinced.

"Get in the car. I'll bring you back to your cycle when we're done so your it won't track the trip."

*　*　*

Her car took them west, eventually turning along the coastline past a deserted beach so infrequently visited that Vera had forgotten it existed. They turned off the highway and abruptly took a sharp right turn, back toward the city. A few blocks later, the car turned left, and headed into a narrow canyon with a landscape unlike anything Vera had ever seen. Lush trees towered overhead, almost like a rainforest.

"Look," she said to Chase, as they got out of the car. She pointed up to a flock of large red birds with patches of yellow and blue across their shoulders. They were perched high up in the canopy of a large tree, fluttering their wings.

"Parrots," she whispered. "These used to be people's pets, but before that they came from the tropics. I saw a documentary on them."

They held hands with fingers interlocked and walked up a driveway next to a post with the number 861 on it. Vera guessed that the post had once held a mailbox.

They stopped momentarily at a gate until a voice welcomed them over a speaker with a "come in," and the gate swung open. Vera could feel her pulse beating in her fingers, which were pressed firmly against the back of Chase's hand. The sidewalk felt like it went on forever, climbing uphill to the elegant but compact bungalow above.

The door opened before they reached it. Aneeka greeted them, dressed in black pumps and an indigo-colored flowing dress with a plunging neckline. Her short, upswept hairstyle accentuated her delicate ears, each adorned with a jade earring hanging down in a teardrop shape from a sterling silver top. Vera gawked for a moment at the matching jade pendant, which dangled from a long silver chain around Aneeka Randall's neck like a piece of history. Her gaze fell upon Aneeka's incandescent eyes, as she wondered if the gemstones were real. She expected a Noodle search to pop up, helping her identify and price the jewels but for some reason nothing appeared on her MyndScreen.

"Ahem," Chase sputtered, squeezing Vera's hand uncomfortably hard.

"Come in," beckoned their hostess. She walked them to a room on the side of the house, with large picture windows looking up the canyon into the trees. A small blue device sat on a desk, with two white wires coming out of it, each ending in a round disk.

One wall was entirely covered with shelves, each stacked completely full of books. The desk and accompanying chairs were made from what looked to be real wood, with yellow whorls of grain swirling across the brown aged oak. The chairs had tan leather seats and backs, with soft creases and just a few scratches blemishing the surface. A rich, silk carpet covered the floor, with hues of scarlet, plum and emerald green. Behind an ornate ironwork grate, flames rose from logs nestled in a brick fireplace, sending a smell of hickory smoke into the room.

Chase ran his fingers along the walls, which were covered in a brass mesh that reminded Vera of the chicken wire surrounding Aldo's community garden. The thin strands of metal softly reflected the shine from a 20th century lamp perched on the desk. A map of the Chinasia region hung on the wall, but with different political boundaries than those familiar to Chase and Vera. A golden statue of a creature, sitting cross-legged and with the head of an elephant, a bulging belly, and four human arms, rested on a stone pedestal by the window. One of his outstretched hands held a lotus flower and another a tusk.

"My office," announced Aneeka. "The walls are electrified. It creates a Faraday cage, which blocks MyndScreen transmissions. We can talk here without interruption." Vera watched as Aneeka rubbed the jade pendant hanging from her neck — a nervous tick perhaps.

Another woman, who seemed to be a servant, brought in a tray with three glasses of wine and an assortment of real cheeses. *So, this is what it's like to live as part of the High Establishment.*

Vera took a glass and slowly sat down. Chase walked over to the books. "Where did you get all these?"

"I find some through online auctions, but you have to be careful there," replied Aneeka. "Most are from Paris. There are little stands all along the river there that still sell old things ... like books."

"May I?" Chase asked, pulling down one with the words "Poems by Roberta Willon" written on the black spine in gilded letters. It was next to a book titled *The Fountainhead.*

"Of course," Aneeka responded. She pivoted to Vera, who sat starstruck on the wooden chair. "So. The item you bid on is here," she motioned to the desk, fingered her necklace, then paused. "Is that the only reason you came?"

Chase sat down next to Vera, stepping on her toes in the process. Startled, she looked at him crossly and then turned her head back to Aneeka.

"No. That's not all," Vera said, her voice cracking initially but growing stronger by the end of the short sentence. She recalled Chase's words from the desert. *Sometimes you have to go big.*

Aneeka sipped her wine and slowly crossed her left leg over her right. Her eyes twinkled and a slight smile split her lips. "Well? Tell me...."

"We are here to join the Sisterhood." Vera ignored the painful itch on her elbow. "We believe it exists and that you are a member, perhaps even a leader. We are tired of a world where too much of everything means too little of anything is real, where we are so inundated with episodes and jingles and ads and facts and flavors and gladiators and chatter and news programs and celebrities and lies and fashion and music and even the truth that we have lost the capacity to think for ourselves. It's not so much that we *want* to join the Sisterhood, but that we *need* to. Our sanity, our joy, our sense of purpose depends upon it."

"Wow," said Aneeka, softly as she took another sip of wine. She looked at Chase, who was shifting in his seat and glancing down at the book he still held in his hand. "And you?"

Vera's breathing stopped.

It's a trap. She'd just walked into it, and now Aneeka Randall was luring in Chase. She gripped the wooden arms of her chair and shot him a look of panic. Chase felt the pages of the book flip through his fingers.

"Yes. Me too."

The silence was devastating as Aneeka peered into their eyes.

"OK, then. I can help you."

Vera exhaled.

"You realize that the road you are embarking on will almost certainly lead to your death, exile, or upgrading. That none of us, not even the most committed, have a final plan for toppling the Establishment. The struggle alone gives us purpose, and this is enough. You realize it's hopeless, don't you?"

"Yes," Vera replied, sounding more confident than she felt.

"You understand that most of us have lost so much capacity for creative independent thought that we barely know the world we are living in — let alone how to change it. Objectively speaking, we cannot perceive what we are up against because we are completely immersed inside it. We must act more on faith than on facts."

"We understand," Vera replied.

"You understand that much of the infotainment we consume shields us not only from joy and insight but also from pain, sorrow, fear, hatred? To experience reality, you will experience feelings that will be new to you and possibly unbearable. Are you willing to do that?"

"Yes."

"You will need to cut yourself to inflict pain and soak in its sensations. You will need to starve yourself for days on end, purging what little food you do place into your body until you are thin, emaciated, and weak. You will experience hunger, deprivation, lacerations, bruises, aches, vile smells, intolerable sounds, sensations of drowning, and pitch blackness that will make you feel more alone and afraid than you can even imagine. Are you willing to do that?"

"Yes."

"The periods of pain will be punctuated with days, even weeks, of joy where your heart will feel like it is about to burst only to then experience the emptiness of sorrow and loss when it deflates."

"We know."

"Your MyndScreens will attempt to distract you from these unpleasant sensations. It is possible, indeed likely, that your experiences will create metadata points that will target you for immediate upgrades. If you consent to that, you will have left the Sisterhood. It will be over. Do you understand?"

"Yes."

"You may be called upon to engage your colleagues at work, your neighbors, your families. You may need to disrupt their MyndScreen transmissions. You may be asked to lie, cheat, and steal. You may be asked to kill. Are you sure you're ready to do that?

Vera thought about the serene look in the radical protester's eyes as he was facing deportation and near certain death. "Yes."

"You may reach a point where you need to disable your MyndScreen permanently by whacking your skull with a ball-peen hammer. If you do it wrong, you risk debilitating brain damage. Are you certain you are capable of that?"

"I'm certain."

"We may provide you with new identities, new jobs, new lives. You may need to disfigure yourself, altering your face through reconstructive surgery or pharmaceutical injections, altering your retina through biorobotics, altering your body shape through liposuction or contour enhancement, altering your hair color, your nose, your smile, your fingerprints. Are you willing to do that?"

"Yes."

"We may need to relocate you to different cities, perhaps different countries. We may need to separate you, sending you to different locations with no guarantee that you will see each other again."

"No," Chase blurted out. He looked at Vera and back at Aneeka Randall. "No," he repeated more softly, but still resolute.

"Chase is the one thing that is real in my life," Vera said, after drawing in a deep breath. "If I let that go, I'll have lost the only thing I believe in. The only reason to resist."

Aneeka Randall gazed at them both.

"Understood. Your love for one another will give you strength. You may hold onto that, if you choose."

"What happens next?" Vera wanted to know.

"You will leave here together, but part as soon as you can, and try not to think about one another. That would almost certainly trigger metadata records on both of you. Devise a plan to meet each other as a matter of routine habit, so that it happens without your anticipation or planning. Wait for instructions from us."

"That's it?" asked Chase.

"You can begin your journey toward independent thought by reading a book, *The Book*. It will describe, as best as we know, how we arrived at our current predicament. It details the Great Saturation, the Secret War, how MyndScreen transmissions began, and the underlying structure of Globalia's economy and security. Perhaps it will spark some ideas as to how we might get out from it. You should read it in a place where you are beyond MyndScreen range, not only to avoid metadata trackers but you'll find the content is rather dense, and it requires your undivided attention. It's a difficult read."

"There is only spotty MyndScreen transmission in this canyon. When you get out to the highway, each of you must run a Noodle search for something called MyMind26. It's a privacy app that will self-install once you click on it and accept the licensing permissions. It won't bar all transmissions or emergency signals, but it will block the metadata trackers for at least a month or so until it becomes outdated or compromised. You can read *The Book* safely when you are running the app."

"You have it here; *The Book* I mean?" Chase asked, eying the shelves.

"Downtown, near the Department of Information, there is an old building at the corner of 5th and Grand. It's called a library and it has thousands of books all sitting on shelves just waiting for someone to read them. I'm going to give you a piece of paper now with the name of one of those books. Look at the name while we are in this Faraday cage and then immediately put it out of your mind — it's not that memorable. Fold the piece of paper and put it someplace you are likely to forget about it. When you run across it again, do not open it. Take it to the library, and hand it to the librarian without looking at it or thinking about its title or contents. This will require discipline."

Aneeka ripped a sheet of thick, vellum paper from a leather-bound tome on her desk. Vera winced — it seemed a terrible thing to destroy such a sturdy book. She unscrewed the cap on a bottle filled with a black liquid and dipped an eight-inch long stick with a sharp metal end into the bottle. Using the instrument to scribble on the paper, she wrote:

"A People's History of Globalian Thought and Truth — Revised and Updated Edition, by Bernice Wohrn." Vera watched Aneeka's lips pucker as she blew a stream of air over the wet ink. When the page dried, she flipped it around and on the backside wrote, "Don't read this. Just hand it over."

"You will cut your right thumb with a razorblade while you are shaving your armpits the morning before you go in. Show them the cut when they ask to scan your thumbprint at the library check-out desk. They will then ask you to fill out a form instead. Use my name and my address, as these will soon become obsolete." She paused, only briefly. "We will meet again only on the other side, in a world that has no drudgery."

Vera stood up and took the piece of paper, all the while looking straight into Aneeka Randall's eyes. She folded it and stuck it into her purse. Chase stared at the carpet and shuffled his feet.

"Don't forget this," Aneeka laughed, handing Vera the iPod she had purchased in the auction. "Meditation will indeed clear your mind, if that's what you really want."

"I do," Vera smiled.

Aneeka Randall gave her an unexpected farewell hug. Vera took in the scent of honey and jasmine blossoms on her skin and closed her eyes a moment. Then, she turned quickly and left, with Chase following.

When they had firmly closed the doors to Vera's car, Chase exploded. "You've got the hots for her! You just signed away our lives because you have a crush on Aneeka Randall."

"Don't be ridiculous. Why ever would you say that?"

"C'mon. You two were gazing into each other's eyes the entire time we were there. And, you were checking out her cleavage — don't think I didn't see."

"I was just admiring her necklace, Chase. Women do that sort of thing. Don't be jealous. We were there because it's the right thing to do, and you know it! Don't you get all squishy on me after all your big talk in the desert about taking risks," Vera fumed.

"Are you kidding? Did you hear what they're going to do to us, or were you just making goo-goo eyes with her the whole time? Bulimia. Cutting. This is bad stuff, V."

"She's obviously survived it, and we will too. And I wasn't making goo-goo eyes. I admit that she's attractive and that I feel drawn to her. But that's only physical chemistry. You're the only one I love. The only one I've ever loved."

She had shared too much. After that, there was no convincing him.

They argued for about ten minutes of the drive back to Chase's motorcycle before sitting the rest of the way in silence. Vera's head ached. This wasn't supposed to happen. Just as her resistance was coming together, her world was falling apart.

Chase got out of Vera's car without saying a word. As she watched him drive away, an empty ache swelled inside Vera's abdomen. She understood why people had abandoned physical romance for virtual sex.

As her upper incisors pinched down on her lower lip, a thought drafted itself in her Chatterfeed: "Reality bites." Impulsively, she hit send and found a chorus of immediate agreement.

Phoebe chimed in. "Boy troubles?"

Vera replied with, "☹."

"Men are from Mars, Vera. And if you believe in space aliens, I've got some real estate in New Mexico to sell you."

When Vera finally arrived home that evening, she saw the petals from the tulip Chase had given her had become shriveled up, dry, and brittle. She gathered them carefully and added the shards of flower to the potpourri she had purchased from the Vue woman, taking a moment to inhale its fragrance and let it waft around her apartment.

* * *

The morning sky was low and gray, providing an uninspiring background for the whirring delivery drones that buzzed through the air on Vera's ride to work. Electric driverless buses hummed along the streets, making screeching sounds as they came to each stop to pick up Vue passengers. The electronic billboards on the sides of the buses scrolled through the usual litany of ads: "Announce Your Individuality with a New Line of Fashion; Check Out the Latest Flavor of Pepsoilent; Watch *Big Mother* — Reality Like No Other! by Timeless Warning — Amusement is Peace." The jingle played itself in Vera's head.

City Hall Plaza was abandoned as Vera walked from the parking garage to her office. Not even the squirrels were out today. Her shoes made clacking sounds on the concrete that seemed to fill the void. She stopped at a bakery and purchased a Pepsoilent bagel with strawberry-chocolate-cream-cheese-flavored spread and devoured it when she reached her desk.

Her assignments that day were not appealing:

"How many different outfits did the first woman president wear during her tenure in office?

How many views did viral cat videos earn during their peak years of 2015–2020?

How much did starvation in Africa decline from 2025–2045?"

The latter question would be easy enough; Vera could find reputable experts, who could provide facts that she could easily compile and send for condensation and verification. The first two questions would require her to conduct some automated counting, sorting, and addition herself. It wasn't difficult, but it would take time. By 4:20 p.m., she had not yet finished the first assignment but had compiled the data she needed for the second one. There had been 6.2 trillion views of viral cat videos during the five years in question.

She took a break.

Vera went to a downtown café and selected a triple-sized mocha-butterscotch-chocolate-chip-caramel iced coffee flavored beverage and took a seat near a jumbotron screen after the drink extruded from the vending machine. The jumbotron was playing a somewhat interesting episode about celebrity home makeovers. Vera watched as Lolita McNamara chose from among 533 yellow fabric swaths to recover her sofa, with accompanying options for new curtains.

Out of the corner of her eye, Vera thought she spotted a familiar face.

Len Coughman, one of the SuperBards of the 2020s, had never been slim, but the person Vera stared at must have weighed 400 pounds. His burgundy wheelchair scooter was pulled up as close as his belly would allow to the table, but the distance was still great enough that the man kept his two-liter Pepsoilent coffee beverage in his chair's cup holder rather than reaching forward to place it on the table. A quick Noodle search confirmed that the man's portly face was indeed Coughman's, based on some celebrity photos Vera found that were no more than five years old. His cheeks had ballooned since the photo was taken, and his neck now protruded well past his chin. Based upon the stretch marks and sag to his skin, she guessed he had recently been even fatter.

Coughman had been known for his pithy biting poems about truth, pain, and intolerance. Timeless Warning had made him into a SuperBard by chopping the poems into single lines and then promoting them heavily in the Chatterfeed.

I wonder if he's still writing poetry? Vera mused. It didn't look like it. Coughman gazed blankly at the jumbotron, or perhaps he was just watching something on his MyndScreen. He was so unaware of his surroundings that Vera didn't feel the least bit bashful gawking at him.

After several minutes, Vera worked up the nerve to approach him. "Hey, you're Len Coughman, aren't you?" she asked, somewhat shyly. "Can I buy you a brownie?"

"Sure," he responded absentmindedly. "Do you want an autograph?"

"That would be wonderful." Vera returned with two hash brownies. She fumbled in her purse and found a piece of paper. It was the note that Chase had left on her windshield, with directions for how to meet him in the desert. The backside was blank, so Vera handed it to Coughman for his signature.

"Have you got a pen?" he asked. "I haven't had one in years."

She was stumped for only a moment and then went up to a vending extruder and ordered a shot of straight-up pomegranate syrup (normally used to flavor lemonade) while printing a plastic fork from a protruder. She broke off all but one tine of the fork and took them back. Coughman dipped the fork tine into the syrup and scrawled his name on the paper.

Can you sign it "For Chase?" she asked.

"Chase?" he queried.

"Like the bank. It's for a friend who's a big fan."

"Sure. Whatever."

It was sticky, but it worked — sort of. His signature stained the paper but then spread out like an ink-blot, leading to a fat, fuzzy image of his name. It would have to do.

"Tell me," Vera asked, "How did you do it? How did you manage to be so creative?"

"I'm not sure," he replied. "I really... I just don't remember. It couldn't have been that hard." He took another bite of brownie.

Vera tried again. "Where did the words come from, that you wrote?"

"Where do words come from?" Coughman seemed puzzled. "You hear them all the time." He motioned to the jumbotron, which he'd been staring at during the whole conversation. "Which fabric do you think she's going to choose?"

"I don't know," Vera said, sounding rather deadpan. "But, I'm not sure I care. You don't think that's really her house anyhow, do you?"

"Now that you mention it, I suppose not."

The conversation paused.

"There's no use thinking too much about what's real and what isn't. Say," Coughman piped up, "Have you been following what's going on with *Big Mother Gets Real*? There's this guy from Cincinnati who's joined the show. He's got ten pet iguanas at home. Ten!"

Vera threw the rest of her brownie in the recycling and walked out the door.

As she got into her car, a thought formed on Vera's Chatterfeed:

"Moderation in all things, even the truth."

She gave it some consideration before hitting send. *Could there be too much truth?*

It was the truth that property values had increased in neighborhoods surrounding the SuperBards, but did it matter? It was true that viral cat videos had been viewed 6.2 trillion times from 2015–2020, but was that fact obscuring or revealing the truth? It was true that the guy from Cincinnati on this week's *Big Mother* episode had ten iguanas at home, but who on earth could possible care? *Coughman, that's who.*

Somehow hitting "send" to launch the phrase into the Chatter felt like a waste of effort. Vera deleted the thought.

* * *

She wasn't hungry when she got home, nor did she feel like watching an episode. Even meditation felt like it would be too exhausting. As she stepped out of the car, she hit upon the idea of going for a walk around her neighborhood.

It seemed like a good plan, but the first challenge was to find a way out. The elevators from the parking garage led only to the residence floors, none of which had access to the outside. Vera saw a pedestrian-sized door on the wall across the garage, but when she approached, she was deterred by a sign saying, "Fire exit only. Alarm will sound."

The concrete of the parking garage felt cold, even through the soles of her shoes — a classic pair of tan leather-looking flats. The air felt both damp and dusty. She heard the screech of car tires as one of her neighbors turned up the ramp.

That was it! Vera just had to walk down the ramp, the way the cars came in. After listening carefully to assure herself that there were no additional cars coming up the spiraling rampway, Vera ventured down. She reached the ground level and after ducking underneath the security gate, found herself outside.

But where to walk? Unlike downtown or the older Vue neighborhoods, there were no sidewalks. Vera stepped up on top of the curb and carefully walked down the curved driveway that led into Magnificent Estates.

It was not yet entirely dark, but the landscape lighting was already shining upwards on the identical palm trees that lined the entrance. The skies remained overcast, but now the whir of drones had been replaced by the cacophony of a flock of crows. Vera admired the uniform green grass leading up to the curb and extended a fingertip to feel the bark of a palm tree. It was smooth, like plastic, and its trunk went straight into the grass, with no surrounding dirt.

I've seen these trees every day for years and never stopped to wonder if they were real.

Leaving the curb, she walked forty feet across the artificial lawn toward a statue in the middle surrounded by plastic bird-of-paradise flowers. She'd ridden past it in her car every day for years, yet never given the figure much notice. It depicted a thin man in antiquated clothing who was leaning slightly forward and holding a cigarette in his hand. Vera reached out and tapped the bronze-colored statue — plastic.

She inspected the pedestal that the statue was mounted on. It looked like marble but was, of course, plastic. The entire structure was so lightweight it had been staked into the ground to keep it from blowing over in the wind. Upon the pedestal, she found an inscription molded into the plastic and painted in gold letters:

"If liberty means anything at all, it means the right to tell people what they do not want to hear — Eric Blair."

Vera was quite certain that neither she nor her neighbors had ever noticed the statue, let alone read the inscription. *What use is the freedom to say something that nobody listens to?*

A pang started somewhere deep inside her as she realized that what she wanted more than anything was someone who would listen to her.

Vera's MyndScreen flashed to life with a news alert:

"A nefarious evildoer regime in Chinasia has been overthrown after tens of thousands of protesters chanting, "Freedom is Free!" surrounded a presidential motorcade and ground it to a stop. The crowd was angered by a recent mobility tax, which placed a surcharge on each mile driven to pay for road maintenance. Protester signs claimed the tax was a violation of their freedom of movement. The mob grew so large and unruly that it physically lifted up the president's limousine and threw it into a nearby river, drowning all its occupants. The regime's president, Emanuel Goldstream, was a hated figure in Globalia. He had blackmailed, tortured, and murdered hundreds of journalists — all to the apparent delight of his supporters who regularly paraded in the streets. Globalian foreign policy experts said the sudden revolt was completely unexpected given the suppression of infotainment transmission in the region."

How did they do it? With no free press, no MyndScreen transmissions, how did the resistance make itself heard?

A gentle breeze blew one of the plastic bird-of-paradise flowers against the back of her hand, reminding her of the tulips in City Hall Plaza.

How can I get him to hear me?

The sun had gone done now, and the sky was turning the color of graphite. The fake palm fronds rustled slightly in the wind, shimmering from the reflection of the lights below. A seagull screeched somewhere in the sky above.

Mrs. Manquin was getting out of her car as Vera walked back into the parking garage. She gave Vera a puzzled glance, as if she couldn't quite discern what was odd about Vera's pedestrian entrance but knew something was amiss.

"Hi," Vera offered, hoping to break the spell of confusion. "How are you doing?"

"Oh, honey, it's been a hectic day. Reginald got teased because his sneaker delivery got delayed so he had to wear last week's shoes to school. Of course everyone noticed, because the kids all have fashion-tracking apps in their MyScreen helmets. He was like a walking target for cyberbullying all day. He kept bombarding me with Chatter posts linking to the shoes he needed, so I went out to see if I could find a store, you know an actual store, that had them in stock."

She blabbed about her troubles the whole way up the elevator ride, as Vera nodded politely and listened. Just as the doors opened, she stopped and said in an uncommonly sincere voice, "You know, Vera, thank you for asking. It's been ages since someone asked me how I was doing and then actually listened to my answer."

Vera stood alone in the hallway as Mrs. Manquin's door closed behind her. She pinged Phoebe in the Chatter, "Got 🕑2 talk?"

Chatter replied with a standard rejection notice, "This account has been deactivated due to suspicious bot-like behavior."

* * *

Several days passed where Vera did not see Chase. She began staking out his motorcycle in the parking lot, but, however long she waited, he never arrived. Her days in the office were filled with routine research about trivial topics.

Each morning she strained to get out of bed. Her MyndScreen coaxed her into the morning physical jerks for exercise, but she declined its invitations to enjoy the sensual pleasure afterwards of the MyMassage lounge. A constant, dull ache filled her abdomen that abated only slightly when she ate.

Twice Vera mustered the energy to attempt meditation, this time with the aid of the recordings on the iPod to guide her. They were helpful in keeping her on track, but both times she unexpectedly had to stop when tears began slowly streaming down her cheeks. At the end of one session her body let loose an uncontrollable sob, so much so that she was startled.

She spent her evenings watching episodes of *Big Mother the Spy* and drinking Pepsoilent red wine. It was a buddy cop show where Big Mother partners with a transgender multi-ethnic immigrant who was raised by an abusive mother with an addiction to clove cigarettes. Together they team up to root out Fear Mongers operating in the Australian region. Anything was better than *Big Mother Gets Real*. Anything was better than sitting in silence — alone.

One day after work, her car asked if she wanted to stop for a coffee at the café she'd begun frequenting on her ride home. Sure, she decided, almost automatically. The café was offering a special sale price that she was certain was higher than the price she'd paid last week, but when she asked about it the salesclerk said that nobody else had complained. As Vera picked up her supersized caramel-apple-cinnamon-lavender Pepsoilent cappuccino from the extruder, she noticed the old Vue women she'd conversed with a few weeks ago sitting idly by herself. Vera waved and walked near the woman as she went toward the tables.

"Do I know you?" the Vue asked.

"Never mind," Vera replied. "I must have mistaken you for someone else."

Her MyndScreen issued a breaking news report:

"Unnamed sources have leaked the fact that a congressional candidate's husband has been photographed sunbathing in the nude along with a calico cat. Calicos are well-known to be raised by members of the Sisterhood, leading to speculation among many political experts that the candidate herself is a deep-state agent for the insurrection against the Establishment. The candidate had no comment when asked, and her spokesman refused to confirm or deny rumors that multi-colored cat fur has been seen on the bushes outside of their home."

Vera decided to drink her beverage outside, while ambling through the Vue neighborhood. Within a few minutes, she was back at the rundown strip mall where she'd purchased the potpourri from the flower shop. The pale-skinned woman was there, still wearing a bright blue scarf around her graying hair.

On a half-empty shelf on the side of the shop, Vera noticed some potted plants with delicate flowers protruding up about three inches above a bed of round dark green leaves.

"They're violets," interjected the shopkeeper, answering her unstated question before Vera's MyndScreen completed its Noodle image search. "The blue ones represent faithfulness, the purple ones royalty, I forget what pink stands for."

"Thanks. They're pretty. Say, what's your name? I've been here before, but it never occurred to me to ask."

"I'm Ellen. It means light. Thanks for asking. And you are?

"Vera. I don't know if it means anything. But I'll take this one," she answered, picking up a blue violet.

"Careful not to overwater them. The leaves will turn mushy and jellylike, and the whole plant will die before you know it. Just a few sips once a week will do it. Every two months give it a really good watering, and then let the soil go completely dry before watering again. It's easy."

"Excessive sustenance is as lethal as desiccation," a familiar voice startled her from behind.

"Thanks for those, Aldo," said the smiling shopkeeper, taking a cardboard box full of cut zinnias from him and placing them into an empty vase.

"Selling flowers from the garden?" Vera asked. "I guessed you were more of an anti-profit guy."

"There is nothing wrong with exchanging real things of value, especially things you helped create."

"That makes sense. Aldo, have you ever been in a situation that you knew didn't make sense, that wasn't rational, but you felt like you should embrace it anyway?"

"What you feel is not always rational, but what you feel is as real as what you think," he replied as he walked out.

Vera shrugged.

"What are these pots made of?" she asked Ellen, feeling the heavy, terra cotta texture in her fingers and admiring the earthen red color. She was certain it wasn't plastic.

"Why, that's a clay flower pot. Haven't you ever seen one? They help the soil breath. There was a time when that was the only sort of pot you could buy."

Vera picked out a blank greeting card with violets on the front from the nearly empty rack by the cash register. She didn't bother to argue this time with the shopkeeper's requested price.

Vera took the plant home and stared out the window at the late afternoon sky. The sun would soon dip behind the horizon but if there was one truth she was certain of, it was that the sun would rise again the next day. Nothing could be more permanent, more true, more faithful.

Taking out the card, Vera used her protruder to manufacture a red felt-tip pen. She wrote:

Roses are red, violets are blue,

As long as the sun shines, I'll only chase you.

She tucked the card into the envelope and sat down to meditate. After exhaling a long breath, Vera's mind relaxed. She didn't need the iPod.

*   *   *

The next morning, Vera left the violets and card underneath the rear tire of Chase's motorcycle.

He can't not see that.

When she returned at the end of the day, both the plant and cycle were gone.

The following day, Vera found a note under her windshield wiper:

"I'll B the 1 chasing U V. This Saturday, tell your car to take you to the Santa Anita Chariot Racetrack to watch the Gladiator 500. Once parked, get out and read the rest of this note (but not until then)."

Vera's smile was irrepressible. She stashed the note in her purse and got into her car.

*   *   *

On Saturday morning, Vera's MiOtto whirred along the freeway for nearly an hour before pulling into the parking lot of the Santa Anita chariot racetrack. There was a line of cars waiting to get into the parking lot, but passengers were patient as they watched a pre-race program on their MyndScreens in the comfort of their air-conditioned vehicles and prepared to place their bets.

When Vera got out of her car, she dug through her purse looking for the directions from Chase and found three folded pieces of paper. One looked like the note

Chase had left on her windshield and a second was the autograph from Len Coughman, which she'd been saving to give to Chase at the appropriate moment. A third, written on heavier parchment, said "Don't read this, just hand it over."

The Book!

Vera had envisioned reading the book together with Chase, not only to further their relationship but because she felt like she needed someone to serve as a co-conspirator in whatever adventure she was undertaking. But his jealous attitude toward Aneeka Randall had thrown off Vera's plan. Resolving to head to the library on Monday, she stashed Aneeka's note back in her purse.

Vera opened the first note, from Chase, and read the rest of it.

"Walk through the stables and armory and then walk directly away from the center of the racetrack on a worn-out road (your MyndScreen navigation app will label it Gate 7). Cross the street and walk to an abandoned fountain. Look left, toward a forest, and go there."

As she entered the horse preparation area, Vera smelled the pungent, grassy aromas coming from the stalls. She couldn't see the horses, but she overheard two Vues who groomed the animals bragging about what they would do with their winnings should their chariot team prevail, or at least survive the day.

Vera found an asphalt roadway full of potholes, but had a hard time getting cars to stop as there was no crosswalk.

She eventually just ran through the traffic, forcing driverless cars to dodge her and slam on their brakes. Looking up she approached an enormous white tile basin, filled three inches deep with greenish water. Real marble walls some twenty feet high stood on either side, protruding into the pool to prevent her from walking around it. Vera kicked off her shoes, rolled up her pant legs, and waded through the murky, algae-filled water, taking care not to slip on the slick bottom that she could feel with her toes but not see.

The grass had been overgrown for years and was filled with dandelions — mostly yellow but a few already forming white blowballs. Vera picked one and instinctively blew the seeds away. As she watched them float off into the distance, she saw a green thicket of tree branches, an odd sight amidst the decaying sprawl of a former suburbia that now consisted largely of ranch homes with their windows boarded up and shingles slowly peeling from their roofs.

After seventy-five steps through the trees, Vera arrived at a small pond. Looking across it, she saw an intricate wooden building with peeling white paint, on what looked to be an island. A three-story pagoda-styled bell tower rose from its center, no more than fifteen feet across, capped by a hexagonal cupola with a red-shingled roof and an ornate rounded wooden spire half-broken on top. Gingerbread woodwork graced its front eaves. The house was surrounded by a wrap-around porch with a cross-beam railing. On the porch, the silhouette of a motionless figure dressed all in white gazed out over the pond. Next to him was a dark-skinned smaller statue of a man with jet-black hair, wearing a matching white suit. Then men stood like human-sized paper dolls, eerily motionless yet with lifelike detail.

Vera hiked quickly to the right, following the shoreline of the pond. After a short distance, it became clear that the house was not on an island but rather a small peninsula. As she approached, she saw a confusing sign.

Welcome to Fantasy Island?

A voice startled her from behind. "Be careful what you wish for. The devil comes not in a red cape but disguised as everything you've ever wanted."

Vera spun around frantically to see Chase holding his belly with suppressed laughter.

"You asshole! You scared the wits out of me!" Vera exclaimed while wrapping both arms around him. "I'm sorry. I mean, about everything."

"I believe you. I'm a bit sensitive about these things. It's OK."

"What's with the creepy cottage that isn't really on an island even though the sign says it is?" Vera asked.

"My company filmed an episode series here about 75 years ago," Chase said. "It was called *Fantasy Island*. I ran across it in some archives when I was working on a similar concept a few years back. The figures on the porch are the two main characters, Mr. Roarke and Tattoo. People come to the island to fulfill their dreams, but there's always a twist so it doesn't work out like they wanted. You know, sort of a 'too much of a good thing' trope. The rest of the arboretum has been abandoned for years, so we have the whole place to ourselves. Let's go." Chase picked up a woven wooden basket unlike anything Vera had ever seen.

On top of the basket lay a wreath of tiny blue flowers on light-green stems that Chase had braided together in a circle while waiting for her to arrive. Each flower had exactly five matching petals, no bigger than a ladybug, with a bright yellow round center. He placed it on her head like a crown.

"Forget-me-nots. They're beautiful!" Vera noted, recognizing the flowers from a nature episode she'd seen recently.

Chase removed his 180° sunglasses and placed them on a nearby rock, with the lenses pointing away and the temple-cams focused directly back at them. He gave Vera a long kiss and then placed his arm around her waist and asked her to look at the glasses. Using his Sunglass180° app, he snapped an image of the two of them onto his MyndScreen, with the aging wooden house and its two cutout figures in the background. He sent the image to Vera through the Chatter with a note, "And forget U I will not."

Holding hands, they walked past another wooden structure that was leaning slightly to one side — evidence of decades of wood rot. They soon came to a pond of stagnant water directly underneath a rock outcropping. A rusting sign labeled it "Meyberg Waterfall," suggesting the pond had once been fed by a stream running down the rocks. By the water's edge, a large black stone had letters etched into its polished front surface: "Silence is the sleep that nourishes wisdom — Francis Bacon."

They sat down facing each other on the grass, with their hands clasped between them and their knees bent up at forty-five-degree angles. As she leaned forward and gazed into his eyes, Vera noticed the patterns of his irises, changing from dark blue around the edges to a lighter blue and even gray as they reached the dark center of the pupil. The sunbeam behind her head reflected off his corneas and into her pupils where it produced a sparkling image on her retina. She wanted to make an impressionistic painting of it, capturing the color and light but more so the serene, joyous feeling that the moment was producing deep within her.

"Chase, I need you to know that what I feel about you and what I think about the Sisterhood are two totally separate things, two different parts of me. I am drawn to the Sisterhood, to Aneeka, to its mystery and its importance. I think about it a lot, it's something that weighs on my mind. I admit that, and sense it makes you envious, resentful even." She grabbed his forearm, holding it firmly. "You are not something I think about with my mind, but something I experience with my whole body every waking moment whether you are with me or not. It feels like you are a part of me, or at least something I want to be a part of me. Does that make any sense?"

He just smiled. After a minute had passed, he responded, "I believe you. Even if I don't always understand you, V, I will always believe you. That's what matters."

After a long while, their backs began to ache, and they needed to change from their seated their positions. From the basket, Chase produced a thick cotton picnic blanket, two brown glass bottles with metal caps on them, and sandwiches made with real ham, cheese, and bread carefully wrapped in white paper.

"Where'd you get these? And what's in the bottles?" Vera asked.

"There's an old deli in my neighborhood that still sells non-extruded food. The ingredients are getting harder to find, so they've jacked up the prices. But, my job has some perks. And these," he said, producing a bottle opener from his pocket, "are bottles of real beer."

Vera ran her fingers through his hair and caressed his cheek. "I brought something for you too." She produced the autograph, penned in extruded pomegranate syrup. "It's hard to read, but its Len Coughman's signature, for real. Did you see my Chatter message that Timeless Warning is credited with reinventing poetry?"

"Reinventing and ruining you mean," he said. "Real poets pen stanzas, not autographs. But, I'm glad you were missing me."

"Constantly," Vera whispered, moving her fingers to his lips following quickly with her lips and tongue. She pulled him over and then on top of her and lost herself in his embrace.

When they came to a respite, Vera lay naked on the picnic blanket, her head nestled in Chase's armpit. She inhaled his scent, not entirely pleasant but distinct. With her fingers, she studied the contours of his pale-skinned, hairy abdomen and pectorals — not hard as rock but still pleasingly firm. His body was imperfect and yet simultaneously everything she could possibly want.

When they sat up to drink the beers, Vera looked more closely at the pond. Noticing the same large green water lilies that had been floating in the desert pool, she looked coyly at Chase. "Have you been here before — I mean, with other women?"

"Yes. Does that make it less meaningful for you?

"No," she said, truthfully. "But it explains how you know so much." She paused. "You're far more pleasing than my husband ever was. He did what he thought he was supposed to from watching movies rather than what felt right — like he was guided by instructions instead of instinct."

"I was married too," he said, caressing her arm. "My wife was killed in a car accident on her way to meet someone she'd encountered through the Virtual Sex Liberation League. A drone fell out of the sky and landed right in front of her car, causing it to career off an overpass. Or, at least she thought she was on her way to meet someone. Her lover turned out to be just a bot — she was cheating on me with an avatar. They … they gave me her recent MyndScreen searches as part of the autopsy."

Vera didn't know quite what to say, yet she felt a guilty ping of satisfaction.

A black-headed grosbeak whistled and chirped in a tree branch above them. Vera stared at its cinnamon-orange breast and wondered if it had a mate.

"I've been with others since," he continued. "They've all eventually been upgraded and moved to entertainment homes, so I've learned how to play the game. How to avoid getting trapped. That's why I have the tattoo. To remind me to be careful and to trigger predictable responses that protect those I love by making their MyndScreens behave in routine patterns. I know it's reckless — for both of us. But I can't stop. I need you to be careful too — this whole Sisterhood thing could end it all and make this, make us, a distant fantasy."

"We'll be careful. We won't stop. And, we'll hold on to this, right now, forever." She squeezed him. "But part of that means living in the real world — and doing that automatically puts us outside the system, outside the Establishment, living with risk. That means we keep moving forward with whatever the Sisterhood might entail, beginning with reading that book. I can't do it without you, and I can't not do it. Deal?" she smiled.

"Deal."

CHAPTER 9

Two weeks later, Vera awoke determined to take the next step. Her head was aching, so she took a PainZapper pill before entering the shower. Slowly, deliberately, she shaved her armpits, feeling the cut of the blade severing each hair as she drew it across. Her skin stretched a bit under the razor as the hairs pulled before they cut.

Vera switched the razor into her left hand and took a deep breath. Slowly, she slid the blade edgeways down the length of her right thumb. A bright red line, thin as a paper's edge, appeared on her thumbprint and then a stinging sensation shot through her thumb. Vera winced and instinctively thrust the thumb into her mouth, taking in its salty metallic taste.

The bleeding wouldn't stop. She let the water wash it away continually for several minutes. Vera could now more carefully observe the sensation instead of writhing away from it. The pain was undeniable, but it was bearable. She was not afraid.

The bathroom began to smell like a swimming pool, with the sharp smell of chlorine wafting up with the steam of the shower. Vera realized that the recycling filter was removing the color of the blood from the water along with the soap scum and hair it normally captured, and then chemically treating the water as it recirculated through her high efficiency shower system. Vera asked her bathroom fiber protruder to make a bandage, thankful she'd downloaded a design for one after the encounter with the chili can lid.

The library stood impressively, if desolately, against the deep blue sky overhead with puffs of white clouds on either side of the faded gold, red, and blue mosaicked pyramid that crowned the top of the antiquated building. A small spire pointed upward from the top of the pyramid, but Vera couldn't make out what it symbolized as its color had worn off.

It had been a challenge to prevent herself from anticipating the event. Aneeka Randall had warned against thinking about the title of the book, for that would signal the metadata crawlers that she was interested in the Sisterhood.

But more than the book, what pre-occupied Vera's mind was Chase. Her thoughts returned to him nearly every waking moment. When his name flashed into her mind, it triggered a cycle on her MyndScreen that was becoming as predictable as a *Big Mother Gets Real* episode. First, her bank account popped open and presented her available balance. Then, she thought about their encounter in the desert while ads for Las Vegas casinos popped up incessantly. She recalled the arboretum and saw opportunities to place bets on the upcoming gladiator races in Santa Anita. In her mind, she saw the photo image he'd taken of the two of them standing in front of the set for *Fantasy Island* with his 180° sunglasses. Her thoughts lingered there a moment, and she admired the crown of forget-me-not flowers in her hair before her

MyndScreen kicked in with another infotainment announcement or Chatter burst that broke the trance. But within minutes, there it would be again. *Chase. Bank. Vegas. Fantasy Island. ...*

"Love." There, she'd said it, if only to herself.

Vera approached a colossal door made of thick glass encased in heavy brass. It was topped with two monumental stone statues of people from a bygone age. It felt as though they were peering down at her, watching her every move — already aware of what she was about to do. Beneath them, men rode on horseback in what Vera imagined was an early precursor to the gladiator events.

Higher up on the building, in English, the word "Shakespeare" had been carved into the stone. Vera remembered the name from her high school studies and guessed he must have been the architect who designed the library. Letters etched above the doorway spelled out an ancient wisdom in a language Vera did not understand.

Will The Book *be written in Effispeech, Mid-Century Modern English, or an even more antiquated dialect that I won't comprehend?* She took a deep breath and waited for the doors to slide open. When they did not, she noticed small raised letters on the brass handle of the massive door. *Push.*

She pushed, feeling the weight of the door slowly give way as it pivoted on strong metal hinges attached to the side. The cold sturdy handle of the door twisted beneath her palm as she walked into the building.

The entrance was cavernous, with vaulted curved ceilings arching more than fifty feet above her. The walls were covered with ornate paintings and mosaics using vibrant colors unlike anything Vera had ever seen. The hard tile floors had intricate patterns of their own and were buffed to a shine so brilliant that they reflected the beams of light streaming in through the high-mounted windows. Vera felt her heart pounding inside her ribcage as her heels clacked off the floor and echoed through the chamber with each step she took.

"Why, hello," came a voice from behind a large wooden desk at the far end of the atrium. "Pretty, isn't it?"

A petite woman with light gray hair and darker gray plastic spectacles peeked at Vera from behind the desk. Vera was startled at first, but then approached the librarian slowly, trying hard not to appear overly anxious.

"Hello. Yes, it is quite pretty. I've never seen anything like it. I'm here, … I'm looking for a book."

"Well, you've come to the right place. We've got lots of them. Anything special you have in mind?" the librarian asked, cheerfully.

Vera returned the smile while opening her purse, fumbling for the piece of vellum parchment Aneeka Randall had given her. She found it at last. *Don't read this, just hand it over.* Vera followed the instructions, unfolding the note as she presented it.

"Ah, yes," said the librarian, knowingly. She typed on an archaic keyboard and spun a computer screen around for Vera to see. "This one," she said, pointing to a book depicted on the screen with a simple blue cover and the words, "A People's History of Globalian Thought and Truth" in capital gold letters. With the push of a button, a machine spit out a small piece of paper with a picture of the book cover and an inscrutable code of fourteen letters and numbers on it. She handed it to Vera.

"You'll find it on the third floor, section 984."

Vera took the slip of paper and headed to the elevators; the doors of which appeared to be made of real wooden panels. On the third floor, she saw a seemingly endless row of bookshelves, each with a sign containing a three-digit number. Dozens of empty wooden tables were lined up neatly across the silent room. Vera imagined they were for people to sit and read, but not a single chair was occupied.

She walked slowly through the stacks, leaving a faint trail on bindings as she dragged her right index finger along their dusty spines. Vera liked the feel of the yellowing cellophane that wrapped each book cover and the crinkle it gave when she pressed them. At long last, she found section 984, then the shelf that corresponded to the first six digits on her slip of paper. Slowly, she ran her finger along each book until she found it: *A People's History of Globalian Thought and Truth.* It was right next to a similar looking book titled *A People's History of the United States.*

Her hand shook a bit as she took *The Book* down from the shelf. The cellophane seemed less yellow than the surrounding volumes, but as Vera flipped through the thick sheets of paper, she noted that the pages of *The Book* were dog-eared and occasionally torn. Wohrn's work felt heavy, substantial.

Although nobody was watching, Vera rushed quickly out of the stacks. Instead of waiting for the elevator, she hopped on a downward escalator. She'd never ridden such a curious metal moving staircase and marveled at the black handrails moving along with her as the steps groaned beneath her feet. She gazed up at whimsical chandeliers depicting flowers and birds while reflecting that the conveyance allowed her to go down gradually while still observing her surroundings, unlike elevators that closed you off from the world. She walked down the final ten steps, accelerating her descent. At the bottom, she walked steadily back to the librarian's desk and handed her the book.

"Looks like you've found it," she smiled. "I just need your right thumbprint to check it out."

Vera looked down and saw her bandaged thumb. She held it up for the woman.

"Ah, I see, dear. Well, just give me your address and I can check you out manually."

"861 West Rustic Road," Vera replied, almost automatically. *She suddenly yearned to be there, to see Aneeka Randall, to ask her questions. To feel....*

"Alright, dear. It's due back in three weeks. Enjoy it!"

"I hope I will." Vera swallowed a lump in her throat and rushed toward the door.

On her drive home, a newsflash appeared on her MyndScreen announcing that the war on a cabalistic Evildoer regime in Chinasia was winding down. This was fortunate, a leading security expert explained, because it would allow the Globalian military to focus more resources on battling Fear Mongers, who had increased their attacks in Europe recently.

Vera grimaced. Last week, the Department of Information had tasked her with producing verifiable facts about fatalities from Fear Monger attacks in the Italian and French regions. She found that while the number of incidents had increased, the number of fatalities had gone down because each attack was significantly smaller in scale than before.

Further, the *Two Minute Spate* had reported just last week that The Tribunal of Educates had ordered another

200,000 Globalian troops to be stationed along the Pajikistania border, a known Evildoer regime in Chinasia. That was hardly a "winding down" of the war.

Globalia remained at war with Chinasia, Vera realized. *Globalia has always been at war with Chinasia. But for whatever reason, the Department of Safety and Security is switching its perception management focus to the war against the Fear Mongers, whom Globalia has also always been at war with. Why?*

When she got home to Magnificent Estates, Vera was anxious to begin *The Book.* But all she could think about was food.

She had no appetite for any Pepsoilent dinner option. After spending twenty minutes browsing through menus on her MyndScreen, nothing seemed the least bit appetizing. Instead, she had an intense craving for pork chops. She couldn't remember the last time she'd eaten real pork chops, probably not since she was a little girl at her grandmother's house. But she suddenly just had to have one.

Where to find such a thing? Every food court she could think of would quickly and efficiently produce a tasty pork-flavored dish from an extruder, but none would be able to cook real meat.

She poked Chase on the Chatter.

"Hi there," he smiled.

"I need pork chops, like right now. Real pork chops."

"I'm doing great, how are you?" he grinned, toying with her.

"OK, OK. How are you Chase? I miss you. But really, I'm starving."

Chase thought for a minute while gazing at the freckles on Vera's face that displayed prominently on her MyndScreen profile image.

"It's absolutely delightful to hear you, my love. I'll be there in twenty-five minutes. If it's pork chops you want, then pork chops you shall have. Dress nice. Watch some *Big Mother Gets Real* while you're getting ready."

Where are we going? How does he know all this? Vera hurried to pick out a new wardrobe. She opened a MyndScreen window and began playing the evening's *Big Mother* episode, although it literally made her feel a bit sick to her stomach. In a multi-tasking window, she picked a flowing red sundress with spaghetti straps at the shoulders and matching red pumps and lipstick. After sending the dress and shoe order to the instant fiberweave delivery service, she did her hair. Her protruder spit out the lipstick along with a string of white balls on a thread looking almost exactly like pearls, which she clasped around her neck. She stashed the lipstick in her purse, in case she needed to freshen up later.

Standing on her delivery balcony in her disposable underwear waiting for the drone to bring the dress, she looked out over the city and wondered how others were spending their evenings. *Was everyone going to watch 'Big Mother'? Would some just skip it and go for a walk?* There wasn't a single person out on the streets. Vera thought about the ambling figures she'd encountered on her trip to the hardware store and tried to guess what they would be doing tonight.

Chase sent her a Chatter post when he had arrived in the parking garage of Magnificent Estates. She rushed down to meet him, barely able to contain her excitement and frustrated she couldn't make the elevator go any faster.

"Don't you look glowing," he said, taking her hand as they got into her MiOtto.

"So, where are we going?" Vera asked, as the car drove past the plastic statue standing proudly in the artificial lawn.

"I thought it was time I took you on a proper date," he replied as he sent the address to her car. "We're going to a High Establishment bistro that serves real food."

Traffic was heavy, but Vera and Chase occupied themselves holding hands and kissing in the back seat while simultaneously running the same romantic comedy on each of their MyndScreens. After nearly an hour, the car dropped them off at a non-descript yellow stucco building with small windows and a sign out front saying *Michaels de Angelinos*. A smiling host asked for their name and performed a credit check off Chase's thumbprint before telling them it would be a twenty-minute wait for a table.

Half of the tables were filled with couples staring vapidly at each other in empty silence, scraping their silverware against the ceramic plates in awkward clinks. A few may have been conversing with their dinner partner (or somebody else) on the Chatter, but most were engrossed with an episode on their MyndScreen. The remaining tables had either solitary diners perusing the menus or glancing at their palms, or a group of four people sitting quietly.

A live musician crooned an old-time song while playing a real piano:

"We'll met again, not sure where, not sure when, but I know we'll meet again some sunny day..."

Tuxedoed waitstaff scurried back and forth. The diners appeared unfazed by any of the activity; their thoughts were elsewhere.

Vera took in the smells. The fresh baked bread coming out to every table floated an incomparable aroma that made her smile inside. The scent of onions sautéing in olive oil streamed out from the kitchen along with sizzling sounds from the saucepans. The smells were dizzying so she leaned against Chase, ostensibly to steady herself but also because it just felt nice. Right above the maître d's head, Vera noticed a cobweb.

The restaurant had only five entrees on the menu, simplifying their choices among options that all sounded delicious. They both ordered the house special — a large salad of mixed baby greens, toasted walnuts, and pomegranate seeds. Vera chose pork chops glazed in plum sauce accompanied by roasted sweet potatoes with black truffles and rosemary for her entrée. Chase ordered roasted duck served with wild rice and asparagus. The waiter recommended a bottle of merlot to accompany the meal.

Vera's mouth salivated as they placed the salad in front of her. It looked and smelled differently than any Pepsoilent dish she'd ever eaten. The pomegranate seeds exploded with flavor and juice that excited her tongue, but their texture was chewier than she was accustomed to. Her jaw ached a little after she swallowed it.

Vera was halfway through her pork chop while Chase still nibbled at both the first course and main entrée. He preferred to take a bite of duck, followed by a bite of salad to cleanse his palate.

Her hunger satiated, Vera turned to conversation — breaking the restaurant's awkward silence that now famished her intellect.

"I got *The Book* today. I can't wait to start reading it," she whispered, sipping her second glass of wine.

"Oh?"

"You know what's wrong with the world?" she continued, more loudly. "People are so stupid they believe anything they hear. Today on the news they reported that Globalia is winding down the war with Chinasia and this means we can concentrate on the increased threat from the Fear Mongers. But it's not true. We're not winding anything down, we'll just hear less about the war in Chinasia but it will go on and on and on. And the threat from the Mongers hasn't gone up. There've been more attacks in Europe, but overall the number of people killed by Mongers is fewer than last year. But people just swallow it, accept it, and go on with their lives as if nothing has happened. If only people were more informed."

Chase chewed his duck and took a sip of wine, gazing intently into her eyes. Some of the other guests were now looking their way, evidently finding eavesdropping on a real conversation more interesting than whatever was playing on their MyndScreens.

"Perhaps the trouble is not that people are ignorant, but rather too well-informed to believe anything," he said calmly. "To fool someone, you just have to say something outrageous — a statement people know isn't true, but which still grips them because it is too shocking to forget."

"That's crazy. If you know something is false, why would it bother you? I'd just ignore it."

Chase ripped a piece of bread, glancing around the room at the High Establishment members who seemed not to appreciate how special the experience of dining in a real restaurant was.

"Did you like your salad?" he asked.

"Of course, it was delicious. But you're changing the subject!"

"Excuse me, just let me look something up."

His face went blank as he ran a Noodle search, disengaging from the conversation. Within half a minute, a smirk spread across his face and his twinkling eyes reengaged Vera's.

"Watch this," he implored softly. She was expecting him to send her a video through the Chatter, but what happened was far more shocking.

Chase cleared his throat. He picked up a piece of mesclun green from his salad plate and then dropped his fork on the marble floor, sending the lettuce up into the air with a loud clatter. "Oh, my god! People are saying they found a tarantula in their salad at some restaurant! I'm never coming here again."

Two couples at nearby tables turned their heads to see what the commotion was. A man asked his wife, "Did he just say he found a tarantula in his salad?"

"That's impossible," his wife sneered. "It's one thing to find a fly in your soup, but there's absolutely no way a tarantula is going to sneak onto a salad plate." Soon, the debate was spreading. *Did tarantulas even live in Los Angeles? Wouldn't they die in the refrigerator where the salad was kept? How could both a cook and server not see such a thing even if one did manage to get in? Were they actually poisonous?*

Chase then sent a post into the Chatter: "Just heard someone at Michaels de Angelino's found a tarantula in his salad. I myself noticed a cobweb near the entrance." A startled look shot across a man's face who was sitting across the room from Vera, out of earshot and disengaged from the growing commotion. She noticed him push his salad plate toward the edge of his table while closely probing it with his knife.

Within minutes, the maître d' took action, but the damage had been done. He cleared away the cobweb and brought the chef out to personally tell each table that there had never been a tarantula spotted in Michaels de Angelinos, that he had trained for seven years with the most acclaimed chefs of France, and that he staked his reputation on the exceptional quality of the real, soilgrown food served at the restaurant. While food grown in the dirt theoretically could have been exposed to pests, it was inherently superior to extruded food, which was both sanitary and bland. The maître d' produced a copy of the restaurant's health inspection report, demonstrating a spotless record. He showed their glowing reviews from several restaurant critics and ratings from the top gastronomical guides.

The guests politely told the chef that they had the utmost confidence in him and of course it was outrageous to suggest that such a thing could happen. Still, nobody touched their salad.

Finally, the maître d' approached Chase and Vera. "Our chef thanks you for coming tonight and is granting you dinner on the house. Let me show you to the door." It wasn't a request.

When they walked outside, Vera jammed her elbow into Chase's rib cage. "That was the most embarrassing moment of my life!"

He smirked and tried to hold her hand, but she was having none of it as she directed her car to come pick them up. He turned and faced her squarely, lifting her chin gently with the tip of his fingers so that she could not avert her fiery gaze.

"Vera, my love. What I said was technically true. I had just seen in my Noodle search that somebody once claimed to have found a tarantula in their salad at some restaurant somewhere. There really was a cobweb. People were smart enough to know it was absurd. They could see with their own eyes that there was nothing but salad on the plates in front of them. And yet, once they'd heard it, they lost their appetite. They doubted the chef, they doubted the health inspection report. Informing them of the facts didn't help because their doubt is the problem, not their credulity."

"And I lost my appetite, too, thank you very little," she fumed. "That was the best food I've ever had, and you ruined it before we could even order dessert!"

"Well, I did say I'd never eat there again. That will turn out to be true." He smiled before turning serious. "Vera, Michaels de Angelinos is not the real world. It exists only to cater to the High Establishment, to place them in a bubble that is removed from reality precisely so they can blissfully ignore how the rest of us live. They dine on soilborne food that nobody else can afford while their companies run ads telling us that real food is unsanitary because it comes from the dirt. If you want to fight the Establishment, if you want to join the Sisterhood, you can't do it by only reading books. We just engaged in our first act of civil disobedience — and you got a free pork chop out of the night. C'mon, you have to admit it was kinda funny."

Vera got into the car and slammed the door. It took quite a while before she grabbed his hand on the ride home.

* * *

As they approached Magnificent Estates, Vera proposed a rapprochement. "I'll forgive you for humiliating me in the nicest restaurant I've ever been in, if you come up and read *The Book* with me. If you like it, you can stay all night." She raised an eyebrow and took out her lipstick to deepen the red pout of her mouth.

"That sounds tantalizing, but the data miners would then record that we'd spent the night in the same proximity. That's not a problem in and of itself, but it would mean that if either one of us was upgraded, the other would be targeted too. Besides, we're supposed to read the book somewhere that doesn't have MyndScreen transmissions."

"Wait, the app! What was the privacy app Aneeka told us about? We were supposed to download it when we left but you got all worked up with your stupid jealousy fit, and now I can't remember what it was called."

Chase gave her a frozen stare.

"I'm sorry, I just mean … " Vera paused.

"It's OK. I know what you mean." Chase dropped his shoulders. "It's called MyMind26. I remember it because we met on the 26th day of the month."

Vera had forgotten the date that they met. Or, perhaps she had never known. At any rate, it was good he'd remembered. She thought it would be better if the datatrackers didn't notice two identically timed downloads at the exact same location.

"OK, I'll go upstairs and download it now. You take a walk around or something, and then download it here in ten minutes. Then come find me. I'm on floor 23. Go check out that statue over there. Some dead guy I'd never heard of."

Chase got out of the car and watched as it drove around the gentle turn into the parking garage of Magnificent Estates, imagining how the seat of the car pressed against the curves of Vera's body as it carried her around the bend. Only once Vera was out of sight did he turn around, noticing that her lipstick had fallen to the ground as he got out of the car. He picked it up and put it in his pocket.

Walking over the artificial grass, he felt a squish beneath his feet. The recent rains had soaked through drainage holes in the turf and saturated the ground underneath. Each step made a gurgling sound as he approached the bronze-colored figure Vera had pointed out. The pose of the man — leaning forward with one hand on his hip, the other holding a cigarette — made Chase feel as though he were being admonished.

He thought about Vera, upstairs with *The Book*. He wasn't sure he wanted to read it, although he was confident he knew what it said. To acknowledge it would mean he could no longer ignore it; he'd be compelled to do something more than cheat the system at its own game. While he had enjoyed his prank at the restaurant, he wasn't sure he was willing to risk taking the next step.

Aimlessly, he walked closer to the statue and read its inscription:

"If liberty means anything at all, it means the right to tell people what they do not want to hear — Eric Blair."

A wry smile of recognition spread across his face. "Orwell. … Your warning was all too easy to heed," he said aloud, wondering if the statue would hear him.

"Is the problem that we heeded him too much?"

Chase looked twenty feet past the statue and saw a man wearing a cowboy hat and a black collarless shirt sitting cross-legged on the ground in the shadow of a palm tree. He was so still and quiet that Chase hadn't noticed him.

"Orwell warned of government becoming too powerful, controlling our thoughts, suppressing our freedom. But as it turned out, the infotain firms used our worship of Orwell to cripple government and grab power themselves. The Tribunal of Educates exposed Orwellian doublespeak, so instead of twisting the truth, the firms just bury it in a sea of trivia. Rebels are at liberty to tell people things they don't want to know, but nobody can hear their dissent above the din and nobody believes the few things that manage to penetrate their filters. We are free only to consume what the Establishment gives us, not to create a world for ourselves."

"And you?" asked Aldo. "What would you create?"

Chase stared at the motionless figure and then looked up at the moon above, thinking about what lay ahead. He knew there must be stars in the sky, but even though there were no clouds, he couldn't see them. The nearly full moon, combined with the lights of the city, overpowered starlight that was millions of years in the making. A slight breeze sent a chill up his spine. Thrusting his hands into his pockets, he found Vera's lipstick. He took it out, thinking about her lips, thinking about *The Book.*

After several minutes of contemplation, Chase bent down and crossed out some letters on the statue's inscription with the red lipstick. He wrote other words above them. His graffitied quote now read:

"If ~~liberty~~ autonomy means anything at all, it means the ~~right~~ *duty* to ~~tell~~ listen to people ~~what~~ that ~~they~~ you do not want to hear."

After admiring his handiwork a moment, he glanced down at the stakes holding the statue into the muddy ground. With relatively little effort, he pulled the plastic statue over, yanking the stakes out with it. Bending down, he took the sharp end of a stake and dragged it along the Astroturf, cutting it in the shape of an X. He lifted the statue overhead and spun it, plunging the figure's head through the X and into the mud below. He pushed and twisted and pushed until it was stuck — an inverted statue with its defiled pedestal poking up in the air.

Stepping back in satisfaction with his arms folded across his chest, Chase ran a Noodle search for MyMind26 and selected "download." He granted the app permission to install on his MyndScreen. As it did, he walked toward the parking garage of Magnificent Estates.

*　*　*

Vera welcomed him inside with a long kiss. She had changed into gray sweatpants and a loose-fitting pink T-shirt and held her ceramic cup with green tea in her hand. "Come, sit," she said, pulling his arm toward the couch. Chase lay down with his feet up on the armrest and his head resting in Vera's lap.

"You've got some weird people hanging out in this neighborhood, V."

"What do you mean? I've never noticed any. Anyhow, what did you think of the statue? Did you notice it was fake? I guess they were too cheap to use real bronze."

"Yeah, but it's funny they used his real name, which nobody knows. It's almost like whoever put the statue there didn't want us to know it was George Orwell, so they hid the truth by using his actual name."

"Who's George Orwell?"

"You know, the guy who wrote *1984*. Didn't you read that in high school?"

"Maybe. Sounds familiar. I think I found it pretty boring so I probably just downloaded an e-study guide. How do you know all this?"

"I read books. Or, at least I used to. Nobody does anymore, even though you can walk into the library and get any book you want for free. Anyway, let's read yours."

She picked up *The Book* from the end table, and began reading aloud, "A People's History of Globalian Thought and Truth by Bernice Wohrn. Here's what the Table of Contents says:"

INTRODUCTION

CHAPTER 1 FORMATION OF THE GLOBALIAN TRADE ZONE

CHAPTER 2 INTRODUCTION OF MYSCREENS AND MYNDSCREEN TECHNOLOGY

CHAPTER 3 THE GREAT SATURATION

CHAPTER 4 THE WAR UNSEEN

CHAPTER 5 THE RISE OF INFOTAINMENT AND THE MAKEWORK ECONOMY

CHAPTER 6 TECHNIQUES OF PERCEPTION MANAGEMENT

CHAPTER 7 PROCEDURES FOR ENTERTAINMENT HOMES AND MYNDSCREEN UPGRADES

CHAPTER 8 THE GROWING MOVEMENT TO RESTORE CREATIVE THOUGHT, EMOTION, AND REALITY

"We'll just do the introduction tonight. Are you listening?"

"Of course, my love," he replied.

HUMAN THOUGHT HAS ATROPHIED TO THE POINT WHERE A MAJORITY OF THE WORLD'S POPULATION IS NO LONGER CAPABLE OF GENERATING INDEPENDENT CREATIVE IDEAS. LACKING THESE FOUNDATIONAL CHARACTERISTICS FOR SELF-GOVERNMENT, WE HAVE ENSLAVED OURSELVES TO A RULING EDIFICE THAT PROVIDES SUBSISTENCE LEVEL NUTRITION TO OUR BODIES BUT HAS LEFT OUR MINDS AND SOULS STARVING. THIS BOOK DETAILS HOW SOCIETY ARRIVED IN THIS CURRENT SITUATION AND WHAT MANY ARE DOING TO LEAD US TO A DIFFERENT FUTURE. IT IS NOT FOR THE FAINT OF HEART, THE EASILY DISTRACTED, OR THOSE WHO PREFER PLEASANT STORIES TO DISTURBING TRUTHS.

"What do you think?"

"Orwell's book was disturbing fiction. But it felt true to many who read it back then. Keep reading."

THE GLOBALIAN TRADE ZONE, WHICH EVOLVED INTO PRESENT-DAY GLOBALIA, WAS FORMED IN REACTION TO THE FAILED NATIONALIST MOVEMENTS OF THE ERA SPANNING FROM 2015 TO 2025. PEOPLE WHO HAD PREVIOUSLY BASED THEIR IDENTITIES AND SENSE OF SELF-WORTH ON THEIR OCCUPATIONS, SOCIAL GROUPS, AND HOBBIES REVERTED INSTEAD TO IDENTITIES PRIMARILY BASED UPON THEIR COUNTRY AND ETHNIC ORIGIN. THIS SHIFT OCCURRED AS MANY OCCUPATIONS THAT HAD PROVIDED A TANGIBLE SENSE OF ACCOMPLISH-

MENT THROUGH PHYSICALLY CREATING A PRODUCT (STEEL, AUTOMOBILES, APPLIANCES, HOUSES) WITH ONE'S HANDS WERE REPLACED WITH SO-CALLED SERVICE ECONOMY JOBS WHERE A WORKER SPENT TIME ON THE PHONE AS A TELEMARKETER OR COLLECTION AGENT, A CASHIER AT A SUPERSTORE, OR A WAREHOUSE WORKER AT AN ONLINE RETAILER. THESE NEW, SERVICE-ECONOMY JOBS ENTAILED LITTLE MEANINGFUL INTERACTION WITH OTHER PEOPLE, OR TANGIBLE OBJECTS THAT WERE THE PRODUCT OF ONE'S LABORS.

THE SHIFT FROM A MANUFACTURING ECONOMY, WHERE PEOPLE MADE THINGS, TO A SERVICE ECONOMY WHERE PEOPLE SOLD THINGS, TO AN INFORMATION ECONOMY WHERE PEOPLE EXCHANGED FACTS AND ENTERTAINMENT, PROVIDED DRAMATICALLY LOWER INCOME LEVELS TO WORKERS AND FEWER OPPORTUNITIES TO ENGAGE IN LEISURE ACTIVITIES SUCH AS HUNTING, FISHING, HIKING, TRAVELING, BOATING, AND USE OF RECREATIONAL VEHICLES. PEOPLE HAD LESS TIME AND MONEY TO DEVOTE TOWARD SOCIAL INSTITUTIONS SUCH AS CHURCHES, ROTARY CLUBS, BOWLING LEAGUES, AND LOCAL CIVIC GROUPS. THESE ACTIVITIES ALL DIMINISHED AS A SOURCE OF IDENTITY, REPLACED BY NATIONALISM THAT HAD BEEN STOKED BY VIOLENT ATTACKS FROM HOSTILE ORGANIZATIONS AND INDIVIDUALS KNOWN NOW AS FEAR MONGERS, KNOWN AT THE TIME AS "TERRORISTS." TERRORISTS WERE INTERESTED IN PROVOKING WARS OF NATIONAL AND RELIGIOUS IDENTITY. THE TERRORISTS MADE PEOPLE FEARFUL OF THOSE WHO CAME FROM OTHER COUNTRIES EVEN THOUGH THEIR MILITARY CAPACITY TO HARM SIGNIFICANT NUMBERS OF PEOPLE WAS DEMONSTRABLY SMALL. FORMER U.S. PRESIDENT FRANKLIN ROOSEVELT HAD SAID, "THE ONLY THING WE HAVE TO FEAR IS FEAR ITSELF." THE TERRORISTS WERE ARMED WITH MEAGER WEAPONS BUT THEY USED THEM TO PROVOKE AMPLE FEAR, WHICH AS ROOSEVELT PREDICTED PROVED BY ITSELF TO BE ADEQUATE FOR THEIR PURPOSES.

"Gee," said Vera. "This thing would be easier to read if it wasn't screaming at me in all caps."

"Some people think yelling is more persuasive. Louder is always better, you know?"

Vera used her eyes to scan the written pages onto her MyndScreen, where she then used the AbodeShift app to convert the text to a more readable font, and then continued reading from her screen:

> The rise of so-called nationalist demagogues in several countries at the beginning of this era led to an inevitable pattern of repressing participatory democracy at the domestic level. Nationalist parties and politicians held fleeting plurality support, but lacked broad and sustainable majority support. Their ideas ultimately could not withstand reasonable critique, common sense, or the test of time. Nationalists clung to power by preventing those who disagreed with them from participating in politics, through techniques known at the time as "voter suppression." Nationalists distracted voters who were disadvantaged by their policies by stoking hatred and intolerance toward outsiders, those who were different, and other countries, which led to an increase in both international and domestic tensions. Nationalist strongmen portrayed themselves insincerely as populists, or champions of common people. In fact, their sole objective was personal power and enrichment. True advocates of common people turned against the demagogues.

> While there had been bouts of bigotry and intolerance throughout history, the ethnic, racial, and religious xenophobia that arose from renewed nationalism around the globe broke out into a full-fledged international

war, now known as World War Unseen. While there were dozens of news accounts each day about the war, it went largely unnoticed by most populations in the Western world. There were a great number of injuries, as even the human soldiers who played a supporting role reloading and repairing the fighting machines and drones were subject to attack. Veterans were maimed for the remainder of their lifetimes, but these wounds did not garner the same level of media coverage and public outrage as fatalities. There were relatively few military funerals or events that allowed the public to witness the ramifications of the war firsthand.

During the same period, citizens in the United States and other industrialized nations were heavily inundated with entertainment and "news" (which consisted of information that was sometimes correct, often inaccurate, and mostly irrelevant.) With the widespread adoption of personal MyScreen technology in the 2020s (usually in the form of entertainment helmets), most people spent the majority of their waking hours consuming large amounts of low-quality information from a host of sources. MyScreens and other entertainment helmets blocked out surrounding real-world distractions while allowing people to watch personalized news, comedy, drama, and sports programming as well as enjoy music, video games, and engage one another in what was called social media (similar to today's Chatter).

A genre known as "reality" TV programming had risen to prominence during the late 20th century, although contrary to the name there was little, to nothing, real about it. People were carefully cast and auditioned as actors who were subsequently placed in entirely artificial situations and given incentives to behave in highly unusual ways. As viewers grew accustomed to the contrived scenarios of the programs, producers continued to innovate with new and increasingly surreal storylines in which to place the actors. Some programs became dangerous, leading to the gladiator sports competitions of today as well as strategic elimination programs such as *Big Mother Gets Real*. The entertainment value of a series increased proportionally with the level of physical or emotional risk and strain that people were subjected to during the program. People knew the programs were contrived, so eventually the term "reality" came to take on the meaning of "fake."

"Oh my God," Vera exclaimed.

"Yes, very disturbing. But, at least the reality show producers understood that if they wanted people to pay attention to something, they needed to make it interesting. If the Sisterhood really wanted people to read and absorb this diatribe, they could have learned something from those shows. I mean, it doesn't really matter if it's true if I can't force myself to pay attention to it." Chase turned over to his side. "But go on, keep reading."

People needed little information about government actions and elections because they had little responsibility for governing. During previous periods of history, voters actually paid money to read newspapers that provided useful information in determining which candidates they would support in the elections process. By the 21st century, however, the vast majority of elections were forgone conclusions. Individual voters perceived, correctly, that their own decisions were of little impact. They therefore had little incentive to acquire information about voting decisions, or to vote in the first place, and they stopped purchasing newspapers. Candidates combatted voters' lack of interest with paid advertising, which replaced the information readers once sought out with information candidates wanted them to hear.

Elections were held in geographic districts. People increasingly lived in proximity to others who shared their political, religious, and cultural views, leading some historians to conclude that North Americans self-sorted themselves into homogenous political districts. This process of self-sorting was somewhat exacerbated by a process then known as gerrymandering, where politicians drew political boundaries around like minded-people so as to ensure their own election. Other historians theorized that people's political views were strongly shaped by their surrounding citizens, who shared common employment opportunities, education levels, and ethnic backgrounds. Whether geography attracted people of similar views or proximity itself created the similarities, the end result was elections that were essentially predetermined, with the candidate of the political party most similar to the geographic district easily winning.

People surrounded themselves with like-minded friends socially as well as geographically. Through internet media applications, people shared information about their own lives with others who had similar interests, such as cooking, hiking, or as fans of a musician or sports team. They formed networks of people with similar interests, including political interests. These networks provided people ample access to political views that were redundant with their own. These opinions and facts were shared in such prolific amounts that little time or mental energy remained for considering contrary political views on the few occasions when somebody would happen to run across them.

In the rare instances of a geographic boundary with a somewhat even balance of political views and a correspondingly high probability of a contested election, voters began to rely almost exclusively on highly skewed and inaccurate sources of information — namely political advertisements funded and produced by the candidates themselves. Only candidates who adopted the views of the wealthiest interests and corporations were able to present their information to the electorate in sufficient volume and repetition to break through the clutter. Any attempts to reduce the clutter through limiting the amount of money spent on political ads was rejected by a precursor to the Tribunal of Educates (known as the Supreme Court) as Orwellian censorship of free speech and the trampling of the individual by authoritarian collectivism. Spam filters were ruled an un-

constitutional restriction of corporate or political speech.

Candidates learned that the more outrageous a statement they made, the more likely it was to be repeated — even if it was later proven to be inaccurate. The torrential volume of low-quality information in circulation during this era therefore rewarded candidates who were the most inflammatory, while candidates who offered more nuanced, detailed positions received little attention. They were deemed invisible, or unviable, candidates.

In the extremely rare cases where the geographical districts and massive information imbalance failed to predetermine election outcomes, rules dictating how government operated prevented any real changes from taking place even after a landslide election altered the balance of power. Political losers could prevent the winners from accomplishing any of the promises they had campaigned upon through procedural obstacles in the legislatures. If legislative obstruction failed, parties who had been vanquished both in electoral contests and legislative debates would simply nullify any substantial policy that managed to pass through judicial fiat. Elections became meaningless rituals where people participated only out of habit, guilt, or boredom.

As a result of predetermined elections and gridlocked government, voters rationally concluded it was a poor use of time and mental energy to consume information about candidates and public policy unless it was highly entertaining. The popular sentiment was summed up by a letter to the *Punxsutawney Herald*, urging the nearly bankrupt paper to eliminate its front section of news coverage and triple its comic pages, weather, and other features:

> "Why bother depressing ourselves reading all the bad news about our government when there's nothing we can do about it? Far better to enjoy life and spend time reading the sports and entertainment sections."

The lack of demand for factual, relevant, and substantial information led to a dramatic decline in a discipline that had been known as journalism. Newspapers found it costly to hire reporters who could provide eyewitness accounts of events or investigate claims made by politicians. The "news" industry came to outsource its fact-finding work to public-relations firms who were on the payroll of the corporations and politicians that were the subject of news coverage. This greatly lowered the cost of content creation for news providers, albeit reducing the authenticity of information that was presented to the public.

As it became less credible and necessary, the "news" also simply became less interesting. The routine reporting from World War Unseen was boring in comparison to the large variety of comedy, drama, mystery, "reality," and infotainment programming that was readily available to people. Further, inaccuracies in news reporting about previous wars and other domestic topics led viewers to conclude that most news sources disseminated nothing but falsehoods. People used the technological tools available to them at the time to screen out information they perceived as dull, depressing, false, or irrelevant — which meant that essentially all news reporting of the war went into a black hole of obscurity.

In order to remain financially viable, news programs, which had previously contained journalism or coverage of topics such as wars and elections, gradually replaced their content with entertainment. News shows became more prolific, but they contained increasingly longer segments on sports, celebrities, weather, and gossip, topics that were intriguing to people but which they also exercised little or no control over. By the height of the Great Saturation, not a single widely viewed "news" program in Western industrialized nations contained any journalism or information that could be used by a voter to base a public policy opinion upon.

"Chase, Chase." She nudged him. He had fallen asleep.

*　*　*

The next several weeks passed blissfully. Emboldened by their MyMind26 blocking app, Chase and Vera spent more and more time together. They often met up for lunch, taking walks in the park where Chase had first plucked the variegated tulip. They drank cups of real coffee and bottles of real beer, while engaging in the art of conversation.

"What are you thinking about, my love?' he'd ask.

"I'm trying to remember something," or "I'm wondering how they got away with it," would be her answer, leading to an exchange of questions and partially formed answers. Sometimes she'd just say, "nothing," and that was OK too. For Vera, as each day passed what she was thinking became less important than what she was feeling.

More than a few times, Chase had spent the night. They indulged in delusional conversations of spending a life together, away from the city, away from MyndScreen transmissions, away even from the Sisterhood. Maybe they didn't need to rebel if they could simply escape. Vera secretly hoped they could engage in insurrection and escape simultaneously. She thought, possibly, that one even required the other.

It was the notion of spending a lifetime with Chase that prompted Vera to recall her past — specifically her previous marriage. Although marriage laws in California had been liberalized to allow multiple simultaneous marriages, Vera did not want to go that route. If she was going to propose to Chase, she wanted first to track down her legal husband and get a clean divorce. Surely, he wouldn't object. She probably wouldn't even need to travel to Brazil to find him. She'd just locate him in the Chatter — unless, that is, he had blocked her.

For the first time in many years, Vera reminisced about her wedding. Quite frankly, she remembered very little of it, but she pulled up some images in her Mynd-Screen archives that made it look rather pleasant. She was dressed in a flowing white gown with her hair done up in a twirl and her hands encased in long white satin gloves. Many of the bridesmaids hadn't been able to attend in person, but there were head-sized screens mounted on poles surrounding the wedding couple that allowed them to participate virtually.

He didn't look bad either. He wore a tuxedo that was in fashion at the time and had a practiced smile that made for great photographs.

In the image, they held a bouquet of white roses, their hands joined around the stems. Vera had kept them for a few years in a closet, but she threw them out after the thin plastic petals became brittle and cracked.

Vera was distressed at momentarily forgetting his name, but breathed a sigh of relief when she ran across an archived Chatter post from his parents that was clustered with the images:

"Congratulations, Gary and Vera. Love, Mom and Dad."

What about my parents? They hadn't attended the wedding, of course. Vera wondered where they were now. She hadn't seen them since she was taken away to the foster home, but she suspected that they would have eagerly accepted a MyndScreen upgrade once the technology became available as a way to avoid the pain of her brother's death. She thought they would have had enough money to afford placement in a decent entertainment home. It shouldn't be that hard to find out which one, although it would mean contacting each home individually — and there were thousands in the area. *Perhaps they could meet Chase.*

She began running Noodle searches on their names, finding hundreds of possible matches and social media profiles, so that she wasn't certain which were real people and which were bots. She started pinging some in the Chatter, but usually got no reply and when there was a response it was usually a recommendation to try a new flavor of Pepsoilent. She looked for client rosters of entertainment homes in the Los Angeles region, but found that information blocked for privacy reasons.

Vera looked at her thumb, still recovering from its cut. *Would I be able to prove who I am to an entertainment home? Will my parents remember me? Do you still have memories if you've been upgraded? Will I even recognize them?*

* * *

That evening, Vera continued reading *The Book* to Chase, who promised he'd try to stay awake.

> During the 20th century, authoritarian regimes in Asia achieved remarkable stability over periods lasting several decades by successfully controlling public perception through censorship of the press, torture of opposing candidates and journalists, mass incarceration of political dissidents, and large-scale government propaganda campaigns. In the short run, these regimes killed, tortured, and jailed millions of their own citizens and created a perception of inevitable and permanent authoritarian rule. In the long run, these "Orwellian" tactics ultimately failed in every regime that employed them, for three principle reasons.

"Ah, OK. Maybe Wohrn is onto something here," Chase chimed in.

> First, by jailing journalists and shutting down news organizations, repressive autocrats created a chasm of political silence. The government-produced propaganda was contrived and uninteresting compared to what had been less predictable journalism. As a re-

sult, propaganda was unable to successfully fill the vacuum left by chilling the normal marketplace of ideas. In the abysmal silence, dissenting voices found ways to be heard through quiet techniques as simple as reading books out loud around kitchen tables, underground poetry slams, folk music festivals, punk rock concerts, and hand copied manuscripts of books smuggled outside of national borders for overseas printing. Once information was digitized, it made sharing even easier and suppression even less practical. Moreover, the widely observable clampdowns tended to make dissenting voices more credible and powerful even while they were quieter. If the government didn't want you to hear something, it seemed more enticing and likely a threat to their power. If it was threatening, it therefore was deemed true.

Secondly, regimes that propped themselves up by suppressing public opposition eventually weakened themselves by creating bureaucracies filled with incompetent and corrupt men and women. Government officials gained power through connections and connivance rather than through winning over hearts and minds or demonstrating an ability to accomplish a task. While authoritarian regimes could capture and maintain power through a charismatic strong man, these dictators eventually sickened and died. They were replaced by weaker, less engaging people whose primary attribute was to be acceptable to the broader governing elite. These anemic leaders emerged as consensus choices amid competing power blocs within the government and were therefore by design not too towering figures individually. Authoritarian regimes stagnated and began to rot from within.

Finally, these so-called Orwellian regimes found themselves unable to compete economically or militarily with countries that shared ideas more widely. Stagnant governments built missiles that crashed into the ocean and drones that flew off course. As the industrial revolution gave way to the infotainment economy, the inability to share information, art, culture, and ideas forced repressive regimes to rely more and more upon pirated infotainment, patents, and designs from outside their orbit of control. The avenues for spreading these pirated ideas also allowed for the spread of dissenting political views.

By the 21st century, regimes that had previously controlled information through censorship began adopting techniques already in use by western multinational corporations and marketing agencies to manage information flow in a way that appeared less heavy handed. Information deemed hostile to the regime was tolerated in public, thus removing some of the legitimacy and excitement it once held when it was treated as contraband. Rather than censoring unfavorable information, modern regimes simply made opposing views more difficult to find while simultaneously filling the vacuum with infotainment that was far more interesting, engaging, and accurate than 20th century propaganda. Articles that would previously have been banned were now published in obscure journals that almost nobody read and were dismissed by mainstream news outlets as fringe, alternative, or radical.

"Hey, look. Somebody else highlighted the important parts." Vera noted, while she continued to read every single word.

In turn, multinational economic entities used the same method to manage information in countries that had previously enjoyed more robust public policy debate in order to gradually wean populations away from political discourse. In places that had never experienced overt censorship, the truth slowly drowned amid a sea of distraction. Rather than uprooting the truth, which left seeds of information in the soil ready to sprout again and again, powerful interests overshadowed veracity with weeds of drivel that deprived it of sunlight and water. These societies, now known as "Entertarian Regimes," have proven far more stable than 20th century authoritarian governments.

One distraction technique developed by Entertarian rulers is known as the "Trivial Leak." When information surfaced that was unfavorable to a corporation or government figure, instead of censoring that information, the targeted entity "leaks" accurate information about another topic to a news reporter. The leak often is of a salacious nature, involving an illicit romance between public figures, a moral faux pas such as gambling or prostitution, or details of a family member's

embarrassing statements or photos. Because
of the perception that the leak is something
that the Establishment is trying to conceal, it
rapidly becomes widely known. The public
obsession with the leaked trivia then sup-
plants the information that was problematic
to the Establishment in the first place.

Vera stretched her arms above her head. "When will
they get to the part about the Sisterhood?"

"I don't know. What was is it that *The Book* said about
gerrymandering?"

"I can't remember, something bad I think."

"The thing is, this book dumps a whole lot of really
important information on you, but it doesn't engage you.
A good book should show, not tell."

Vera returning to reading.

World War Unseen continued to obscurely escalate until it reached the nuclear stage.
Missile defense systems prevented all but a
few nuclear attacks in the United States and
Europe, most of which were delivered by
driverless cars or luxury yachts. Other regions
that lacked missile defense shields were hit by
a dozen nuclear strikes within the course of a
few weeks. The mass destruction, particularly
in the countries of Australia and South Africa,
brought an end to the war for two reasons.

"Can't they include some maps? I want to be able to
visualize all of this," complained Chase. Vera kept on.

First, the war became directly visible to people who had previously failed to notice it.
Citizens all over the world began experiencing

significant hair and tooth loss from radioactive fallout. Ash and soot fell from the sky for a period of weeks. A five-year nuclear winter brought on by ash in the atmosphere temporarily halted the process of global warming and created dramatic changes in weather patterns that were directly observable to people without requiring journalism or the news media to report on them. Blizzards ravished cities that had never previously seen snow. Rainfall diminished as ocean temperatures fell. When the soot eventually fell from the atmosphere, global warming ramped up again at a more rapid pace due to the higher levels of carbon dioxide produced by mass forest fires that had been sparked by the nuclear explosions.

Secondly, the loss of nearly a billion consumers had a negative effect on the earnings of multinational corporations, which had heretofore profited handsomely off the war. Corporate revenues from arms sales, privatized prisoner-of-war facilities, and mercenary services were more than offset by economic losses due to the sudden obliteration of a significant portion of the global customer base. Insurance companies went bankrupt trying to cover claims arising from the war and ensuing climate disasters while seeing a sudden drop in subscriber premiums. Petroleum companies saw entire oil fields obliterated by nuclear explosions. Agribusinesses were unable to grow crops due to diminished sunlight and the cold temperatures of the nuclear winter. Raw materials became unavailable for manufactured goods.

The combined forces of a greater public awareness of the formerly unseen war and unprecedented corporate financial losses quickly brought the conflict to an end. Governments around the world could not resist the demand for peace by both their citizens and corporate constituents. Nationalism eased, charity blossomed, and the world entered a period of retrospection about how such an atrocity could have happened in the first place.

An international trade agreement known as the Piese Treaty (after its key negotiator Justinian Piese) at the end of the War Unseen created a global structure to manage security and economic stability with more authority than the failed world government structures devised in the 20th century. The Piese Treaty left nation-states intact while converting their elected governments largely into ceremonial posts similar to the old European monarchies. This would allow for periodic bouts of populism or patriotism to run their courses without disrupting the world economy or military infrastructure.

Countries that had previously been part of what was thought of as "The West" consolidated into what is now known as Globalia. Countries that had experienced governments built upon authoritarian-style censorship (primarily, but not exclusively in Chinasia) formed an economic partnership that Globalia labeled the "Evildoer Bloc." Individuals and religious fanatics in regimeless regions (primarily in Africa and the Middle East) that affiliated with neither Globalia nor the Evildoers bloc have become breeding grounds for Fear Mongers. They continue to engage in acts of violence against the more powerful regimes as a means of keeping their impoverished populations focused on external enemies.

Since the early 21st century, Globalian nations have been in a constant combat with both the Evildoer bloc and various Fear Monger groups. The Globalian Establishment refers to the situation as "low-intensity conflict." At various periods, Globalia has allied with an amenable Evildoer regime or a specific Fear Monger organization around discrete objectives where they share a common enemy. In all cases, rational military leaders in both the Globalia and Evildoer regimes take precautions to keep fatalities from exceeding certain acceptable thresholds, which they ensure receive modest attention in the news media — but not too much. The low intensity conflict creates a constant churn of news coverage, which instills a sufficient sense of anxiety within the Globalian population. This conflict entices people to accept mandates from the governing structure and prevents the return of utter complacency as with the War Unseen, but avoids creating so many fatalities as to rouse the population into revolt.

Globalia is managed by an international council known as the Tribunal of Educates. The Tribunal was initially formed to adjudicate issues pertaining to global economic stability, trade, and physical security. The Educates soon extended their jurisdiction over issues such as wages, the rules for international trade, product safety requirements, the definition of liberty, pollution rights, intellectual property rights, military and counter-terrorism efforts, immigration, taxation, atmospheric carbon management, and resource extraction.

The Piese Treaty stipulated the initial lifetime appointees to the Tribunal of Educates from leading legal, military and economic experts. Ever since, the Educates replace any vacancies on the Tribunal themselves by choosing from a pool of highly credentialed and qualified scholars who are certified by the top twenty universities and management-consulting firms in Globalia. The oversight and endowment of those universities and firms, in turn, is provided for by a levy on the top fifty multinational corporations.

The self-perpetuating Tribunal was thus protected from the vicissitudes of populism and the uneducated masses, who were not deemed capable of voting in their own economic interests or of maintaining global security. The Educates' mission is not to govern based upon erratic and irrational popular whim but to dispassionately interpret the original Piese Treaty and ensuing Tribunal Doctrine. Its members view themselves, therefore, as "originalists."

Nation-states that existed prior to World War Unseen remained intact with their previous boundaries and were initially permitted to rule locally on issues of social, religious, and sexual practices such as marriages, fornication, reproduction, bathroom use, prayer in public places, prostitution, use of alcohol and drugs, punishment of petty crimes, and the like.

Vera put down the book and yawned. She saw Chase had again fallen asleep. *He's right, it is dreadfully boring.* If this was how the Sisterhood communicated, maybe their revolution wasn't going to be that much fun after all. Still, she was determined to get through it.

> To cope with the massive famine that had been created by the war and the ensuing nuclear winter, the Globalian Establishment employed technology to cheaply manufacture abundant amounts of lab-grown soyalgent food products consisting of soybeans, lentils, and algae. Soyalgent contained all the nutrients required for human sustenance, was efficient to mass-produce, and was essentially flavorless.

> In exchange for lifetime patents on the technology and a two-hundred-year exclusive license for producing flavor enhancements, two multinational corporations (Pepsoilent and Cokaid) agreed to provide free basic nutrition in the form of unflavored soyalgent to every person in Globalia and to some inhabitants of the Fear Monger territories as well.

> It took several years for the post-war economy to regain prosperity after the nuclear holocaust. Not only had the war decimated the global consumer base, technology had advanced so significantly that adequate amounts of food, shelter, and clothing could be produced with the efforts of only five percent of the Globalian labor force. While these

technological advances were initially viewed as beneficial, they entailed some significant downsides.

Manufacturing was primarily conducted through robotic factories and the advent of home plastic protruders, initially called 3-D printers. Automation handled the manufacturing of consumer goods, structures, and clothing with only a tiny workforce needed to design, maintain, and refill the protruders and robotic assemblers. Food production was primarily handled by extruders that flavored, texturized, and heated the base soyalgent product into literally thousands of different food forms. Most modern homes, at least for the Establishment, are equipped with personal extruders. Restaurants have been largely replaced by vending machine extruders that produce soyalgent meals and drinks on demand and with near zero labor costs.

These technological advances served the useful social purpose of preventing the mass starvations that had existed prior to the war and had been a primary driver of violence. Prior to soyalgent, an endless supply of young men and women had joined a host of terrorist organizations and faith networks that promised them glory, salvation, and sexual satisfaction in a future life as well as food for their surviving families if they sacrificed themselves in acts of suicidal butchery. The extremely low cost of unflavored soyalgent made basic food available to starving populations and helped reduce, but not eliminate, cult-like organized terror. It also helped alleviate the famine caused by the War Unseen itself and accompanying huge variations in climate that had made traditional agriculture all but obsolete. With the advent of genetically modified organisms, soybeans, lentils and algae could be produced even while heirloom crops perished in the nuclear winter.

But the newfound abundance of readily accessible consumer goods and nutrition exacerbated an economic problem that had been developing for decades. With only five percent of the workforce needed to produce all of the food, shelter, and clothing required for every person on Earth, what was everyone else supposed to do? The immediate post-war economy provided no way for the vast majority of people to earn a living, leaving them with a mundane subsistence of survival on the unflavored soyalgent dole but with no meaningful purpose in life.

Vera's MyMind26 app sent her a Chatter alert that her MyndScreen had been inactive for 47 minutes. She promptly opened up an episode of *Big Mother Nature* and ordered an outfit for the next day. Only then did she return to *The Book*.

The Tribunal of Educates solved the problem of surplus labor by creating a system known as "Makework." Members of the wealthiest segment of society, known as the High Establishment, had a surplus of wealth that they had been aggregating over several generations. Rather than paying Globalian taxes, High Establishment members were encouraged through tax incentives to spend their wealth on an array of unnecessary Makework jobs that made life more pleasant for the High Establishment and kept workers occupied.

High Establishment members built large estates, requiring dozens of gardeners, security guards, house cleaners, maintenance staff, interior decorators, remodeling consultants, car washers, horse groomers, pool cleaners, yacht captains, and personal celebrity chefs who could create meals out of real food grown on the property. The tax code gave High Establishment members incentives to own and manage not just one estate, but multiple compounds at locations around the globe. They hired personal masseuses, dieticians, acupuncturists, manicurists, butlers, valets, publicists and beauticians, all of whom provided services that were not essential to the core global economy other than the fact that they provided disposable income to those who did the Makework. An army of lawyers, accountants, investment advisors, lobbyists, hedge fund managers, stock traders, and consultants were employed to maintain and grow the financial assets of the High Establishment while producing no tangible products themselves.

The disposable income that middle-class Makeworkers received allowed them to purchase enhanced flavors of Pepsoilent or Cokaid, generating profits for the High Establishment executives and shareholders who could then provide more Makework jobs. Makework also created consumer demand for a rebounding infotainment industry, which became the primary engine of the Globalian economy. In a seemingly virtuous cycle, people added value to the world economy not from their labor, but due to their ability to purchase information and entertainment, measured in "views." This class of people, valued principally for their consumption potential rather than the fruits of the labor, became known as the "Vues."

In addition to infotainment, Vues had sufficient disposable income to enhance and individualize their own appearances. The fashion industry revived with the advent of disposable clothing, created instantly by hyper-local, on-demand protruders using synthetic fibers. Constantly discarded garments provided a means to clothe indigent populations through reuse and recycling centers. Hairstyle and makeup fashions changed on a daily basis, allowing a person to reinvent their personal characteristics frequently and minimalizing nationalistic identities. This generated another line of profits for the High Establishment, allowing for the creation of more Makework jobs.

Makework wages also provided a consumer base for another leading component of the post-war Globalian economy: pharmaceuticals. Drugmaker corporations had suffered greatly from the loss of more than a billion customers during World War Unseen. There simply weren't enough Establishment members to provide a viable customer base. Profits fell as patents expired on many of their core products. The revival of the post-war economy brought new life to pharmaceutical firms by creating income for people to spend on life-enhancing drugs. The Department of

Prosperity also financed research into the ever-evolving diseases that plagued mankind, especially in the wake of significant radiation levels that lasted for decades after the war. This research was given to the pharmaceutical companies, sparking a whole new product line that was patent protected.

Built upon Makework, infotainment, fashion, and pharmaceuticals, the world economy grew tremendously and eventually surpassed its prewar levels. During this time, the Establishment learned to smooth out cyclical depressions in the Globalian economy through strategic advertising, which helped to stimulate additional purchasing of enhanced soyalgent and infotainment. It was not necessary to give corporations an incentive to advertise, but the sheer abundance of products and infotainment led to a corresponding profusion of advertising that became self-defeating.

Even before the War Unseen, the enormous volume of advertising, which financed the larger still magnitude of infotainment, began to fuel what is now called the Great Saturation. The Great Saturation, in turn, had enabled World War Unseen by masking its consequences for several years until the war escalated to a point where it affected most people's lives directly. The Tribunal of Educates realized that, for both economic stability and public safety, it needed a system to manage the overabundance of information that caused the Great Saturation.

The Tribunal recognized that while information was plentiful, the capacity of each person's brain to absorb that information was fixed. This created a condition that economists termed "Mind Scarcity." Human beings' ability to process information had become a scarce resource just like gold, petroleum, and clean water. Using the principles of marketplace economics, the Educates produced a doctrine that addressed Mind Scarcity by putting a price on information. Information that was highly valued would be profitable in the global economy; hence it would be able to pay a usage fee on information transmissions. Information that was not highly valuable to the world economy would be unable to pay the price of transmission. People's minds would then be free to focus on what was economically valuable.

This Tribunal Doctrine of Mind Scarcity Pricing became a key tenant of Globalian law. Corporations, and even individual people, were at liberty to disseminate any information, entertainment, or political speech that they wanted so long as they paid the Mind Scarcity user fee. This fee became incorporated into all advertising price structures, and the concept was enshrined in the simple slogan:

"Advertising Frees Speech."

The corollary to the Doctrine of Mind Scarcity was that economically worthless information should not be allowed to saturate people's attention. Communication that cost little to disseminate such as protest rallies, lawn signs, leafleting, petitioning outside of post offices, and door-to-door volunteer canvassing were restricted and eventually banned. Ordinary posts in the Chattersphere that had no economic value were pushed to the bottom of news feeds so as to ensure they would not interfere with information that had paid the Mind Scarcity fee.

In addition, the overwhelming amount of information produced during the Great Saturation caused advertisers, infotainment producers, and ordinary people to become much more efficient in their use of language. In a gradual evolution to what is now known as Effispeech, people began replacing words with phonetically similar single letters. In a pattern similar to Egyptian hieroglyphics, words were replaced with symbols. Effispeech allowed advertisers to cram more meaning into the limited bandwidth they had paid for with their Mind Scarcity fees. It also allowed people to more rapidly and efficiently convey an emotion or opinion in their Chatterfeeds. Eventually, it had the effect of greatly diminishing the number of words in circulation compared to what was used in Mid-Century Modern English. Nuance and meaning declined as many words became extinct and human thought simplified. Conversely, the alphabet expanded greatly since people needed to learn the meaning of new symbols in addition to letters.

Establishment members also added new words and phrases to the lexicon as a way to assert authority or expertise. For example, instead of saying that there was a good reason for a governmental law, a lawyer or judge would say there is a "compelling state interest." Or, instead of saying that judges should carefully examine laws and weigh their pros and cons, legal scholars would say that laws need to withstand "strict scrutiny." Doctors used phrases such as "irritable bowel syndrome" to describe stomach pains. Military leaders spoke of "collateral damage" instead of "killing people." This genre of speech became known as Expertalk.

As the elites in positions of authority departed further and further from common sense, the volume of Expertalk expanded greatly as a technique for obscuring the truth. The goal was to project sufficient confidence and re-establish badly damaged public trust by using words that most people did not understand. By speaking obtusely, Establishment members projected an image of intellectual superiority and implied that the Vues should simply trust difficult societal decisions to qualified experts. Ultimately, however, the technique was more successful at convincing Establishment elites of their own superiority than it was in persuading the Vues, who simply ignored it.

As free speech became defined as speech that had been paid for by the speaker, and words took on more constricted or conflated meanings, the term "freedom" itself became a narrower concept during the post-war era. In the 18th and 19th centuries, freedom connoted the ability to think as you please and worship as you please, as well as to vocalize those thoughts and religious views. This conception of freedom presupposed an ability for autonomous thought.

However, in an era of mass starvation and deprivation following the nuclear holocaust, freedom came to mean the ability to feed, clothe, and house oneself. Political and legal experts at the time opined that a man who is hungry cannot possibly be free, for he is enslaved every waking moment by the all-consuming task of finding his next meal. Hunger physically coerced people toward doing whatever was needed to alleviate it, even if it meant going against their professed moral codes and political convictions. Further, social scientists and brain researchers were finding data that cast doubts on whether any thought was truly autonomous in the first place. Ideas appeared merely to be reflections of others' thoughts a person is exposed to. If autonomous thought didn't really exist, the imperative for protecting it became less compelling in the face of mass starvation.

Freedom thus became conditioned upon economic prosperity. The Globalian economy guaranteed freedom by providing adequate unflavored soyalgent food to every man, woman, and child. The huge volumes of frequently discarded fashion items ensured free used clothing to the world population. Ensuring profits for the pharmaceutical industry so they could continue to produce life-enhancing drugs was deemed essential for freedom. Threats to economic stability, especially any action that jeopardized flavored-soyalgent sales and the Makework system that enabled them, became seen as threats to freedom itself. The Tribunal of Educates issued a series of doctrinal rulings aimed at stabilizing and guaranteeing profits for the major Establishment owned corporations. These rulings all relied upon a simple principle:

"Prosperity is Freedom."

Vera thought back to the poor people she had seen on the streets while going to the hardware store. They were not prosperous, but they were smiling, laughing and dancing far more than any Establishment member she'd ever encountered. *If prosperity is freedom, shouldn't it make you happy?* She read on.

Pepsoilent and Cokaid were allowed (even encouraged) by the government to test and manipulate the fat, sugar, and salt content of flavored soyalgent in order to make the products highly addictive. Once people became hooked on any given brand's formula, they could eat nothing else.

The Globalian Establishment soon came to recognize another advantage of the Makework/infotainment economy that emerged after World War Unseen. Most people in Globalia, even the lowliest Vues, could afford ample levels of infotainment and flavor-enhanced soyalgent so as to keep them continually satiated and amused. This led to several beneficial developments for the Establishment. People who were constantly entertained found little energy to commit crimes, engage in labor strikes, or conduct political protests. Day-to-day conflicts between people diminished with the overall decline in social interaction. Spousal abuse and domestic violence plummeted. Petty theft and muggings became almost nonexistent. The domestic tranquility brought about by the infotainment economy lead to a final governing principle used by the Educates:

"Amusement is Peace."

Further research by social scientists and leading experts found that people were even less likely to become violent when they were sexually satiated and provided with plentiful doses of natural herbs. The advent of virtual sex, facilitated by MyScreen helmets and physical aids such as vibration lounges, which massaged both men and women in sensually pleasing locations, brought about a decrease in rape and sexual abuse charges. It also led to a revolt among some religious conservatives and people known as Luddytes, who thought it undermined humanity. Followers of Omar Ludd, who promoted a back-to-the-land approach of survivalist hunting and gathering, rejected the entire premise of free soyalgent and infotainment-based amusement. Religious conservatives resisted early twenty-first century laws legalizing cannabis in much of the western world, which fueled a similar backlash worldwide.

Many reactionary regions banned not only marijuana but also alcohol and tobacco. In the name of world peace and economic stability, the Tribunal of Educates expanded its jurisdiction into matters of sex and drugs by preempting any state or regional laws that barred pornography, virtual sex, vibration lounges, or mind-calming drugs including to-bacco, marijuana, alcohol, and Prozac™. "Amusement is Peace and therefore there is a compelling governmental interest to ensure that amusement is legal," ruled the Educates in an oft-quoted doctrinal ruling.

Vera, however, was not exactly amused by *The Book*. But all the talk about Pepsoilent and Cokaid was making her hungry, even though she'd just had dinner two hours ago. With only a modest feeling of guilt and hypocrisy, she whipped up a cherry-cheesecake portion on the Pepsoilent protruder and indulged in a break. *There's only so much knowledge a person can endure without life's little pleasures,* she told herself. In between bites of cheesecake, she resumed *The Book.*

The infotainment economy significantly in-creased its capacity to produce "peace" (amusement) and "free speech" (advertising) with the invention of MyScreen technology in the 2020s followed by MyndScreen capability. The first MyndScreen was successfully im-planted in an injured Navy pilot, Stephen Ostin, whose vision and hearing had been damaged when he was on leave during the War Unseen. A Fear Monger had conducted a suicide mission into a nightclub where Ostin was partying with friends who were taking live videos to share on social media. The Fear Monger simply walked through the metal de-tectors at the entrance, took a wooden baseball bat out of his overcoat, and smashed Ostin's skull so hard that his eyes popped out.

The national horror at seeing the upper third of Ostin's head hemorrhaging blood and brain sparked the top Navy brass to attempt a surgical procedure that had been heavily researched by a defense contractor but not yet conducted in humans. The Navy justified both the risk and the expense of the procedure by noting it had spent hundreds of thousands of dollars training the pilot, whose skills were better than 90 percent of his peers in the armed forces. The surgery, which was broadcast live, produced the highest Vue ratings of any program at the time.

Military surgeons implanted a medical device into Ostin's head that connected directly into the parietal lobes of the brain. The device could receive RedTooth™ signals from video cameras and microphones attached to a pair of sunglasses worn by Ostin, which concealed his disfigured eyes. The breakthrough technology, which enabled the success of the subsequent MyndScreen implant, was its ability to power itself by converting glucose found in blood sugar into electrical energy by use of a tiny fuel cell.

Soon, improved MyndScreens could also receive data input from healthy human eyes and ears by tapping directly into nerve connections. However, sensations of touch and smell travel through different neural passages so as of yet they have not been integrated into MyndScreen technology.

Vera recalled what Aldo had told her in the garden. A MyndScreen "cannot detect what you feel with your hands or with your heart. It cannot detect what you smell. You must build your reality, your truth, upon more than your sights and your thoughts, for those can betray you."

He must be blind! That's why he was feeling my face and smelling my breath. But why didn't he just get a MyndScreen implant and stream visual data with a sunglass cam? Or maybe he did. Is Aldo a misplant?

Subsequent innovations allowed the brain implants to receive signals not only from users' own eyes, ears, and sunglass cameras but also from transmissions by 11G cell phone towers. This allowed soldiers to receive live battlefield data and satellite imagery directly into their MyndScreens. The military and police applications were enormous, and elite Marine troops, Navy Seals, and SWAT units began receiving routine implants as part of basic training.

After two years of exclusive use in the military, a few high-profile celebrities launched fundraising campaigns to provide Mynd-Screen implants for children who had been born deaf or blind. The celebrities collectively received a Nobel Peace Prize for their contribution toward bettering human existence. The technology then spread from disabled people to healthy ones that were able to afford it.

After a few unfortunate mishaps, a medical protocol was established that dictated devices could only be implanted once a child reaches thirteen years of age and has had appropriate development of the cerebral cortex. Nonetheless, the cost remained prohibitively high and the procedure was not covered by any health insurance corporations.

Funding for widespread MyndScreen implants developed in the late 2020s when an information-provider company, Noodle, agreed to fund brain implants for every Establishment member between the ages of thirteen and thirty. Noodle's business model allowed it to recoup its initial investment through a lifetime of advertising revenue generated by ads directly streamed into the MyndScreen. Hedge-fund investors deemed those not part of the Globalian Establishment unlikely to have adequate lifetime purchasing power to pay for the MyndScreens, so most Vues to this day have not received an implant. They continue to use the older MyScreen helmets, which, from the advertiser's view, are less effective because they can be removed. Corporate leaders are currently working on economic models that would allow for MyndScreen implementation in the entire population of Globalia.

As MyndScreen technology and programming improved in the 2030s, Timeless Warning became so adept at transmitting amusement that some of its customers literally did nothing all day other than consume infotainment on their MyndScreens. This view consumption was compatible with the Globalian objective of prosperity so long as the customer had accumulated enough wealth over their lifetime to pay for permanent placement in an "Entertainment home" that could take care of their daily needs. Entertainment homes have been gradually replacing the dismal "retirement" or "assisted living" facilities that plagued North America in the 20th century. By providing constant amusement for the remainder of a senior citizen's life, the homes ensured clients were stimulated, well fed, and contributing to the economy. The need for personal care at these facilities was greatly reduced through carefully dosed soyalgent and pharmaceutical injections, made directly into the guest's bloodstream. This maintained health and also allowed for automated bathing and mechanized bowel-movement management. The MyndScreen infotainment was so compelling, and nutritional delivery so unobtrusive, that most guests didn't even notice when they were being fed or washed.

The catatonic state that entertainment home guests lived in provided them with a great deal of freedom, amusement, and prosperity. However, it did create an economic problem for Globalia. Some of the Establishment members, who were quickly winding up in entertainment homes, were among the five percent of the population that were actually needed to keep the economy running. Establishment members produced the infotainment, designed the robotics and drones, and constantly created new designer fashions and soyalgent flavors to fuel the consumption upon which global prosperity depended. If the rate that entertainment homes grew in the mid-2030s were to continue, experts projected that soon there would not be enough Establishment talent to keep prosperity on track. Further, Noodle was worried that its younger audience of MyndScreen implants would enter infotainment comas at middle age, before they could engage in sufficient lifetime purchasing to pay off the costs of their initial implant surgery.

The Tribunal of Educates solved this problem by issuing doctrine stating that all entry-level MyndScreen software programming needed to allow the viewer to retain at least forty percent of their independent-thinking capacity. This required MyndScreen programmers to either limit the duration of infotainment over the course of a day or only partially consume a viewer's attention span — leaving the ability for multi-tasked organic thought. However, once a viewer had accumulated enough wealth to pay for a lifetime annuity in an entertainment home, their MyndScreen software could be upgraded — upon their consent — to consume one-hundred percent of the viewers' attention span at all hours of the day.

"Wait a minute," Vera interjected. "If Renaissance Mercernary now owns both Timeless Warning and a chain of entertainment homes, they make double the money when people upgrade."

"I could have told you that. Pretty smart business model, eh?" Chase retorted as her commentary woke him. "Let me tell you, these guys ain't dumb."

"This is messed up, Chase. Listen to this, it's talking about people like us."

The requirement for consent and wealth accumulation ensured that there would be a sufficient number of educated Establishment members with pre-upgraded MyndScreens, who therefore were capable of some levels of creative thought. This was not only important for the economy, but for the ongoing function of government, the process of holding selections, and the creation of infotainment news. Establishment experts viewed regional selections (previously known as elections), which took place in the pre-existing nation-state boundaries, as a critical perception management tool for venting populist anger and providing legitimacy for the Globalian regime.

Despite, or perhaps because of, the ample supply of nutrition and amusement, pockets of resistance rejected the new technologies. Religious cults of radical Amish extremists refused to allow their thirteen-year-olds to accept MyndScreen implants. Political agitators used Chatterfeed technology to spread anti-Establishment messages questioning the assumption that Vues should live rather empty lives doing Makework jobs entirely to provide luxuries to the upper Establishment.

Spurred by new realities of MyndScreen technology and growing Luddyte opposition, Establishment members in government and corporate leadership embarked upon a public-private partnership of perception management. A lifetime of bliss and amusement was something to be earned, not considered a human right, much to the consternation of some social-rights organizations that pushed for universal MyndScreen upgrades to be financed directly by the government. Flavored Pepsoilent and Cokaid were heavily promoted as superior to soilgrown food, even while Establishment members continued to have their private chefs use soilborne produce grown in gardens and farms on their private estates. Some of the larger, more exotic estates became known as plantations, primarily for their ability to grow heirloom food made from plants.

In order to prevent another outbreak of invisible wars and to re-establish a modicum of credibility to the infotainment news industry, the Tribunal of Educates created the *Two Minute Spate* through a doctrinal ruling. This ruling required the Department of Information to produce two minutes of verifiable facts about important world matters every day. Viewers were assured that all information broadcast during the *Spate* had been thoroughly researched and fact-checked. Dissidents who had lost all trust in the Establishment and begun to question the very legitimacy of Globalian rule were convinced that they could depend upon the *Spate* for accurate reporting.

In exchange for exclusive MyndScreen broadcasting rights, Timeless Warning Corporation was required to carry the *Two Minute Spate* at least twice daily as part of its 90-minute news program, with the remaining 88 minutes to be filled with advertisements, entertainment, weather, gossip, bombast, and unsubstantiated facts and allegations. By mandating at least some factual transmissions — without censoring any other speech — the Tribunal claimed it was safeguarding the truth and protecting independent human thought while enabling self-government. The *Two Minute Spate,* combined with the policy of delayed

MyndScreen upgrades, was thought to forever solve the problem of the Great Saturation, where it became impossible for any informed public opinion to form due to a complete inundation of entertainment and lies. All people would now have a common set of accurate facts that could be used as the basis for public policy debate. The regular ritual was also thought to ensure that educated Establishment members would maintain an attention span of at least two minutes, the amount of time needed to follow the essential news.

The combination of the *Two Minute Spate* and carefully metered advertising have maintained peace, freedom and free speech in Globalia (using the accepted metrics measuring peace by consumption of amusement products; measuring freedom with production indexes; and measuring free speech by the rate of return on advertising dollars.) Thanks to these perception management techniques, Globalian society is remarkably stable, with levels of domestic and international violence considerably lower than historical averages.

However, beginning in the mid-2030s, problems began cropping up at the individual level that threatened the entire Globalian economic and security model. After several years of MyndScreen viewing, some users began experiencing side effects — including boredom, depression, hyperactivity, fatigue, epileptic seizures, anxiety, hyperventilation, and in some cases even suicide. Experts at the Department of Entertainment were unable to determine why only some individuals were prone to these symptoms, known as Mynd-

Screen Side Effect Syndrome, or MSES, so they began an exhaustive clinical study of the problem.

To conduct the study, government scientists at the Department of Entertainment partnered with Noodle and Timeless Warning to devise tracking software that measured how long a patient had viewed a singular MyndScreen episode before the program lost their interest. Lack of attention was a strong indicator of boredom, and it also seemed to correlate highly with other MyndScreen side effects. In addition to the medical research value, this tracking was also useful to help price advertising accurately, so Noodle was willing to keep financing further research.

"That's where the SpeidrWeb trackers came from," noted Vera.

"Can't they add in some timelines and graphics to make it easier to digest all this," Chase complained. "Anyhow, what next?"

There appeared to be a correlation between MSES and people who were raised in a household that was so poor it could not afford basic infotainment such as the cable TV services of the early 21st century, let alone MyScreens or other more advanced amusement opportunities. It was these people, those who had been under-stimulated in their formative years, who were most prone to side effects once they became prosperous enough to afford either a MyScreen or MyndScreen device. However, that didn't explain everything. Most early MyndScreens had been installed in members of the Establishment, who had been raised in economically prosperous families. They experienced side effects at an even greater rate than the Vues, so childhood amusement poverty couldn't be the entire problem.

Government scientists are now studying another theory — that people who experienced a real-life trauma such as an automobile accident, death of a loved one, or sexual abuse as a child were more likely to develop MyndScreen side effects. Their trauma has forced them to experience reality, which then continues to exert a stronger pull over their lifetimes than even the most compelling infotainment.

"What's wrong,? asked Chase, noticing Vera had stopped reading. *I must have loved my brother.*
"Nothing. I'll keep reading."

Whatever the cause, experts at the Department of Entertainment developed a three-pronged cure to ameliorate MyndScreen side effects. The first approach was to treat the patient with pharmaceuticals that would calm the mind, which in many cases had become over-stimulated by MyndScreen activity. Overstimulation has been shown to cause many of the side effects including anxiety, depression, and hyperactivity. To date these drugs are administered either orally, by injection, or via inhalers. These techniques often require an additional person (parent, caregiver, etc.) to administer the drug, as the patient is unable to recognize and diagnose the side effect. MyScreen manufacturers are currently working on a helmet that includes an integrated aerosol spray canister that could automatically administer a pharmaceutical dose whenever its wearer exhibits signs of side effects.

A second treatment for MyndScreen side effects is to enhance the level of amusement being provided to the individual. During the early 2040s, the quality of entertainment suffered as it became hopelessly dull and predictable. Likewise, news programming was dreary, with nothing really "new" occurring. It was one thing for reporting to be useless, but news programs were still expected to be interesting.

The Department of Entertainment, working in public-private partnerships with Noodle and other metadata tracking firms, developed a technique of content enhancement that was more successful at holding patients' attention than regular MyndScreen programming. Through providing government subsidies to infotainment firms such as Timeless Warning, the Department encouraged production and distribution of this enhanced content, targeted at individuals who had been identified by data tracking as "at risk" for side effects.

Enhanced entertainment content included Chatter applications that were intentionally designed and rigorously tested to addict users to the platform, using psychographic data to design social feedback rewards that triggered release of the pleasure hormone dopamine in the brain. Successful productions such as *Big*

Mother Gets Real, dramas with top-rated celebrities, and some of the more extreme gladiator sports competitions, which included a high level of risk and occasional death, were another form of enhanced content. News enhancement included stepped up coverage of Fear Monger attacks or other highly gruesome events that were difficult even for the most hardened mind to ignore. The Department had no need to create these gruesome events as they occurred on a daily basis around the world. It was simply a matter of ensuring that abnormally gripping real-life events were broadcast more frequently to the MyndScreens of patients who were experiencing side effects.

"They've ID'd me 'at-risk,'" Vera whispered, recalling the news reports she had seen about puppy decapitation and high-school Fear Monger attacks. Chase had fallen back asleep.

The perpetual war with Evildoer regimes served this purpose as well. Most of the war was carried out in carefully managed low-intensity conflicts that primarily involved drone strikes, robotic soldier assaults, and the like. Footage from the robots proved sufficiently interesting for most MyndScreen viewers as well as the entire Vue audience. But for those with side effects, the Department of Entertainment would occasionally feature war atrocities involving actual fatalities, rapes, and kidnappings of innocent non-combatants on either side of the conflict as part of the news coverage preceding the *Two Minute Spate.*

These enhanced news content features had the intended effect of keeping the wars against both Fear Mongers and Evildoers a perceived reality, preventing the conflicts from becoming entirely invisible as the War Unseen had been. When viewers were constantly living in an environment of real but distant fear, they were more apt to pay attention to the news programming produced by the infotainment firms and suffered fewer side effects.

When both pharmaceutical treatment and enhanced programing therapies failed to help a patient suffering from MyndScreen side effects, the case was referred to the Department of Prosperity. Economic research had shown that when side effects became too widespread in a region, it produced a devastating economic collapse. People stopped paying any attention to MyndScreen programming and began having conversations with other people in coffee shops, bars, public parks and living rooms. These conversations tended to further reduce MyndScreen content views. People began engaging in economically worthless activities such as taking walks, going to public parks, participating in open "mic" music or poetry events, or playing physical games such as soccer, shuffleboard or bingo. These pursuits cut into the profitability of both MyScreen and MyndScreen gaming software. Consumption of flavored soyalgent products also plummeted as people increased their consumption of heirloom food in bouts of sentimentalism and nostalgia. They even consumed fewer pharmaceutical products.

The Department of Prosperity was concerned that if untreatable outbreaks of MyndScreen side effects became too widespread, the entire global economy would collapse. This would mean Pepsoilent and Cokaid would face bankruptcy and no longer be able to provide free unflavored soyalgent to the world population. Mass famine would break out, leading to a dramatic increase in violence and playing into the hands of Fear Mongers. It was conceivable that the constant low-intensity conflicts would escalate again into a nuclear-level war.

To prevent such a calamity, the Department of Prosperity partnered with Mercernary General Hospitals to create a program of subsidized MyndScreen upgrades. Funded by a tax on book sales, art galleries, yoga studios and museum fees, the subsidies covered the costs of Entertainment Home care for anyone suffering from MyndScreen side effects who had not yet achieved enough wealth to pay for an upgrade on their own.

The Department also trained a network of therapists who could treat people experiencing MyndScreen side effects. In order to keep Establishment members in the workforce for as long as possible and to minimize the expense of subsidized upgrades, therapists first attempted to treat the side effects with pharmaceuticals or enhanced programming. Only when these failed did the therapists move to the third treatment of subsidized upgrades.

Vera realized that while she was reading the words, she was not comprehending them. They skimmed the surface of her brain, but they were too dense to penetrate her oversaturated curiosity.

She needed a break.

CHAPTER 10

Vera awoke to a nauseous stomach.

She stumbled to the bathroom, thinking a drink of water might settle the disturbance. It had the opposite effect. Heaving from the soles of her feet up through her innards, she vomited into the sink.

How strange. It's not even seven in the morning, and already I'm sick of the world. Is this a side effect of too much information?

Prompted by the thought, her MyndScreen ran a search and delivered several articles under the topic "morning sickness." She selected one:

"Morning sickness is not uncommon among women in their first trimester of pregnancy. It usually subsides after..."

Pregnancy?

She immediately ran a Noodle search, "Signs of being pregnant." Dozens of articles appeared along with ads for birth control pharmaceuticals and home pregnancy test kits.

She frantically checked her MenstraManage™ app to see the last time she'd had her period. Vera's mouth gaped open at the result, "Seven weeks." There were several alerts the app had sent to her Chatterfeed that she had hadn't bothered to open, presuming they were just the routine messages or promotional offers that the app frequently sent out. She had been so caught up in her resistance that she hadn't noticed what was happening, or not happening, with her body.

Tremors of panic, joy, anxiety, and excitement swept through her, followed by a return to nausea. She went back to the bedroom to lie down. Too overwhelmed to think clearly, she sent in a Chatter note to her work saying she wouldn't be in that day.

Breathing deeply, Vera tried to calm her heart rate using some of her meditation techniques. She suddenly felt like there was something alive inside her, moving, but when she placed her hands over her tummy it felt the same as it always had. She stood up and looked in the mirror, first head on and then sideways.

Same.

Should I call my doctor? Should I tell Chase? What will it feel like? Am I up for this? How did this happen when we weren't even doing IVF? How can I know if I'm ready? Will he be there for the baby? He seems pretty cheesy — almost like a caricature. How do I know who he really is? Is he just putting on an act, playing a game?

The questions kept coming. Answers did not.

She began researching the early stages of pregnancy. As she read, she couldn't resist the ads that popped up and began browsing shopping sites on her MyndScreen for baby clothes. *They're adorable!*

There were home protruder designs for pacifiers, cribs with surround sound speakers, disposable bibs with prints of bunnies and strawberries, and the cutest little socks imaginable. Each item listing suggested other similar products and she spent hours devouring information about babies, pregnancy, preschools, the role of strong fathers, and immunizations.

By the afternoon, Vera had decided to tell Chase. She could not do this alone — he'd need to be on board. *But how?*

Vera was adept at asking questions, but her emerging creativity was at a loss for ways to break such important news to someone she loved.

I need an idea.

Her empty mind produced none.

Oh, what's the point? I'm no good at finding inspiration.

While her brain was stuck, her MyndScreen sprung to action:

"Inspiration Point. This pleasant 2.6-mile hike begins at the historic home of Will Rogers in Pacific Palisades and ends at Inspiration Point."

What was it The Book *had said about hikes?*

Vera sent Chase a note via Chatter, "Run a Noodle search on Will Rogers. Enjoy the first three links that appear with his witty quotes. Then, choose the 8th link. I'll meet you at Will Rogers State Park at 6 p.m. There's something I want to tell you — V."

Vera arrived an hour before the appointed time. When she got out of her car, she looked down upon an overgrown field. A few bushes of manzanita were surrounded by tall grasses, which were drooping sideways, bent down from recent rains and wind. A slight breeze rustled the leaves of the trees, interrupted frequently by the dull roar of overhead airplanes. She saw the yellow dandelions in bloom, along with some white blowballs, just like at the fountain outside the arboretum. A rotting wooden sign read "Polo Field." Vera thought that it must have once been branded by the Ralph Lauren clothing company — although she saw no logo and there didn't seem to be much sponsorship value in an overgrown plot of grass.

Above the field was a dilapidated ranch-style home, its windows covered with plywood and roof shingles crumbling from years of alternating heat and ice. Vera slipped off her sandals and walked barefoot through the weeds, letting them tickle her ankles. She pulled away some vines from a stone monument near the house with the inscription:

Advertising makes you spend money you haven't got for things you don't want. Will Rogers, 1931.

She inhaled the mint-like, sanitary scent of eucalyptus trees mixed with another, earthier, aroma that she had recently encountered, though she couldn't quite remember where. The smell grew stronger as she walked up beyond the house to an area surrounded by white plastic fencing. She picked dandelion blowballs as she walked.

A strange sound pierced the air, something like a car's screeching brakes combined with a haunting clown laugh in a horror movie. Vera looked up and saw the creature.

A horse. A real horse!

Vera had heard that High Establishment members kept horses along with a personal staff of breeders, trainers, farriers, and veterinarians. She approached the monstrous animal with some trepidation, eventually working up the courage to touch its soft muzzle. The horse let out a quieter whinny and stared at Vera with eyes of deep black ink. It snorted and sent her dandelion seeds flurrying into the air.

"You know, horses are smarter than people. You never heard of a horse going broke betting on people, did ya?" A voice with a strained folksy drawl shot out from behind her. She spun around.

Chase!

Vera threw her arms around him, squeezing him tighter and longer than usual, with the sandals she held in her right hand rubbing up against his shoulder. Still in character voice, Chase asked, "Don't you think you'd better put those shoes on missy? We can't have you walking around barefoot and pregnant."

"What?" Vera exclaimed, pushing herself back from his clutch so she could see his face.

Does he know?

"It's just an expression. Long ago men used phrases like that to keep women from having an equal opportunity to work — you know, back when work was something that people needed. It may even have been said by Will Rogers. I know for sure he said that thing about horses."

"But, …. I am, Chase. I am pregnant."

The words rang like a bell in the fog.

"OMG! That's amazing. I can't believe it!" His voice returned to its normal tone as an irrepressible smile spread across his face.

Vera exhaled and then let out a little shriek as she gasped for breath. She had not been sure how he'd respond.

"Believe it, Chase. I'm certain of it." She kissed him while he stood in shock. "C'mon, let's go for a walk." She put on her sandals, then grabbed his hand and began walking up the trail of decomposed beige granite and reddish dirt.

The path was washed out in several places due to the heavy rains. They picked their way around decaying prickly pear cactuses that had split open during the nuclear winter and not recovered. They both were breathing hard when they reached the top of the trail and stopped for a moment to gaze at the ocean, smelling the moist, salty air.

"It's so big," said Vera, suddenly feeling quite small. Chase put his arm around her shoulder as they walked to the edge of a lookout point.

"Chase, I want to be with you always. I want to raise this baby with you. But first, I need to find my husband and make a clean divorce. I want to find my parents, or at least find out what happened to them. I need to discover who I am, before I can join with you and bring someone else into the world. I … I love you, but … but I'm not quite sure I'm ready to really love anyone. I will be though. I know I will be."

"I believe you," was all that he said while looking into her eyes and stroking her cheek.

"I'm afraid, Chase." The words kept pouring out. "Afraid that this baby will one day forget me, not even know or care where I am — just as I have forgotten my parents. That would be more than I could bear. Before I can be a good mother, I need to be a good daughter. I need to recapture my past so that I can control my own future. I need to remember, so that I won't be forgotten."

Chase held her tight, not saying anything. He then looked over her shoulder and saw an old wooden bench, with an inscription carved on it:

"Do not let the behavior of others destroy your inner peace."

He smiled and led her to the bench. They sat, taking in the distant ocean breeze. For a long time, they just sat.

* * *

The weeks passed quickly as Vera immersed herself in information about pregnancy. There were hundreds of "what to expect when you're expecting" articles, videos, and interviews to take in. She became fixated on nutrition, augmenting her Pepsoilent diet with vitamins, supplements, and real soilborne food that Chase helped acquire. She upgraded her bathroom fiber extruder to have extra capacity to produce disposable diapers on demand.

Her MyndScreen was inundated with ads for lactation devices, infant car seats, baby-sized MyScreen helmets, and belly speakers that could play brain-stimulating music and words through a mother's abdomen to ensure Einstein levels of intellect in a newborn. Some experts were recommending the use of a crib screen, which mounted on top of a crib facing downward. They could display images of mobiles or pictures of a mother's face while playing soothing lullaby music to newborns to help them sleep through the night.

Who knew you needed so much stuff to have a baby?

Vera watched episodes on C-sections, birth defects, ectopic pregnancies, and the dozens of things that can go wrong during gestation. She worried and obsessed about it nearly every waking moment, leaving little time for other concerns. She visited her doctor, who ran multitudes of tests and provided Vera with more than two-dozen handouts, videos, and exercise instructions along with the standard liability disclaimers that contained thousands of Expertalk words in fine print. Vera tried reading them at first, but gave up after several pages. Her sleep became erratic. Sometimes she was up at two in the morning, other times she slept ten hours straight.

She downloaded a MyndScreen app with week-by-week plans for the number of steps she should take on walks and the number of prenatal exercises to incorporate into the morning physical jerks. Her doctor prescribed three different pharmaceuticals to prevent birth defects, ensure healthy pregnancy, and improve the chances that the baby would have blonde hair like Chase. Vera wondered how anyone had managed to give birth prior to all this technological support.

She went through the motions at work and was no longer preoccupied with whether any distinct fact she researched was relevant, helpful, or true. She just ensured it was accurate and sent it on up the chain of command. One day she noticed her friend Symeon wasn't in the office. *Must have been upgraded. I always thought he would be.*

At the doctor's yet again, she had an ultrasound with images from her abdomen beamed directly into her MyndScreen. A grainy, alien-like figure lay encased in black fluid surrounded by a gray sac. The doctor zoomed in on a small dot that was blinking on and off like a computer cursor.

"That's the heart beating," said the doctor.

The baby. It's real.

* * *

The next morning, Vera received a notice from the public library indicating she owed $525 to replace her long overdue book. *The Book!* She'd completely forgotten about it amid all the excitement of her pregnancy. In looking through her thousands of old Chatterfeed messages, she saw that she'd missed three previous notices from the library.

How did they track me down? She wondered. *I never even gave them my name.*

She made plans to meet Chase for a picnic on the beach, promising herself they would at least finish the introduction and wondering just what the library would do if she never returned it. She had given them Aneeka Randall's address. *Would they go there, looking for it? What will happen to Aneeka?*

After work, Vera ordered a picnic blanket for instant delivery and took it, along with *The Book,* down to her MiOtto. She rode to Venice along the beach highway and an ad popped up on her MyndScreen for a pre-packed crab picnic, along with the usual fine print disclaimer "Advertising Frees Speech." She had read that crab was high in protein and iron, so figured it would be good for the baby. The car circled the block while Vera went inside.

A middle-aged man greeted her at the door. By his black hair, and wide tan face, she thought that he might be of Vietnamese descent, and then wondered if there were crabs in Vietnam or if you could learn anything important about a person by where they came from.

He told her how to find a 20th century instructional video on her MyndScreen with a dowdy blonde-haired woman detailing how to do your own outdoor crab boil. Within a few minutes, Vera emerged with a large enameled steel pot containing four live crabs, two ears of corn, a plastic shaker jar of seasoning, four bottles of cold beer (two of them non-alcoholic), instant cloth napkins, a pair of tongs, two faux-wooden extruded mallets for breaking open the crab shells, a box of matches, and a small bag of charcoal briquettes.

She met Chase at the empty parking lot on the beach. A white lifeguarding drone buzzed slowly up and down the coastline. It looked a bit like a flying squid, with long padded arms dangling below in the event it should need to pull anyone out of the water. But a rescue was unlikely. Not only was there nobody on the beach, there were no footprints in the sand other than those of the seagulls.

A rusting sign said in faded letters:

> NO GLASS CONTAINERS
> NO ALCOHOL
> NO LITTERING
> NO FIRES
> NO CAMPING
> ENJOY YOUR DAY

Vera stared at the sign, but Chase just shrugged his shoulders. "Eh, what's the worst thing that could happen?" He started carrying the pot toward the sand.

For Chase, this was just another opportunity for daily rebellion against "The System," thought Vera. She wasn't sure that drinking beer around a beach fire really counted toward membership in the Sisterhood, but she *was* really hungry. She followed with the blanket and *The Book*, looking out over the orangish sky as the sun dipped down toward the horizon. Listening to the sound of the waves gently breaking against the beach, she looked toward her left at the rotting pillars of what had once been the Santa Monica Pier. The beach was considerably more narrow than it had been when she was a child, but still nice enough.

While Chase made a pit in the sand and lit the charcoal, Vera spread the blanket and brought out *The Book*.

"I got an overdue notice on this today from the library. I thought we'd better at least finish the part we were reading. Maybe we can check it out again once the baby is born."

"OK, my love, if you insist. Read away." Chase picked up a handful of sand and let it seep slowly through his fingers.

"Why do you always call me, 'My love?' Is it just an expression?"

"I guess it is. … I'm sorry. It's a phrase I use a lot in my writing for the studio. I suppose it's become a habit. Have I cheapened the feeling by using the word too glibly?" Knowing the answer, he looked down at the sand for a moment.

"Words matter. If we're going to make anything matter again, we must start with words. That means using them in the right amount, at the right times."

"OK, OK. So, now that I've destroyed the meaning of the word for you, how can I convey my feelings?"

"Look at me."

He obliged.

After a long while, he said," OK, I know that you need to read the book. Even more so, you need me to listen. I know what you need. I'm ready."

As the Pacific Ocean crashed against the shoreline, Vera read:

> The techniques of mind-scarcity pricing, perception management, and treatment of MyndScreen side effects have proven remarkably successful at preserving a stable economic order and increasing prosperity. There remain, however, significant pockets of the world population who live outside of the

infotainment bubble. In addition to the Amish and the Luddytes, who consciously reject both MyndScreen and MyScreen technology, there remain millions of people in rural areas that simply lack access to MyndScreen transmissions. Their relative purchasing power is so low that neither Noodle nor Timeless Warning has been willing to make the investments in the necessary infotainment infrastructure to reach these communities.

Further, there remain some populations of nuns, Buddhists, indigenous peoples, orthodox Jews, yoga enthusiasts, and others who live in proximity to infotainment but have not shown an interest. These demographics have never really integrated into the post-war economy, so their lack of participation has not been deemed a threat by the Department of Prosperity.

The Vues, however, comprise the clear majority of Globalia's population and thereby pose a potential source of economic and political instability. Their consumption of infotainment, flavored soyalgent, and pharmaceuticals are critical to the new world order. Yet, due to incomplete MyndScreen implantation among the Vue population, they remain more capable of independent thought than most members of the Establishment. Some Vues have been known to tire of their MyScreen helmets and remove them for days on end. Others simply forget to keep them charged, so they lose service periodically. For the past several decades, the public-private perception management campaign has been successful in keeping the Vue population sufficiently content. But should this fail, the Vues could rapidly upend Establishment rule of Globalia and precipitate a breakdown in peace and prosperity.

Beyond the populations that MyndScreen technology has not completely reached, there is one particularly threatening source of instability to the Globalian regime — the Sisterhood."

"Chase, listen. This is the part we've been waiting for."

"OK, V. But, if the Sisterhood really wanted people to get what they're saying, they should have made the book interesting. You know, like with characters and a plot. It's not just that it's boring, but when you bludgeon someone with an endless barrage of depressing facts it's just hard to take."

"Facts aren't supposed to be emotional or engaging, just accurate. Important information will not always be entertaining." She plowed forward.

The Sisterhood consists of people who once belonged to the Establishment but have come to view the infotainment economy as fundamentally threatening to humanity. Sisters are willing to risk starvation not only for themselves but for the entire planet if that is the price of weaning the world from complete dependence upon two multinational corporations for nutritional survival. Sisters are willing to endure a life of pain in order to experience a life of joy, to suffer from boredom in order to enable creativity, to ignore or even disable their MyndScreens in order to free their minds to observe reality. These disabling procedures involve forceful blows to the head with a blunt instrument to disrupt the connections between the MyndScreen chip and the cerebral cortex. When done improperly, disabling procedures can seriously injure or kill a person who attempts the procedure by causing a concussion, stroke, or cranial fracture.

It is their proximity to the Vues that makes the emerging Sisterhood such a threat. While the other populations that lack MyndScreens rarely, if ever, come into contact with Vues, Sisterhood members live among them and share technological channels. Sisters who have not yet disabled their MyndScreens can engage Vues through the Chatterfeed as well as through personal encounters in parks, restaurants, workplaces, and entertainment venues.

Because of this threat, the Department of Information and Department of Entertainment have partnered in a massive perception management campaign to discredit the Sisterhood among the Vue population. Whenever there is an accurate fact about any harm done by any member of the Sisterhood, perhaps even unintentionally, it is included in the *Two Minute Spate*. For example, if a car accidentally kills a dog or a rabbit, it is sure to receive prominent news coverage attributing the death to a "reported" member of the Sisterhood. Any sexual deviations among people who lack MyndScreens are meticulously studied and publicized.

Other entertainment programs that aren't constrained by the accuracy requirements of the *Spate* ostracize the Sisterhood conceptually. They are ridiculed for being out of fashion, for eating archaic and unsanitary food, and for not being up to speed with current happenings in reality programs. Since it isn't usually possible to positively identify someone as a member of the Sisterhood, anyone displaying criminal or anti-social behavior is labeled a "likely" or "alleged" Sisterhood member in news reports.

While nobody knows for sure how many members of the Sisterhood there are, the perception management campaign portrays the number as extremely small.

But above all, the Establishment takes great care to ensure that in the physical world beyond MyndScreens the Sisterhood is ignored and ostracized. So long as they remain largely unnoticed by the Vues, even while existing in plain sight, the Sisterhood poses little threat.

The biggest challenge for the Establishment in combatting the Sisterhood is identifying individual members. They do not congregate in any physical location nor do they have any characteristics that mark them as Sisters. This anonymity also presents a challenge for Sisterhood members to organize themselves and find support for their views from sympathetic colleagues. Many Sisters say they instinctively know when they run across another member. Some suggest that facial expressions are the best way to tell. Members of the Sisterhood seem to have more engaged looks on their faces, they make eye contact with others, and seem to have a depth or gleam in their eyes. They smile.

If you are reading this book, you are likely a member of the Sisterhood whether or not you have realized it up until this moment.

This means you are at significant risk.

Establishment corporations are working on facial recognition software that could detect "eye sparkle" and help the Globalian Establishment root out the Sisterhood. Datatrackers put members of the Sisterhood at constant risk of being "treated" for Mynd-Screen side effects. These treatments could render you incapable of autonomous thought by immersing you in a constant world of info-tainment. They could lead to an upgrade, which would mean you would no longer be useful to the Sisterhood or to yourself.

This book elucidates in greater detail the conditions described in this introduction. Your first task is to understand how things have become the way they are. Your second task is to remain cheerful, optimistic, and curious in the face of this discouraging information. Your final task is ...

Everything went dark and silent.

*   *   *

A powerful wind rushed over Vera's head and shoulders. The sound of a lawn mower roared all around her. Regaining consciousness, she opened her eyes to see cars and houses far below her dangling bare feet. Her arms hurt, and she realized she was tightly held in the grip of a lifeguarding drone.

Chase was nowhere in sight, nor was the beach. A foreboding ache developed in her stomach, as if she had just ingested a smoldering cannon ball.

I'm captive.

Delivery drones whirred by in flocks launched from mule trucks down below. The air was cold and dry, rushing past her face. The sudden dips and twists of her lifeguarding drone made Vera's stomach lurch.

The darkening sky turned black as she slowed and dropped in elevation. As she approached a tall skyscraper, illuminated under streetlights she could recognize City Hall, the library, and the park where she and Chase had met. The machine gently placed her on a concrete landing pad atop the high-rise.

As the drone's arms released her, three large men in blue medic uniforms came out of a gray doorway, followed by an automated wheelchair. Above the sliding door, an illuminated screen read, "Prosperity is Freedom."

"Are you OK? Sit down," said one of them, as the chair circled behind her.

"No, I'm not fucking OK. What the hell am I doing here? Where's Chase? Who are you?"

The man stepped toward her, placing the toes of his boots on either side of her bare feet while simultaneously the chair pushed in against the back of her knees, buckling them underneath her. The two other men, standing on either side of her, held her elbows down against the chair's armrests, which then ejected a blue fabric that wrapped around her forearms and locked itself tight to a latch underneath. A lap bar automatically fastened around her waist and bolted in place.

The auto-restraint chair drove forward on its own, through the gray door that slid open as she approached. Leaving the medics behind, she rode down a brightly lit hallway for what seemed like half an hour, passing dozens of doors on either side of her as the chair softly whined with the high pitch of a straining electric motor. Finally, a door opened on the right and the chair drove through. The door closed behind her with a whoosh.

Vera sat alone in a room with smooth, dusty pink-tiled walls and pale-yellow floors that had the dull shine of aging vinyl. She panted and tried to catch her breath, but kept gasping uncontrollably. Frenzied thoughts raced through her mind.

Where's Chase? What are they going to do to me? How long can I withstand them?

She struggled against the arm restraints and tried to break the lap bar by thrusting her abdomen against it. Then she remembered. *The baby. I've got to keep calm.*

Vera inhaled, counted to three, then exhaled slowly. She repeated the exercise five times. She felt the cold metal frame of the chair with her fingertips and let her feet dangle onto the floor. It was sticky.

She could hear a faint rush of air above her head, which she guessed must be coming out of an air conditioning vent behind her. She could feel her heart beating, still rapidly but no longer out of control.

Vera closed her eyes and observed the reddish hue of her eyelids as the bright white light from above bled through them. She absorbed the stone silence of the room while studying the blotchy crimson glow, noticing how it changed intensity as she squeezed and relaxed her eyelids or turned her head away from the light.

Her muscles remembered the last time they had been frozen motionless in an upright, tense position. The previous occasion had left her helpless, paralyzed, and afraid. She had heard a faint hissing of air, but it was almost imperceptible above bleeps and zaps of the *Angry Bugs* game in her MyScreen helmet. She had felt something clinging to her left forearm, squeezing it much in the way the chairs arm restraints held her now. She had meant to take off her helmet and look to see what it was, but she just needed five hundred more points to make her high score. The sounds went quiet and the tugging stopped just before she surpassed her record, everything must be OK. She kept on — the game was amazing, exciting, intoxicating. She reached the level of the centipedes and needed to accumulate enough pesticide in her spray gun before flushing them out from under the rocks and logs. She'd never made it this far before. They moved fast and had fierce pinchers that would bite off your fingers if you weren't nimble.

When the game finally ended, she slipped off the helmet and saw him, lifeless on the couch. His bluish face contorted in a look that seared into her memory, with his eyes still open — dull and pleading. Her brother was dead. At the time, the twelve-year-old Vera had thrown her helmet back on and stared at its blank white screen through her eyelids until her parents found them. Not moving. Not thinking. Just taking in the red hues of the inside of her eyelids.

This time, instead of suppressing it, Vera held onto the image of her brother using the mindfulness techniques she'd learned through meditation. She took in the color of his hair, the light purple outfit he was wearing, the smell of Vienna sausages in the air, and recalled the itchy texture of the stiff embossed velvet sofa, which had pressed against her arms and elbows.

A moan trembled within her innards, erupting out through her lungs and throat in a sob of anguish that echoed in the room. Tears ran uncontrollably down her cheeks. She could not wipe them away, nor clear the snot draining down her nose because her hands were still restrained in the chair. Vera did not run from the pain. She wallowed in it, embracing its full horror. Her shrieks alarmed her, sounding unlike anything she'd ever heard. She was worried she would suffocate from lack of air as she could not control her sobs or pause long enough to breathe. She writhed from side to side, almost tipping the chair over but unable to break free from its hold.

Eventually, it lifted. She felt the saline tracks of tears begin to dry and tighten on her face. She licked her upper lip clean with her tongue and tasted the sweet gooey mucous that had accumulated.

Vera spat onto the floor.

"I'm sorry," she yelled into the room. "I'm so, so sorry. I didn't mean to … I'm sorry." She heaved a sigh and let her head hang forward, dangling from her neck so low that her chin touched her breastbone. She could feel blood coursing through her arteries, pulsing its way to her hands, her fingers. She could hear the thump of her heartbeat echoing inside her head. The arches of her feet ached and her toes curled up against the vinyl floor. Vera had never felt so alive, and it was awful.

Her eyelids looked dark as she pointed her head down, away from the bright lights of the room. Her breathing slowed. Exhausted, Vera collapsed into sleep.

* * *

At eight o'clock in the morning, Vera's MyndScreen woke her with the gentle voice of an automated intake attendant. It surprised her since the MyndScreen hadn't been working the previous night when she arrived. Her neck was stiff and painful.

"Hello, Vera. Welcome to Mercernary General, a mental health center accredited by the Department of Prosperity. You have been admitted because your therapist has determined that you are a threat to your own well-being and also the well-being of others. With your cooperation, we will be able to ameliorate your symptoms and enable you to lead a safe, enjoyable life."

"A threat?" Vera yelled back, even though the attendant was not in the room, present only on her MyndScreen. "How could I possibly be a danger to anyone? And besides, I don't even have a therapist. What the hell are you talking about?"

"You were found on the beach with a hammer while the accomplice you were with was running a Noodle search on how to disable a MyndScreen by smashing the skull with blunt instruments. As a safety precaution, your MyndScreen disabled you by administering a shock to your brain and sent out an emergency distress signal. Fortunately, there was a lifesaving drone in close proximity." The attendant's voice was calm but firm, like a first-grade teacher's.

"We were eating crab. The hammers were for the crab, nothing more. They weren't even real wood, only hard plastic. You can't prove anything." Vera's voice grew louder, but she was not yelling. She felt her neck physically restrain her vocal chords from exploding with rage and focused on keeping a measured tone to her words.

"You have exhibited both a willingness and an ability for self-mutilation, Vera. Look at the scar on your thumb where you intentionally cut yourself with a razor."

"That ..." she bit her lip, realizing she probably should not explain her motivations.

"That was evidence that you were acting on your previous thoughts of cutting and self-endangerment, Vera. We know everything, Vera." Her MyndScreen displayed a video recording of her conversation with Aneeka Randall:

"You will need to cut yourself to inflict pain and soak in its sensations. You will need to starve yourself for days on end, purging what little food you do place into your body until you are thin, emaciated, and weak. You will experience hunger, deprivation, lacerations, bruises, aches, vile smells, intolerable sounds, sensations of drowning, and pitch blackness that will make you feel more alone and afraid than you can even imagine. Are you willing to do that?

Vera watched herself respond, *"Yes."*

"You may be called upon to engage your colleagues at work, your neighbors, your families. You may be asked to lie, cheat, and steal. You may be asked to kill. Are you sure you're ready to do that?

"Yes."

"You may reach a point where you need to disable your MyndScreen permanently by whacking your skull with a ball-peen hammer. If you do it wrong, you risk debilitating brain damage. Are you certain you are capable of that?"

"I'm certain."

"You see, Vera, the only rational conclusion is that you have been harboring thoughts that are dangerous to yourself and others. Further, you have acted upon those thoughts. It is for the protection not only of yourself, but also of society, that we are legally required to admit you to Mercernary General as provided for under the Doctrine of the Educates. But, don't worry, everything is going to be alright. With your cooperation, you will experience a speedy recovery. We have a near perfect record in treating your disorder. Now, please wait here."

It was an instruction Vera could not help but follow as she had no way to leave the room, let alone get up from her chair. She realized that she had an intense need to urinate, but she held the burning sensation inside her. Her neck still ached painfully from having slept upright in the chair.

After what Vera guessed must have been a few hours, the door to the room slid open and her chair wheeled out into the hallway. She entered an elevator, which closed automatically and took her to another floor. The sinking feeling in her stomach suggested she was losing altitude, but there were no buttons or lights to indicate where she was going. The doors parted, and the chair rolled straight ahead, through sliding glass doors, into a reception area directly in front of her.

On three walls of the room hung a jumbotron screen measuring 12 by 20 feet. One was showing a *Big Mother Gets Real* episode, another a gladiator sporting event. Vera didn't recognize the other program — a daytime drama perhaps. There were several tables scattered about the room, with nearly a dozen people seated at them. Both Pepsoilent and Cokaid vending machines stood near the center of the room.

Her seatbelt and arm restraints released, and Vera stood up. She walked across the room, seeing a door labeled "Lavatory," and went inside to relieve herself. After washing her hands, she splashed cold water on her face while listening to the sound it made as it ran through the pipes and faucet. The astringent salt traces of her dried teardrops washed away, and she savored the taste of fresh water on her lips. She inhaled and smelled the hygienic naphthalene scent of urinal cakes, staying longer than she needed to in the quiet stillness of the restroom.

Vera emerged and walked slowly around the edges of the room, gazing at the faces of the people seated around the tables. They looked neither dangerous nor depressed. Most were staring at one of the screens on the wall, waiting.

In a corner, a small man with a contorted face sat cross-legged on the floor. He rocked back and forth with his eyes closed and wrists curled forward while singing in a soft, high-pitched voice,

> *And in the jaded night I saw*
> *A thousand people, maybe more*
> *People talking without thinking*
> *People hearing without listening*
> *People writing poems that voices never share*
> *And no one there*
> *Recalled the sound of silence*

Having spent several hours confined in the chair, Vera paced the room for what must have been twenty laps before tiring. Tables were piled with soyalgent snack food: brownies, potato chips, cheese puffs. The plastic plates beneath the tidbits had a slogan etched onto them that encircled the outer edge: "Prosperity is Freedom."

Periodically, someone approached the vending machines in the center of the room and returned with a cappuccino, soda, or beer. It had been perhaps twenty-four hours since she had last eaten, but Vera did not reach for the food. She stared aimlessly at the floor.

A woman on a motorized scooter stared at the jumbotron playing a daytime drama. The woman's tight spandex shirt could not contain her obese body, which spilled out at the bottom, revealing her navel. She had a shell-shocked look on her face, as if she had stared into an abyss of despair and turned away only after becoming fully anesthetized to every human sensation. Vera watched as she drank a two-liter orange soda from a straw, swallowing a gulp methodically after every three breathes and nervously chewing on the tip of the straw until it was flat and tattered.

Vera tried to get the woman's attention by making subtle eye contact. She thought of asking how she got there, what her life had been like, what she expected might happen next. After a long while, the woman did give her a sideways glance and said simply, "It's over, honey. Everyone consents in the end."

"Vanessa Smith," called out a doctor, wearing a white lab coat as he entered the room. The woman stopped sipping and looked up at him from the jumbotron. "The Situation Room is ready for you now," he continued.

"Already? Are you sure?"

"Yes. It will make certain that you have no regrets. Come with me," and he escorted her from the room.

Over the course of the next few hours, a doctor wearing a white lab coat would occasionally enter and authoritatively announce somebody's name over a loudspeaker, overpowering the din of the competing jumbotron audio systems. They then escorted the person out of the room, often accompanied by two nurses in blue scrubs. Nobody argued or resisted, as there didn't seem to be much point of staying where they were.

Vera eventually grew tired of the chair and instead sat on the floor. She focused her attention on a man who looked to be about fifty years old wearing blue coveralls. She watched him fidget in his seat, shifting his weight back and forth and regularly itching the calf of his left leg. The folds of his garments would stretch and collapse with every breath he took. After carefully observing him for perhaps 30 minutes, she could imagine the sound of air flowing in and out of his nostrils with each breath, although with the noise of the jumbotrons she could not hear it. She judged by the scruffy hairs growing down the back of his neck that it had been at least a month since he'd had a haircut. She wondered what his name was, why he was there.

Several hours later, a wheelchair drove itself in and unbuckled its occupant — a tall man with a receding hairline dressed in a relatively up-to-date pink polo shirt and madras shorts. He stood up and walked around the room, looking at the empty faces seated at the tables.

"Vera!" he exclaimed, sitting down next to her. "By golly, who would have thought I'd see you in here? It's almost like that episode of *Big Mother Gets Real* that takes place in the dentist's waiting room."

Manquin. Good lord, they've even got Manquin. They'll get everyone eventually.

"Looks like I'll be getting an upgrade early," Manquin continued. "Evidently the datatrackers recorded my daughter running Noodle searches for things like "loser dad" and "evil witch mother" just a couple of months after she got her MyndScreen installed. I must admit, I didn't do the best job of keeping things around the house stimulating for her. I'm embarrassingly boring when it comes right down to it, but I guess her MyndScreen will do the trick from now on. And, it means I should qualify for a pre-retirement entertainment home subsidy since they can infer from Marsha's searches that our parenting was detrimental to her health. I guess I'll never miss another *Big Mother* episode for as long as I'm alive. Hey, you want a brownie?" He took a bite of one himself and shoved the plate in her direction. "They're hash. You really should take one!"

"No thanks," Vera replied, watching his jaw bounce up and down as it gnashed the brownie and made his temples bulge in and out with every bite. It didn't take long for his conversation to dwindle as he turned his attention toward one of the jumbotrons.

Turns out he really doesn't have that much to say.

Over the next few hours, Vera stared at the center of the plastic table where she was seated, listening to the competing dialogue and sounds coming from the four jumbotrons and watching her fellow patients gorge themselves on junk food. Nobody seemed the least bit alarmed. It reminded her of the time she was called up for jury service and had to wait all day before being told she would not be picked.

Periodically, an automated chair would wheel in a new person and release them into the room. Later, a doctor in a white lab coat would enter, read off someone's name and escort them out. Vera seemed never to be the one called, but she knew that eventually her time would come. There was no escaping it at this point.

Her lower back ached so she stood up and walked around the room again, methodically counting the steps it took to complete a full lap around its perimeter and then keeping track of the number of laps she had walked. There were no windows in the room, and the jumbotron programming did not correspond to regularly scheduled episodes such as the evening *Two Minute Spate*. Vera lost track of how long she had been there.

She sat down on the floor and leaned her back up against the wall, but was chased away by a middle-aged woman with dark curly hair who said she was blocking her view of the jumbotron. Vera moved to the middle of the room and lay down on the floor, staring up at the ceiling — the only surface besides the floor that wasn't constantly filled with moving images. She could hear the occasional names being called out above the noise of the jumbotrons, but she stopped paying attention to them. *Chase.* She kept repeating the thought in her mind, over and over and over. *Chase. Chase. Chase.*

"Vera?" a familiar voice jolted her attention. Sitting upright and pivoting around, she turned and saw Aneeka Randall walking toward her. She got up slowly.

"They got you too?" Vera gasped. Aneeka had told her that resistance was futile. *Did she know this would happen?*

"Vera, I'm here to help you." Aneeka reached out and gently touched Vera's shoulder with her fingertips, sending a chill up Vera's spine. Only then did she notice that Aneeka was wearing a white lab coat.

"You work here?! That's … impossible." All the air in Vera's lungs left.

"I was assigned to you years ago, Vera, after you were promoted at work. Your new job assignment placed you in an "at risk" category for cognitive dissonance between your professional life and your daily experience. I've been monitoring you carefully, Vera, and you have reached a point where you need therapy to prevent you from harming yourself. Come with me," she said, gently taking Vera's hand and leading her through the sliding doors, into an elevator.

The sudden acceleration of the lift made Vera regurgitate a small amount of stomach acid. Feeling the sting in her throat, she swallowed it back down rather than let Aneeka Randall see her discomfort. She smelled the acrid fumes rising through her sinuses and out of her nostrils.

After a long ride, the doors opened to another floor and Aneeka led them down a hallway into an office. They sat down on opposite sides of a wooden desk, and Aneeka explained, "the cognitive dissonance from your work at the Department of Information exacerbated the side effects you were already experiencing from your MyndScreen, Vera. Your unfortunate encounters with Mr. Hatten then intensified your illness to the point where admitting you to the hospital is our only option right now."

"Chase? You mean Chase? Where is he? What did you do with him?" Vera's voice rose.

"He has also been hospitalized for his own protection. He is already undergoing treatment, you need not worry about his well-being."

But Vera did worry. She looked down at Aneeka's desk, avoiding her gaze, and noticed a placard with black letters etched in brass-colored plastic: "Prosperity is Freedom."

"*The Book*," Vera asked, "what about *The Book*? You told me to read it. It explains everything. It has to be true."

"*The Book* is accurate, Vera, just like the verifiable facts you produced. That is, everything in it except the parts about the Sisterhood, which were embellished." Vera noticed Aneeka broke eye contact and looked at her desk as she said this. "I helped write it, along with a team of co-authors assembled by Renaissance mental health providers. Bernice Wohrn is a pseudonym, there is no official Sisterhood organization, but otherwise the book is authentic."

"But … how … if you know all of those things in *The Book,* how can you be taking part in all this? Aneeka, how *can* you?" Vera stared at a model of a building on a shelf behind Dr. Randall's desk. Its white, curved walls looked like flower petals pointing upward to the sky. The words "Lotus Temple — a gift to SpeiDr. Aneeka Randall from LingerLife Pharmaceuticals" were written on the platform the model was mounted on.

"Expert research has shown, Vera, that a small percentage of people have a curiosity that is so strong it will continue to exert an irrational pull on their attention span until it has been satisfied. Objectively speaking, you had become so transfixed on finding what you call the truth that the only way to relieve you was to offer you the complete information you were seeking in a manner that felt authentic. Now that you have been satiated with this information, it will be easier for you to recover, to be at peace. It is simply a part of our therapeutic process."

"What if I don't want to recover? What if I won't go along?" Vera shot back, knowing in her core that everyone eventually went along, that she too would succumb. She was not prepared to surrender just yet.

"Your therapy leads to an upgrade, doesn't it? That's what this is all about. But you can't order an upgrade unless I consent. Even *The Book* says that. Even your twisted Tribunal of Educates says that. You can't make me. You can't make me. You can't make me!" The strength waned from her voice with the final words, and Vera sobbed, placing her face into the upturned palms of her hands.

Aneeka Randall pressed a button on her desk. "That is enough for today, Vera. I can tell you are upset so I will prescribe some anger management medication. Try to get some rest and relax. It's going to be OK." Two nurses walked in the room wearing blue scrubs, ready to escort Vera out. Before they could, Aneeka stood up and walked around the desk. Vera pushed her chair back and stood up slowly, piercing Aneeka's eyes and soul with her gaze. Aneeka wrapped her arms around Vera and gave her an unreciprocated hug. "It's going to be OK, believe me," she whispered.

Vera was led to a solitary dorm room that contained a vibration lounge, a Pepsoilent extruder, a toilet, a sink, and a small recycling chute. A large video screen on the wall displayed a beautiful ocean scene, with pelicans flying above gently breaking waves. The identical image appeared on her MyndScreen, which had been blank ever since she received her virtual intake interview on it.

Vera closed the MyndScreen window. They couldn't make her watch it, not even here. She instead ran a Noodle search for "meditation." It didn't matter anymore if the datatrackers knew, she was already caught. In fact, she wanted them to know.

Vera couldn't turn off the wall screen, but it was a pleasant enough backdrop for meditation. Clicking on the link she'd found months ago for "ten-minute meditation guide" she sat cross-legged on the floor and concentrated on her breathing, letting go of a minute portion of the rage that burned inside her with each exhalation.

As she focused on her body, Vera felt pangs of hunger with rumblings and bubbles agitating her stomach. Determined not to succumb to their Pepsoilent, she drifted off to sleep, repeating the words *Chase, Chase, Chase* in her mind to distract herself from the discomfort.

She awoke many hours later, feeling a kick inside her abdomen. *The baby. I have to eat for the baby.*

Vera approached the machine and said "plain, unflavored Pepsoilent." It whirred a moment, then swirled out a greenish gray mound that looked like a lumpy pile of ground beef. She lifted the disposable bowl and grabbed a plastic spoon from the cutlery compartment. Vera sat down again on the floor, leaning her back against the padded side of the vibration lounge. She took a bite, but had to spit out the chalky, flavorless paste that mushed up against her tongue.

"Ugh."

She tossed the bowl down the recycling chute and tried again. "Plain Pepsoilent with salt." It was a compromise she was willing to make.

Vera swallowed several bites and drank a glass of water. She then slid back down on the floor to sleep.

The wall screen woke her with an announcement that it was time for the daily *Physical Jerks*. The bubbly host appeared on the screen and began demonstrating the poses and moves for the day, accompanied by the usual upbeat music. Vera's MyndScreen opened a window and played the same program, which she quickly closed. She wouldn't do it, she told herself. They couldn't make her. But, she did get up and walk around the room, counting the paces it took her to travel its small perimeter. *Twelve. Twelve steps.*

Thirty minutes later, the exercise video on the wall screen stopped and the host encouraged viewers to relax in a vibration lounge. Vera's neck and lower back ached from sleeping one full night strapped into the wheelchair and then a second (or was it third?) night on the floor. She lay down on the lounge and winced as it pushed and kneaded her sore spots around the shoulder and lower back. Vera got up before the sensual massage segment began and looked away from the wall screen as it displayed a chance romantic encounter on a Caribbean island.

After a while, her extruder prepared another plate of salted Pepsoilent and sprayed some water into a plastic cup. Vera's MyndScreen opened a window where a calm voice read text that appeared on the screen "Remember 2 take UR anger management pills." The extruder spat out two pills onto the plate. Vera picked them up and tossed them down the recycling chute before eating the food.

Several days passed, or several sleep cycles at least, where not much happened. Vera passed the time staring at the ocean view on the screen, eating salted Pepsoilent, pacing the room during the *Physical Jerks* program, and then sleeping. The pain in her back became severe enough that she was willing to sleep on the massage lounge, changing its position and angle of recline periodically. Her head ached, but she could tolerate it.

One day, an automated wheelchair came through the sliding doors to her room. Vera suspected it would take her back to Aneeka Randall's office. She hesitated.

Vera stared at the chair a long time before touching it to make sure it was real. Suddenly, the chair turned around and departed without her.

It happened again, after the next session of *Physical Jerks*. Again, Vera stared the chair down. And again.

The fourth time that the chair came, Vera sat down.

The chair did not restrain her this time. It just slowly wheeled her out of the room, down a long series of hallways, and into the familiar confines of Aneeka Randall's office. Aneeka was waiting behind her desk.

"Hello, Vera. How are you feeling today?"

"Hello, Dr. Randall, if that's really your name. When I first saw you, you were on the evening news speaking as a legal expert about Tribunal Doctrine. The next time I saw you, you were a member of the Sisterhood, which you now tell me doesn't even exist. Why should I believe you now when you say you're a therapist? For all I know, this is just some dream, or some MyndScreen simulation that I'll drop out of eventually, and you are just some random avatar created by a computer game or the Virtual Sex Liberation League. Maybe I died on the beach, and this is some version of hell or purgatory."

Aneeka Randall shrugged. "Come now, Vera, think about it. It's not so mysterious. You can feel that the metal desk in front of you is real, not simulated. Go ahead, touch it." Vera just sat there.

"You can see that I have a degree in Tribunal of Educates Doctrine, a TED, from Stanford Law School as well as a degree in psychology from Johns Hopkins."

Vera looked at the wall and saw two framed certificates with fancy lettering and metallic round seals on them. *Pieces of paper. So what?*

"It is correct that I appear occasionally on news programs as part of the public therapy aspect of my job. People are much more emotionally stable and healthy if they feel reassured that there is a strong, just, and educated authority that will provide for security and prosperity. I speak publicly to explain and validate that authority and cement Tribunal Doctrine as a permanent fixture of our social and intellectual mindscapes. I never told you I was a member of the Sisterhood, only that I could help you. Your hyperactive imagination presumed I was who you wanted me to be. I, in fact, told you that joining the Sisterhood was futile. Objectively speaking, your decision to go ahead with it was a clear symptom of your illness.

"People need structure in their lives, Vera, an orderly arrangement that then gives them liberty to enjoy the unbounded world of information and enjoyment that is available to us. You have lost that structure, Vera, the essential stability that gives you freedom and that provides for our collective prosperity. It is much more efficient for me to treat the entire viewing population as a group through conversations on news programs that are viewed by millions than to treat individuals, as I'm doing now with you in private practice. But I'm perfectly willing and capable of doing that as well, Vera. You know that, don't you?"

"I don't believe you. You betrayed us. I don't believe in you. You can't make me."

"That's right Vera, I can't. Only you can." Aneeka Randall pressed a button on her desk and stood up. Vera stood also, instinctively. Aneeka Randall walked around her desk. She lifted Vera's right hand and placed it beneath her own lab coat, directly over her heart.

"I am real, Vera. Feel my heart beating beneath your fingertips. Believe me. I can help you if you will let me. But first, you must let go of the other reality that you have invented for yourself."

Vera's mouth became moist and she swallowed to keep from spitting. She looked down, away from Aneeka's face. But she let her hand linger a moment.

Two nurses walked in wearing blue scrubs. Vera sat down without their assistance, and her chair wheeled her back to her room.

After eating a dinner of salted Pepsoilent with a glass of water, Vera still felt empty. She tried eating a second portion, but gave up after a few bites. It wasn't helping.

A black hole had opened inside her body, and it was sucking everything intrinsic to her existence deep into its bottomless confines. Its gravitational pull was relentless, leaving a void that she could not fill.

Vera cried. She didn't know why, she just cried, and cried, and cried.

Thinking back to when she and Chase were at Inspiration Point, she knew that moment could never be taken from her and she vowed to relive it in her mind each day. She would not let it be sucked into that void. She would hold onto it by replaying the memory, repeating his name, recalling the contours of his face and the smell of his hair.

"Do not let the behavior of others destroy your inner peace." That's what the bench had said. She could not be with Chase right now. But she could be at peace if she decided to.

"Amusement is Peace" popped up as a link in her MyndScreen. Vera closed the window.

She cleared her mind and began a session of unguided meditation.

* * *

A few days later, when the automated wheelchair came into her room after the morning *Physical Jerks* had played on the wall screen, Vera sat down. She was no longer afraid. The chair extended and latched its seat belt this time, along with arm restraints and even ankle restraints. Vera noticed that the restraint fabric was crimson instead of blue.

Now what?

The chair wheeled her past Aneeka Randall's office, toward a bank of elevators. After another gut-wrenching ride in the high-speed lifts, she emerged on another floor and was wheeled into a room full of medical equipment. The chair stopped precisely on yellow marks that had been painted onto the floor directly in front of a machine with a white robotic arm. The arm began extending itself toward Vera, aimed at her abdomen. As it got closer, she could see a long needle attached to the end.

My baby. It's going to inject my baby!

Vera's pulse quickened as she strained against the straps that held her firmly in the chair. "Help! Help me!" she screamed and tossed her head back and forth.

The machine hummed as it moved with slow precision. As it approached her belly, the arm veered up and to the right. It pointed directly at the inside of her arm.

"Look at me and you won't feel a thing," said a gentle woman, who appeared suddenly on Vera's MyndScreen. She resisted the urge to close the window and studied the makeup on the woman's face, wondering if she was a video recording of a real person or a computer-generated avatar.

A sharp prick drew her attention back to her arm, where she saw the robophlebotomist had stuck the needle through the red fabric restraint into her forearm. A glass container behind the needle began to fill with blood.

"That's it," said the woman on her MyndScreen in a peppy voice. "I told you it wouldn't hurt. Have a nice day."

That afternoon, the screen on her wall interrupted its normal ocean scene to play a short video of a midwife discussing the risks of pregnancy and the precautions that should be taken. The same program appeared on her MyndScreen. Vera let it run.

The midwife described the options of scheduled C-section birth versus traditional vaginal birth. She noted that while 80 percent of mothers were still choosing C-sections, the vaginal option had become more popular recently with the advent of a MyndScreen diversion app. When combined with the latest pharmaceutical cocktail, the mother hardly noticed the birthing process and could still be alert enough to hold the baby when it first came out instead of having to wait to be sewn back together. This made for much better images to share on the Chatterfeed, and the program showed several examples. Each mother gazed at the camera with a gaping smile while holding up her baby bundled in a white blanket with pink and blue stripes. It looked to Vera like most of the moms were wearing makeup and nail polish.

The following day, Vera's doors slid open, and she expected to see an automated wheelchair enter the room. Instead, Aneeka Randall walked in.

"Hi, Vera. I have the results of the blood test your ob-gyn ordered. Sorry I didn't give you a heads up that it was coming."

Aneeka was not attired in her usual white lab coat. Instead, she had on tight-fitting black leggings and a billowing, low-cut yellow blouse. Vera couldn't help but notice Aneeka wasn't wearing a bra. Maybe she was on her way home for the day, or going out on the town.

"Your doctor says you need to be getting more folate and vitamin D in your diet to help the baby grow. You can take it via injection, pills, or we can just enhance your Pepsoilent extruder. It's up to you."

Vera wasn't excited at the prospect of more needles, and pills seemed artificial. "I'll take the enhancement, I guess."

Aneeka leaned over and put her thumb against a small black piece of glass on the side of the Pepsoilent extruder. "Prenatal boost," she said, and the machine registered the command with a beep. Vera stared at the jade necklace that hung down from Aneeka's neck, the same one she'd had on at the house.

"They taste better with peanut butter or honey," she said, looking up at Vera. "The enhancements I mean." Aneeka flashed her an awkward grin, and Vera suppressed an impulse to smile back.

"Also, your blood pressure is a little high. You might consider cutting down on salty foods — for the baby you know. Sometimes putting yourself first is the best way to help others." Aneeka glanced at the massage lounge. "Do something nice for yourself, Vera, take care of yourself and give yourself some pleasure. It will make you a better parent someday."

"Whatever," Vera responded sullenly. "Thanks." Her pulse did feel like it was beating faster than normal.

"Finally, I brought you some pharmaceutical cream for your elbow. I noticed you've been scratching it raw. This should help. She left a small jar on top of Vera's sink. "Use it sparingly, though. It's expensive."

Aneeka walked out of the room slowly, her shiny black heels stabbing the floor with each step to give additional stature to her physique. She turned her head to shoot Vera a sideways glance over her right shoulder just as the doors were sliding shut. "Bye."

"Bye," said Vera, after the doors had already closed.

That evening, the salted Pepsoilent was inedible. *Must be whatever they added.*

Tossing the dish down the recycling chute, Vera said to the extruder, "Make me a peanut butter and honey sandwich and a glass of vitamin D milk."

In less than two minutes, the machine produced them. Vera chewed the sandwich and relished the sticky peanut butter, the sweet honey and the soft chewy texture of the bread. It was infinitely superior to the salted Pepsoilent she'd been eating. *And besides, it's for the baby.* She would do what she needed to do. She told the machine to make her another one, and she ate every bite.

Vera ran a Noodle search for "prenatal exercises" and found dozens of options. She clicked several, switching from one video to another once she tired of it. *The baby is real, it's the one thing I'm certain of. I'll do everything I can to keep it healthy. I need to keep my mind focused on the baby.*

An ad popped up next to one of the videos. "How to train your baby's memory from day one." It was for a toy design that could be produced on a home protruder system that top-rated pediatricians swore would improve the cognitive functions during the first four months of a baby's life.

Vera wondered if she'd ever have a home protruder again.

What sort of life will I be able to give this baby? Will Chase be there with me?

That evening, her wall screen again interrupted its normal beach mode and began playing a guided meditation video. Vera soon recognized it as the one that had been on the iPod she'd purchased from Aneeka Randall. She'd grown tired of the ten-minute mediation guide she had located on the Noodle search, and she actually preferred this one. Besides, she needed to clear her mind from all the worries of pregnancy that had pre-occupied her.

Vera sat down on the floor, cross-legged, and followed the prompts from the screen.

CHAPTER 11

"Oatmeal, with honey … and raisins … and a little cream," Vera told the extruder.

She devoured it. *For the baby.*

After breakfast, the wall screen began playing a prenatal exercise program. The same program opened simultaneously in a window of Vera's MyndScreen.

Sitting down on the floor, Vera began the stretching, breathing, and pelvic muscle strengthening routine demonstrated in the video. "Inhale, stretch, hold two, three, four and release, two, three, four," cheered the smiling program host, making it look effortless.

While she was working on a butterfly stretch, the wall screen suddenly switched to the regular morning *Physical Jerks* exercise routine. Her MyndScreen switched over as well.

Dammit. I want to choose what I watch.

She closed the MyndScreen window and re-opened the prenatal program she had been watching. It was still paused at the place she'd left off.

I guess that's one advantage of the MyndScreens. You're in control.

Vera kept stretching, focusing on the screen in her head and working to ignore the one on the wall, which continued playing the *Physical Jerks*. The concentration was difficult, but the stretching and floor exercises were so much more appealing than the jumping jacks and aerobic moves of the *Physical Jerks* that she managed it fairly well.

When the *Physical Jerks* ended on the wall screen, Vera felt she'd done enough prenatal exercise for the day, so she ended her routine as well. Her lower back still ached terribly, so it was easy to accept the host's invitation to lie down on the massage lounge. She groaned as it kneaded and pushed her sore muscles and felt the heat seep into her skin. She tarried just a bit as it progressed into the final vibration routine, but got up before it reached its apex. She looked away from the soft porn on the wall screen and closed that window on her MyndScreen.

It was peanut butter and honey again for lunch, followed by an afternoon of daytime dramas on the wall screen. The plots were shallow, but Vera was starting to get drawn into one of them — *The Restless Souls*.

The lead character was stuck in a hopeless marriage and completely unable to perceive that a co-worker was infatuated with him. Vera thought the co-worker would be a far more compatible mate than his wife. He joked with the attractive colleague in the office, saying things like "You're such a talent, my love. Now, please, if you could only get the other staff to be half as clever as you." Vera realized what he did not — that she was only acting clever to win his attention.

He's kind of cute. How could he be so clueless?

Vera had a cheeseburger for dinner, expanding her repertoire of Pepsoilent options. She felt it was important to keep eating. *It's for the baby.*

Days passed. She wasn't sure how many, but they were tolerable. Morning exercises and pregnancy programs. Afternoon dramas. Trying new flavors for dinner.

And so it went.

One afternoon her daytime drama was interrupted by a fifteen-minute infomercial for *Big Mother Gets Real*. Vera turned away from the wall screen as the doors to her room opened and an automated wheelchair came in. She sat down and was taken to Aneeka Randall's office.

"Good morning, Vera, how are you feeling today?

"Fine, I guess, for a prisoner."

"You are held in by your own thoughts and actions, Vera. Only you can change that. Your resentful attitude is not going to help you, it's just holding you back."

Vera scratched her elbow. She stood up and leaned over the desk that stood between them, propping herself up with stiff arms and locked elbows to help hold the weight of her belly. "Aneeka, look at me, listen to me. I know that *you* know what is going on, not just here but everywhere. I can see it in your eyes. I can feel it in my bones. Look at me Aneeka! How can you be complicit in all this? How can you, day after day brainwash people into giving up their lives, giving up their truths, giving up their realities for a world created by infotainment firms? How *can* you?" She jabbed a finger across the desk, almost reaching Randall's arms, which were folded in front of her chest.

"Vera ..."

"Don't 'Vera' me Aneeka! Goddamit. You wrote *The Book*. You know that we're all just living fodder for an infotainment economy that exists only to make greedy multinational corporations richer and to further some fabricated notion of prosperity. Prosperity isn't freedom. Freedom is freedom. Prosperity is gluttony. Freedom is the ability to think for yourself, to have your own feelings, to make your own choices, to experience the real world and accept your own world of beliefs. Freedom means you can know pain, and joy, and love, and fear. You're trying to take those things away from me, Aneeka. You know it. You know it! I *know* you know it!" Out of breath, she collapsed back into her chair and stared at the floor.

"I am no fool, Vera. Yes, I know what is going on. Yes, there are parts of my job that are not always pleasant for me. That's why it's called work and why I'm paid to do it. Believe me, I hate to see you struggling with this, Vera. Yes, it *is* all aimed at ensuring profits and prosperity. Profits are not bad. Profits are good. Greed is good, for it is greed that produces profits, which in turn is what produces prosperity. Yes, there is a trade-off to be made in terms of cerebral autonomy, but that is more than offset by the tremendous choices in fashion, consumer goods, and food consumption that allows the individual to triumph in her own glorious expression. Prosperity enables each of us to express an individuality that was previously unknown to humans. Establishment society is all about elevating the individual, Vera. Do not mistake self-delusional thoughts or so-called creativity for freedom, Vera. My grandparents thought they were free, Vera, but how free do you think they really were after a nuclear explosion annihilated their entire town? There is no freedom for a starving child, Vera. When stability and security break down there is a price to be paid that is far more horrific than the modest cost of enjoying prosperity. So I don't need your lectures about freedom. I know what it's like to live in a world with no profits and no prosperity. There's nothing free about it." It was the first time Vera had ever heard Aneeka raise her voice.

Aneeka slid open a drawer at the side of her desk. She pulled out the Mason jar filled with potpourri that Vera had kept in her apartment.

"Is this what you think is real, Vera? A bunch of rotting flower petals? Somebody made this and stuck it in a jar for you to smell and remember something that may or may not even have happened. How different is that from someone making a program for you to watch on a MyndScreen so you can experience something that has sprung from their imagination?"

Dr. Randall threw the jar against the wall, smashing the glass and sending dried flower petals and orange rind across the floor. Its scent burst into the air, sweet but also slightly musty.

"That reality was temporary, Vera. That reality was manmade — fake. That reality no longer exists for you, for anyone. You can choose to hold on to its memory or you can live in a new one. You can create your own reality, Vera. Or you can let others, with more expertise and talent in the entertainment profession, design a better reality for you; but both will be fabricated."

Vera just sat there, stunned.

Dr. Randall opened another drawer and pulled out an aerosol can. She sprayed it in the air, sending a saccharine, rosy scent through the room.

"There, Vera. If smells are your reality, here are some pretty smells. You can spray it anytime you are feeling nostalgic or want to remember some past reality that you've concocted for yourself. If you upgrade your MyndScreen, it could automatically release this scent whenever those sentimental thoughts run through your mind."

Dr. Randall handed Vera the can then pushed a button. Vera's chair spun around, taking her out of the room. As she passed through the door, she turned her head and yelled back "You can keep your damn chemical spray." She tossed the can at the wall immediately above Randall's head and listened with satisfaction at the clunk it made while bouncing off.

Vera was still shaken up when she returned to her room. She noted that a small, white plastic box with slits in it had been mounted on her wall, immediately above the toilet. Whenever she flushed, the box emitted a fine spray that smelled of citrus, rose petals, and rubbing alcohol. The smell at first made her want to vomit but as the nausea gradually eased, so did her bitterness and anxiety about the whole situation.

The screen on the wall began to play an *International Geographic* documentary on the Mojave Desert. Vera sat down on the massage lounge, dazed, and raised it to an upright position. She watched pictures of Joshua trees, wildflowers, blue skies and giant desert tortoises while a dreadfully dull voice described the previous ecosystem of the Mojave. She remembered driving there; meeting Chase. At least, she was pretty sure that's where it was.

Next was a program where a man with short gray curls and olive skin, dressed in a pure white suit said, "Smiles, everyone, smiles!" to a large hospitality staff while a funny little man with darker skin and jet-black hair shouted, "De plane! De plane!"

"Welcome to Fantasy Island," said the suave host with a flourish as the program cut to a Pepsoilent commercial.

She had beef stroganoff for dinner, with a glass of red wine followed by strawberry shortcake. The next day she had a cappuccino with her honey oatmeal and barbeque potato chips with her peanut butter and honey sandwich. It made her thirsty, so she washed it down with a cherry cola that had an extra prenatal boost.

Days strung together and blurred into weeks. Now there were Will Rogers movies on the wall screen and shows about horses. Then there were more *Fantasy Island* reruns, followed by world cup soccer games from years past. She kept using the eczema cream, which helped. She started taking PainZappers for the headaches and drinking more cappuccinos — they were great for washing down the brownies. They were bringing her real hash brownies now every day, which seemed only to make her hungrier.

Welcome to Fantasy Island.

She had trouble sleeping, but the protruder gave her sleeping pills. Her eyes itched, so they gave her some drops to soothe them.

I will get through this, she thought as she blinked the drops from her eyes.

There was always another hallway to travel down, another episode to watch, another music video. Now, again, summoned for a session with Aneeka Randall for the same conversation, over, and over, and over. More sleepless nights. More blood tests, more supplements, more exercises, more things to learn about infants, more products she would need to acquire.

More food.

Baby.

More wine.
Chase.
More pills.
The Sisterhood.
More cappuccino.
Escape.
More brownies.
Tulips.
Fantasy Island on the wall screen.
Is there anybody out there?
Pepperoni pizza.
Blue violets.
More cappuccino.
The desert.
More wine.
Everyone consents eventually.
Pork chops.
Don't tell me there's no hope at all.
More pills.
I wanna go home.
Sleep.
Baby.
Meditation video.
Numb. I feel numb.
Explosions on the wall screen.
The beach.
More wine. Lots more.
The Book.
Horse movies on the wall screen.
Do not let the behavior of others disturb your inner peace.
Brownies.
Potpourri.
Restless Souls on the wall screen.

Chase.

Silence.

The wall screen went dark. There was a long pause of silence, broken by a song:

Vera, … Vera. … What has befallen you?

Does everybody else in here, feel the way I do?

The voice was plaintive, calm, a little bit hoarse.

Vera stared at the wall screen, but it was black. Was the voice coming from there? The lights went out. It was deathly quiet.

It repeated:

Vera! Vera! What has befallen you?

Does everybody else in here feel the way I do?

Vera slid the massage lounge down to horizontal and thought it must be time to sleep, but sleep would not come.

The lights flashed back on at the same time as the wall screen, blaring loud electric guitars played by bizarre-looking men. The room seemed to spin — Vera braced herself by holding her hand against the wall. She felt the electric base thumping against her chest and the wailing guitars ringing in her ears. The room lit up like a laser show of pink and blue beams of light and the wall screen displayed psychedelic designs that morphed constantly and erratically in a way that glued her eyes to the screen. The spinning was better when she kept her eyes open, but this meant she was bombarded with flashing lights. The dizzy, whirling feeling came back when she closed them. Either choice was torture. For hours it went on, and on, and on.

She passed out.

When she awoke, her head was pounding and groggy. She gulped a supersize cappuccino and took a PainZapper with her honey-cinnamon roll breakfast.

The wheelchair came in and Vera scooted off the edge of the massage lounge into the chair to take the familiar ride down the hallway.

"Hello, Vera," greeted Aneeka Randall. "How are you today?"

"I'm OK. How are you, Dr. Randall?"

"Very well, Vera, thank you for asking. So, what's been on your mind lately?"

"I can't believe Jake is still with his loser wife on *The Restless Souls*, for starters. I know it's not a real-life story, but it's kind of addicting. I just can't wait to see how it will turn out."

"Uh-huh. And?"

Vera fidgeted in her chair and took a breath. She rubbed her eyes, which were still itching.

"Also, I know that the Sisterhood is no more real than *Restless Souls*. *The Book* was appealing to me, intriguing, … fulfilling. I don't blame you for sharing it with me — it's what I was looking for. But I get it now — it was just a story like all the other stories. A documentary I guess, or historical fiction perhaps. I'm not angry with you anymore, Aneeka. I'm not mad at the Establishment. I'm not thinking I'm part of an imaginary group. I won't try to disable my MyndScreen. I won't hurt anyone else. I promise."

"I see," replied Dr. Randall. "That's progress, I suppose. Why, then, are you still searching for escape, Vera? What is the hope you are looking for, Vera? What are you trying to escape from that is driving you to consume so much wine and brownies?"

"I just really miss him," Vera sobbed, suddenly breaking her composure. "I need to see him. I need to touch him. I … "

"Mr. Hatten? You mean Mr. Hatten?"

"Yes. I can't let go of Chase. I won't."

"I see. It sounds like you are still clinging to a past that you invented for yourself, Vera. You keep thinking about others, Vera, when you need to be thinking about yourself. Self-gratification is the highest form of altruism. You need to elevate and protect the individual. To love others, you must first and foremost love yourself and prioritize your own well-being. I know this is hard for you, and I must admit that your case is more difficult than most patients I treat, but you must keep trying. For you to be given a clean bill of health, you need to not only say things that demonstrate your rationality, you need to believe them."

"Chase is the only thing that is real. The only thing that is true. The only thing that makes me sane. I know it, I just know it."

"We can all find our own truth, Vera," Dr. Randall replied. "You don't need to be miserable and stick to one in particular, you can embrace another truth. One that makes you happy. You don't seem happy, Vera. Do you want to be happy?"

Doctor Randall opened a drawer on her desk and pulled out an old-fashioned coffee mug with an iridescent turquois color. "Here, I brought you this. Perhaps it will help ground you." She placed the mug in Vera's lap before pressing the button that sent the wheelchair out the door.

Vera ordered some green tea–flavored Pepsoilent from the extruder in her room and put the mug underneath the spout to fill it. The screen on the wall began playing the ten-minute meditation guide. She watched the steam rise from the cup and noticed there was no chip on the rim. She felt the sides of the cup with her fingertips. They were cool to the touch, unlike the cozy feel of ceramic that has been warmed by the hot liquid held inside.

"Liar!" Vera screamed as she hurled the protruded mug against the wall screen. The tea spattered everywhere but the mug just bounced off the screen and landed on the floor. *Plastic. She was trying to fool me.*

Explosions on the wall screen.
The Sisterhood. Fear Mongers. War.
Air freshener released into the room.
Fresh baked bread.
Pepsoilent bread and butter.
I believe you.
Merlot wine and dark chocolate.
The truth is not statistical or empirical.
Fantasy Island on the wall screen.
We'll meet again, not sure where, not sure when.
Apple-fennel sausage pizza.
She who forgets the past has no future.
Sleep.
Baby.
Hickory-smoked bacon and FarmerFresh™ eggs.
Chase.
Morning prenatal exercises.
Aneeka.
Massage lounge.
Pain.
Vibrations and undulations.
Ah … Ahh … Chase… ohh.

Caribbean island, handsome stranger on the wall screen, tanned six-pack abs, unzipping blue jeans …

Ahhhhhhhh… Chase!

Doublelay™ Potato chips.

Amusement is Peace. Everyone finds peace eventually. It's irresistible.

Silence. Long silence.

Lemon-lime Cokaid.

Gonorrhea.

Restless Souls on the wall screen.

The solution to speech is more speech.

Will Rogers movies.

Advertising Frees Speech.

Dr. Zanders™ Fried chicken.

Fabrizio™ Air freshener.

Baby.

Mocha Caramel Raspberry Cappuccino.

Prosperity is Freedom.

Hash Roca Crunch™ Brownies.

I love U V.

Wheelchair.

Chase.

Hallway.

Information is Strength.

"Hello, Vera, how are you feeling today?"

"Huh?"

"I asked you how you were doing? Are you OK?" Aneeka repeated.

"Yeah. Sure. Fine."

"Vera, what if I asked you what two plus two is?"

"It's four. Two plus two is four."

"And what if I told you that I thought it was five?"

"Five? Sure, whatever. I don't really care. It can be whatever you want it to be. Just leave me alone. Two plus two can be five if you want it to be."

"Vera, remember when I told you that we would meet again, in a new place without struggle and strife?"

We will meet again only on the other side, in a world that has no drudgery.

"Vera?"

"Um, … yes, I remember. I think I do, that is. Was it at the restaurant? The desert?"

"Vera, you are in that place now. It is my professional assessment that you are no longer a danger to yourself or others. You have passed through to the other side of your condition. You are free to leave Mercernary General. However, it is also my professional recommendation that it would be beneficial for you to receive a MyndScreen upgrade. You would be more comfortable that way. I have received authorization for you to be placed in a top-rated entertainment home if that is your choice."

"No. I want to go home."

"Vera, listen to me. You no longer have a home. Your apartment in Magnificent Estates has been foreclosed by the bank to pay for your hospitalization and your pharmaceuticals. Your car has been repossessed. Remember how I told you that the eczema cream is quite expensive? It is considered a non-essential treatment and it isn't covered by your health plan. You have been replaced at your job, Vera, so you have no source of income."

"No!" Vera shouted. "I don't believe you! None of this is real."

"You will be able to decide for yourself what is real, Vera. Our time here is done. You are going to be transferred to the prenatal ward of Mercernary General and will be under the care of your obstetrician from now on as you are nearing your due date. You will be admitted there after waiting in the Situation Room."

"What is the Situation Room?"

"I think you know, Vera. Believe me, I will always remember you fondly." Aneeka Randall stood up and removed the jade necklace from around her neck. She walked around the desk to Vera and gently clasped the necklace around her, caressing her check once she was done with fingers that felt smoother than silk but also cold and rigid. Vera could smell the sweet scent of honey and jasmine blossoms on Aneeka's skin, reminding her of when they had met at her house. "Remember, you can always change your mind and accept the upgrade. Sometimes being selfish can be the best way to help others. I would like nothing better than for us to meet again someday, Vera, even if it's not in this world."

With that, Aneeka Randall pushed a button on her desk and Vera's chair wheeled out of the room.

CHAPTER 12

"Welcome, Vera," a calm voice said as she wheeled into the chamber labeled "Situation Room." "Your doctor will speak with you in a moment. While you're waiting, please enjoy the following promotional video that explains our new MommyForever™ program."

With a whoosh, the doors closed behind her, leaving Vera in the center of a cavernous space with white curved walls thirty feet across in diameter and a high-domed ceiling.

The room went dark, and then the walls lit up all around her, projecting a 3-D image of a newborn baby, cooing adorably. A soft-spoken woman, whom Vera could not see but who seemed to be part of the video, began the explanation:

"Motherhood is the most profound moment of your life. Our team here at Mercernary General will be with you every step of the way to make sure it is an unforgettable experience."

The screen flashed still images of nurses, crying babies, smiling mothers, doctors taking pulses, videographers, florists, massage therapists, and an assortment of hospital equipment blinking and tracking things on moving charts.

"But we understand that childrearing may not be for everyone. If you become incapacitated due to military injury or are ready for retirement into a full-time entertainment home, we're here to help you through that process as well. We'll pair you with a top-rated childrearing firm, so you can rest easy knowing that your little bundle of joy will be well cared for. Moreover, we're thrilled to offer a new MommyForever program to ensure that you will always be in the thoughts and memories of your child. As soon as your precious one is delivered to the childrearing facility, we'll upload your image to their crib screen along with the lullaby song of your choice."

The screen displayed the image that Vera and Chase had taken together in front of the cutout figures of Mr. Roarke and Tattoo, with the dilapidated house at the arboretum in the background.

"As the baby grows, we'll use your image as the background screensaver in their MyScreen helmets. And once they become of age and blossom into their own individual, we'll program your image and a sound clip of your choosing to pop up daily in their MyndScreen. MommyForever gives you the confidence that you will be forever present in the daily lives of your child even if you aren't with them physically. Ask your doctor if you qualify for this exciting new program."

"Hello, Vera," came a different voice, this time from a person who appeared on the screen in front of her. "I'm the obstetrician who will be handling the delivery of your baby. How are you feeling today?"

"I'm fine, really good," Vera responded immediately. "I'm so looking forward to the baby, feeling very maternal and protective — like I could never hurt a soul," she added, wanting to ensure that the system knew she had been cleared from her previous diagnosis.

"That's terrific, Vera," said the doctor, who was speaking into a camera while seated at a desk. There were diplomas hanging on the wall behind him as well as a screen with the logo of Mercernary General. "Now, I know that you had expressed a preference for a traditional birth, Vera, but due to a couple of complications I'm going to strongly recommend that we perform a cesarean instead."

"What do you mean?"

"Well, first of all, Vera, your blood tests positive for exposure to gonorrhea. Your partner, Mr. ah ... Hatten, has also tested positive. While you haven't exhibited any symptoms, as a precaution I believe a C-section would reduce the chances of exposing your baby to the disease. We will also administer a full course of antibiotics to both you and the baby."

Vera used all her remaining willpower to purse her lips and clench her stomach muscles, suppressing a gasp that erupted from within.

"And secondly, Vera, there is the issue of your weight. Given your enhanced size, there are several complications to a traditional birth process that could threaten the life of the baby. It would be much safer, and efficient, to schedule a cesarean."

"What do you mean my weight?"

"Vera, take a look at the wall screen behind my desk," her doctor motioned behind him and the screen flicked on. Vera stared at an image of an overweight woman, with a double chin and thick folds of skin around her neck. "That's you, Vera. You are looking at a live image taken by an in-room camera."

Vera hardly recognized the figure on the screen. As she moved her right arm, she saw the image on the screen also move. A loose flab of skin and blubber dangled down beneath her bicep, jiggling as she strained to raise it above her head. Reaching up, she felt her swollen neck, noticing for the first time how snugly the necklace from Aneeka Randall fit. Pale lips and cheeks were puffed around her chin and dark bags swelled up beneath her eyes. Her hair was long, but it had thinned significantly and it was dull and tangled.

Vera had been aware that her abdomen had grown and her ankles swelled in the recent months, but she had thought that was simply the pregnancy. She hadn't known how long she'd been in "treatment," and the room's wall screen had not included a mirror app, so she hadn't looked at herself in months.

"Stand up, Vera." She pushed down on both armrests of the wheelchair with her hands, leaned forward, and strained to an upright position. After a half-minute, she collapsed back into the chair. She had not only gained weight, but her muscles had atrophied during her treatment.

"You've really let yourself go, Vera, by not attending to the morning physical jerks. You've gained more than a hundred pounds during your pregnancy. Think about if this is the way you want your baby to remember you. More importantly, consider whether you are in the physical condition necessary to raise a baby. There is also the matter of financial security. Given that you have lost your job and your apartment, it is imperative to make a plan for the well-being of your newborn." He paused a moment and rearranged something on his desk.

"Now, I'm pleased to say that I've received a special dispensation from Mercernary General to provide for your situation. There's a new charity fund that has been set up by Wendolyn Palfry and a group of celebrities to help people just like you. If you opt for the MyndScreen upgrade and entertainment home subsidy, Vera, Mercernary General can offer you a special limited-time free enrollment to the MommyForever program as well as placement for your baby in one of Renaissance Childrearing's state-of-the-art centers. That way, the baby will remember you the way you want them to, not necessarily the exhausted way you look when it is born. Lastly, this month we are also offering free liposuction treatment during all C-sections, so your timing is quite fortunate."

Before Vera could shout, "go to hell," the doctor signed off, saying, "I have another appointment now, Vera. Why don't you take some time to think it over and we'll check in shortly?" The screen went dark and Vera felt empty inside.

She stood up and tried to walk around the room, but found it exhausting. Her tummy had ballooned out so much she could not see her feet. Out of breath, she sat back down in the wheelchair and noticed that both her thighs pressed up against the sides of the chair. She wiped a damp misting of sweat off her forehead and looked at her chubby fingers and yellowing nails. Her head ached.

Chase. Chase. Chase. The word ran through her head, conjuring the picture of the two of them from the arboretum. She no longer looked like she did in that picture. *Did he?*

Then it began.

Soft, suspenseful violin music flowed from the walls all around her, which slowly glowed brighter. Momentarily, Vera recognized a scene from within the hospital: the hallways, the elevators. She saw a large woman on a double-wide stretcher that was wheeling into a delivery room. The video zoomed in on the character's face and Vera felt as if she was looking into a mirror. It was her, or more accurately, a computer-generated avatar of her.

She saw her legs braced up in front of her as the character on screen began to yell. A nervous team of doctors wearing masks and hairnets stared at her crotch and told her to push. Suddenly, machines started beeping and images became blurry. She heard a voice shouting, "We have a foot, we need to move people, NOW!"

The stretcher banged through some swinging doors and sped down a hallway as attendants raced by her side to keep up. The screen displayed ceiling tiles passing rapidly overhead as the background music changed to pounding timpani drums and a suspenseful electronic keyboard lick that looped over and over. Doors crashed open in front of her and a needle was pressed into her arm. The room appeared to spin, with images swirling past on the round walls. The screen went dark and the music changed again, this time to a slow organ dirge.

They want to scare me. This is my own, personalized movie designed to frighten me into consenting to a C-section, an upgrade, all of it. It's not real. It's not real. That's what the Situation Room is all about, to find the one situation that will make you submit. I won't do it. It's not real ... I won't do it.

And yet, as Vera swore those vows of resistance, she knew deep inside her that she would succumb.

Everyone does in the end.

After a dramatic pause, the walls lit up again with the face of a grumpy discharge nurse holding a clipboard by her bedside. "Your baby was a breech birth, but the doctors couldn't tell until the last minute because you're so fat," she sneered. "It almost died, but our surgeons are exceptionally trained. They were able to save it but you're going to be very sore for the next few weeks." She handed Vera's avatar the clipboard, which had several pieces of paper and a digital thumbprint reader.

"We named it Randi. You'll be able to pick it up in about a week. For now, it's in isolation and receiving a course of antibiotics. Scan your thumb here to accept your discharge papers."

The avatar stuck her thumb on the reader and Vera was pleasantly surprised that it accepted it even with the scar on her thumb.

They must have updated my ID. Then she remembered that the avatar might not have a scarred thumb. She felt her pulse quickening and scratched her elbow out of habit, although it no longer really itched.

The avatar was driven out to the curb in an automated wheelchair, wearing nothing but a hospital gown. She had no money, no shoes, and no life to go back to.

A window opened on the wall depicting the character's MyndScreen. It ran a Noodle search for homeless shelters and called a car to drive her there. The car-sharing service responded with a notice: "Account closed due to lack of funds."

She tried getting up out of the chair, which quickly abandoned her once she stood. She managed to stumble to a park bench, where she quickly sat down. The video used time-lapse photography, dramatic music, and fast-forward screen shots to depict that several days passed.

Pigeons fluttered about. People walked by without looking until she was picked up by a sheriff's van and taken to a shelter where she was given a cot in a room full of Vues.

Vera sat and watched the personalized movie unfold before her eyes, unable to cry or shout. She felt numb, empty, and resigned to watch events transpire in the way an icicle melts drop by drop until it finally falls off.

Chase. She clung to the word.

Chase.

Chase.

I will remember him. He believes me.

The movie continued for hours. Vera's avatar was eventually given visitation rights to see her newborn, but due to her health conditions and poverty she was deemed unfit as a mother. The baby was placed in a dilapidated, rat-infested childrearing facility, and she was allowed to see it once a month. Her days were filled staring at other indigent people, most of whom had also been recently discharged from a mental health facility.

On Randi's first birthday, Vera's avatar came to visit and saw a familiar man there. He was large, moving only with the aid of a cane to support his weight. He wore gray velour leisure pants held up with a drawstring and a beige T-shirt that fit too tightly, accentuating the profile of his bulging gut. There was a faded tattoo on his arm, but the gaps and stretch marks in the lines made it hard to discern what it depicted. Long tufts of blonde hair were combed over the balding center of his head, meeting the oversized, wrap-around sunglasses that covered half his face. His jowls, covered with five-day old stubble, sagged and bounced a little when he walked.

Chase?

"Hey, don't I know you from somewhere?" the man asked. "Want some chips?" He offered her the bag of mesquite-honey-mustard Pepsoilent potato chips he was munching on. "Hey, did you see *Big Mother Gets Real* last night? Amazing, wasn't it? I can't believe that guy Jarry turned out to be such a jerk, ya know?"

Vera tried to look away from the screen, but it was all around her. She tried to conjure up the image of Chase in her memories, but all she could see was the face of the middle-aged chubby clown from the screen — seared into her brain. She repeated the words *Chase, Chase, Chase,* only to have her past bank accounts pop up in her memory. She longed for the warm feeling in her abdomen when she had been in his arms, but now felt only a frigid hole of emptiness.

Vera's mind fully anesthetized as the movie skipped forward to her child's high school graduation. Wearing a satin black cap and gown, Randi crossed the stage, shook hands with a tall man wearing metal-framed glasses and accepted a black faux-leather binder from him. The crowd applauded along with Vera's avatar, who was looking old and haggard with disheveled, out-of-date clothing. Chase was nowhere in sight, or if he was there Vera didn't recognize him.

As the graduate walked off stage looking proud and smiling from ear to ear, Vera's avatar stumbled forward to give her a hug.

The child gave her a blank stare and kept walking.

"Who's that weird lady?" Randi asked another woman, who was there to shake her hand.

Vera's scream shook the walls. "No more! No more! I consent. I'll take the upgrade. I want the C-section. I want the MommyForever. I consent, I consent, I consent. ..."

She let her head hang down and felt the last of her vigor escape her lungs with a sigh.

The movie faded. Silence. For a long time, there was only silence.

Everyone consents in the end.

"OK, Vera, I think you've made a wise decision." The screen on the wall lit up with the face of her obstetrician. "We'll schedule the C-section for the day after tomorrow and the upgrade for six to eight weeks later. That will give you time to recover from childbirth before the procedure and to bond with your baby before you deliver it to childrearing. You've made the rational choice, Vera, the one that will objectively be the most optimal for your well-being and that of your baby. Happiness is all in your state of mind, you see."

Her chair wheeled Vera out of the Situation Room. She wasn't sure how many hallways and elevator rides it took, but she eventually arrived at a private room in the maternity ward. There was a hospital bed along with a massage lounge. There was no screen on the wall, but for the first time since her hospitalization her MyndScreen was fully operational with no content filters. She opened a window and began to watch *The Restless Souls*.

I can watch what I want to now. I'm in control. No more forced programming on wall screens. I have chosen my own future. It will be amusing even if somewhat inactive. I'm at peace. It's OK. It's going to be OK.

She opened two more MyndScreen windows and simultaneously watched the evening news and a gladiator sports event while *The Restless Souls* episode played. She had missed out on a lot of current events while in the hospital and was happy to start getting up to speed again. A crazed dictator of an Evildoer regime had launched a missile into the middle of the ocean, violating an international agreement it had previously negotiated with Globalia. The Tribunal of Educates was sending a Navy armada to the region as a show of force.

Good. We need to put that madman in his place.

Her Noodle search was working again so she switched to another MyndScreen window to check out a link to a strange new trick that could shrink tummy fat in just six weeks.

* * *

The following day, a nurse came into Vera's room with a tablet computer. "Hi there. I see that you're expecting, and I'm here to help you select options for a childrearing center for your baby and an entertainment home for yourself. But, I can't find any record of your IVF. Where did you have that done?"

"I didn't."

"Really? You mean your child was conceived out of love? How romantic! I can't remember the last patient we had like that, at least among our Establishment clientele."

"Yeah, I thought it was pretty remarkable at the time. But, you know, life is what happens to you while you're busy watching episodes."

She showed Vera a dazzling array of top-quality entertainment homes she could choose from. After clicking on dozens of options, Vera picked one in San Bernardino that looked nice, called Twilight Kingdom.

Next, she chose a childrearing center for the baby: Renaissance Cultivation. It was the same facility used by Wendolyn Palfry and several other celebrities. It had received thousands of four- to five-star ratings and boasted of programs to immerse young people in classical music, the philosophy of John Stuart Mill, Einstein's nuclear physics, and the economics of Milton Friedman all by the age of four. Vera wasn't completely sure what any of those things were, but the expert testimonials about the firm were impressive. Some of its children had tested out of college and gone directly to PhD programs by age eleven. One had already been placed on the Tribunal of Educates and another was a top corporate CEO.

Next, she filled out the electronic forms to enroll in the MommyForever program. As the image her child would see each day, she selected the one Chase had taken with his 180° glasses in front of the cottage at the arboretum. It felt nostalgic to see the image again, reminding her of what they had both once looked like. But, like finding a sports trophy you won as a child when cleaning out a closet decades later, the image didn't have the same emotional attachment it once held. She was stumped when asked for a lullaby or sound clip to play for the baby. She couldn't remember any lullabies from her childhood.

As she stared at the tablet screen, Vera's stomach lurched. She had expected to feel nervous about the procedure, but this was more like the aftermath of a Pepsoilent JalapenoVelveeta™ Burrito Supreme than butterflies in the stomach. She asked the hospital staffer if she could get an antacid. Just as the attendant left the room things felt better.

The discomfort returned when a nurse walked in a few minutes later with a stomach-calming pharmaceutical. Vera wondered if her ordeal in the mental-health ward had made her adverse to all medical staff. She winced as the pain and pressure moved lower in her abdomen.

"Honey, I don't think that's indigestion. You're having contractions. I better call your doctor," said the nurse as she spun around on her heels and headed out the door.

Vera's MyndScreen pulled up a dozen videos about contractions and the birthing process. She skimmed through them, spending five to fifteen seconds on each and concluded that the nurse must be right. She was going into labor.

Maybe I'll get to have a traditional birth after all.

Within thirty minutes, her hospital bed was wheeling her down a hallway. Vera stared at the ceiling panels as they passed over her and wondered if any of this was really happening. It seemed too strange. But then her stomach would spasm again, removing all doubt that this was real. Nothing had ever felt so visceral.

The bed wheeled her into a bright, sterile room that smelled of ozone. Several staff were already there, donning blue masks and green latex gloves. Her bed folded forward, moving her into an upright position, and one of the attendants asked her to lean forward and try to touch her toes. That was nowhere near possible, but two attendants grabbed an arm firmly on either side to help. As she strained toward her knees she felt a sharp stab in her back — directly into the spine.

"Sorry for the prick, but that's the last thing you'll feel," someone said from behind her. The bed lowered her back to a horizontal position and then automated straps came out and bound her arms and shoulders tightly to the mattress. They began scrubbing her belly with a cool gel that smelled of rubbing alcohol, but by the time they were done the icy sensation was gone.

The last thing I'll feel. Ever?

As they hung a blue plastic sheet around her chest, Vera looked up and saw three screens on the ceiling. One screen alternated between showing the weather report in ten different Los Angeles neighborhoods and discount prices for enhanced bathroom fiber extruders to allow you to produce disposable diapers at home. It was overcast and 70–71 degrees everywhere. The pollen, ozone, and particulate matter levels were all within a few points of each other, and the projected times of sunrise and sunset as well as the forecast for sun spot radiation were all identical. Winds were projected to range from 5 to 14 miles per hour except in Santa Monica where they'd be 8 to 17.

The screen on the right was showing spectacular nature scenes from the Hawaiian Islands and playing soft ukulele music. The one in the middle was an educational video from Mercernary General asking patients not to smoke, to heed the directions of all uniformed staff, and to please read the safety instructions for infant care that proceeded to scroll over the screen in eight-point font.

She heard a voice call "scalpel" and lifted her head to speak. A nurse gently pressed her finger to Vera's lips and stuck a contraption around the top of her head that covered her ears and amplified the ukulele music while simultaneously massaging her temples. It felt nice and blocked out a lot of the beeping from the instruments in the room. They stuck a needle in her forearm to attach an IV drip tube.

The center screen on the ceiling, having completed its scroll of fine print, produced a black-and-white livestream video of a curled-up miniature human above the words "Baby Room 3239." Text on the side of the screen flashed the baby's heart rate (130), estimated digit count

(20), along with the number of simultaneous cesareans currently being performed in Mercernary General (2), in all of Los Angeles (7), and across Globalia by the Renaissance Health network (251).

She pushed against the arm restraints and heaved through a contraction. Instead of a baby emerging from below, vomit gushed out her mouth and ran down the sides of her cheeks and back into her throat. They wiped her face and gave her some water to rinse, but didn't release the arm restraints so it felt like she was drowning.

Her neck was sore and stiff from being pinned against the bed for what felt like hours. The ukulele song was playing an endless loop that repeated every forty-five seconds or so. Vera was certain she knew the melody from somewhere, but couldn't remember the words.

Suddenly it came. Without warning, Vera felt intense pressure bearing down all over her. The baby heart-rate number exploded on the center screen, up to more than 190 beats per minute. She couldn't see around the blue plastic curtain, but she was certain somebody had just sat on her abdomen or lowered an automobile-sized weight from the ceiling to flatten her once and for all. There was a tugging and pulling on her ribcage, like a Doberman Pinscher had grabbed hold of the hem of an imaginary skirt she was wearing and was yanking her down toward the ground.

The center screen showed the baby kicking and squirming and then suddenly it was offscreen and replaced by an image of fireworks bursting in the sky. The screen on the right added lyrics to its ukulele riff as children skipped and sang a song about a sunny day that was sweeping the clouds away to a grouchy, green monster in a tin trash can. An air-freshener machine on the wall emitted a puff of mist that had the sweet vanilla scent of baby powder

Vera strained her head up to look past the sides of the curtain and saw a doctor in blue scrubs wiping off her baby with a white towel. They pressed its heel and thumb against a print scanner, suctioned some fluid from its mouth into a glass tube for DNA archiving, and held up a retinal scanner to its eyes before smearing them with a translucent antibiotic gel. The baby writhed and cried.

A mariachi band began playing on the middle ceiling screen. They placed the baby, now swaddled from head to toe in a pink and blue striped blanket, on Vera's chest.

"Ten fingers, ten toes," the nurse announced.

"What's her name?" asked an attendant.

"Ellen," Vera replied resolutely. "Her name is Ellen. Middle name Selah." A photographer snapped an image and immediately sent it to Vera's MyndScreen with the tagline "Vera meets Ellen. #HappyBirthDay!" She would have sent it off into the Chatter, but didn't like the way her chubby face looked with the smears of vomit still on her cheeks.

Another attendant swooped up the baby from Vera's arms and put it down in a motorized crib. As her baby was wheeled from the room, Vera said, "Tell her we'll meet again some sunny day. That's the song I want for her MommyForever program." A nurse typed it into a tablet, "We'll meet again."

They suctioned out a gallon and a half of fat globules from her abdomen before stitching her back up.

CHAPTER 13

*The first cure for a corrupt nation is
amusement of the masses,
the second is war.*

*Both bring a temporary prosperity; both
bring a permanent rot.*

— Frank Hemmingpath

"I'll take a one-liter chocolate cherry cola and a DoubleMint™ Praline brownie," Vera told the vending machine. It had been an exhausting day, and she felt like she deserved a treat.

The baby had finally fallen asleep at the end of a grueling ride out to San Bernardino in the handicap-accessible self-driving van after crying incessantly for most of the trip. When she arrived, Vera had pressed the button to lower and extend the wheelchair ramp but nothing had happened. The door slid open, but without the ramp she had no way to drive her rented burgundy MoveMe™ 6.0 scooter out of the van.

She had been getting back in shape and was pretty sure she could have simply gotten off the scooter and walked outside. But if she did that, how would she get the baby and scooter out — especially without waking the baby.

While she was considering her dilemma, the doors closed unexpectedly and the van began driving off. Using her MyndScreen, Vera was able to hit the "undo" command in the van's operating system to tell it to return to its previous destination.

"Recalculating," the van said, heading around the block. It parked again, and this time the ramp extended properly.

Sometimes you just need a reboot.

Vera wheeled her MoveMe scooter down the wheelchair ramp with trepidation, fearful that the slightest bump or jiggle would trigger another tsunami of wails from the baby. The rental service had outfitted the scooter with an infant crib in the front, right where the handlebar basket would normally be. The extra weight made the scooter a bit less maneuverable, but she was getting the hang of it.

Once out of the van, she resumed the game she'd been playing on her MyndScreen. She hadn't tried it in years, but after a grasshopper bounced off the van's windshield on the highway, she suddenly remembered it. Perhaps the screams of the baby were reminiscent of the shrieks of the houseflies when she shocked them with the game's electronic pest zapper.

Her MyndScreen reported that today's air quality was hazardous for all ages and only then did Vera notice the smell of smoke and a dull haze in the sky. The Santa Ana winds had died down, leaving the fires they had fanned in San Diego still blazing and the air above the Inland Empire of California stagnant and gray.

She had picked the baby up that afternoon at Mercernary General after spending the past week in transitional housing downtown. She'd now spend a few weeks in a hotel before delivering the baby to Renaissance Cultivation. She'd then be ready for her upgrade and retirement to the Twilight Kingdom.

Now that everything was in place, it didn't seem like such a bad fate after all. She'd had the chance to take a few virtual tours of the facility and interview the head programmer, who seemed very nice. He demonstrated the 4-D features of their full body MyndScreen experience, which included vibrations and tilts to the viewer's MyMassage lounge that were synched to the movies they watched as well as an aerosol ScentMaster™ machine on the wall that emitted air sprays corresponding to the setting where the movie took place. So, he explained, a pirate movie would have scents of sea mist in the air while the MyMassage rocked back and forth to mimic the swells on a ship.

One especially appealing feature was the special screen of UV lights mounted inside a plastic frame on a wall in each room. Curtains hung on either side. For twenty minutes a day, the lamp glowed brightly from its virtual window shining perfectly calibrated 7000 Kendall light waves on clients to ensure optimal vitamin D production.

Vera entered the hotel but waited for the baby to wake up before checking in. Once the *Angry Bugs* game had ended, Vera turned her attention to the jumbotron screen in the lobby, which was playing a celebrity news segment. The host, a rather charming looking man of about thirty-two years of age, announced that Delilah Fish's new film would be carried exclusively on premium MyndScreen broadcasts for a week before it was released to MyScreen helmets for the Vues.

Vera inhaled her soda through the plastic straw while reflecting on the day's events.

She had bumped into Chase on the way to Mercernary General to pick up the baby. His motorized scooter was stopped at a crosswalk ten yards in front of her, and she hadn't recognized him from behind. As she pulled up next to him on his left, he nonchalantly asked, "Hey, Vera, how's it going?"

He was wearing gray velour leisure pants and a beige T-shirt that fit so tightly that it accentuated the bloat of his belly. A shabby goatee draped down three inches from his chin while the rest of his face sported what looked to be five-day old stubble.

"I got these new 360°™ sunglasses with cameras that not only face backwards but also each side and straight overhead. They stream into a MyndScreen window that combines all the images and shows me a view of everything around me along with a digital reading of the oxygen content and pollutant count of the air in each direction. And, they keep track of the number of breaths I've taken each day — I aim for 41,000. I was pretty sure it was you when I saw your scooter coming up behind me. What's this?" he asked, pointing to the baby crib strapped to her handlebars.

"Remember, I was pregnant? I'll deliver the baby to the childrearing center in a few weeks. I ... I'm getting an upgrade after that."

"Oh. ... Yeah," he hesitated just a moment. "They got to me too. I was ruined financially after a libel lawsuit by Michaels de Angelinos. It was depressing, and lonely. They bombarded me with movies, and food, and pharmaceuticals. I held out a long time. Too long, I guess — take a look at me now. Anyhow, they finally seduced me with an avatar of my ex-wife. I consented. Everyone consents in the end you know. I'm on my way in now to get the upgrade."

"Whoa!" Chase ducked his head down to the handlebars of his motorized scooter as a pigeon flew overhead and perched on the traffic signal light. "I thought for a minute that thing was going to smack me up side of the head," he chuckled. "I guess I'm still getting used to these new glasses."

There was a somewhat awkward pause.

"The violets you gave me died. My housekeeper gave them a full dose of water each day while I was hospitalized but somehow that wasn't enough."

"Excessive sustenance is as lethal as desiccation."

"Huh?"

The light changed and flashed a walk signal on both of their MyndScreens.

"Anyway, gotta go." Chase said as he motored off.

Vera could have caught up with him. She could have told him that he'd given her gonorrhea, that the baby's name was Ellen, that he had been right about Aneeka Randall all along. She could have explained that she only consented to an upgrade after feeling like she had already lost him and was on the verge of losing her child too. She could have told him that she still loved him, although she wasn't sure what that really meant any more. As she was considering all of those possibilities, an episode of *The Restless Souls* began playing on her MyndScreen. It distracted her long enough that when she looked back at the direction Chase had gone, he had blended in with the crowd on the sidewalk and was out of sight.

CHAPTER 14

Vera took another slurp of her soda and noticed a woman about her age sitting on a sofa in the hotel lobby. She wore an ankle-length plain blue dress over a white long-sleeved shirt and had what looked like a matching blue headscarf covering her hair, held in place by a broad white band around her forehead. Vera at first wondered if she was Muslim, but then noticed a simple golden chain with a large wooden cross around her neck.

The woman was making something out of a ball of string and two pointy sticks that she moved back and forth in her fingers.

"What's her name?" the woman asked, looking toward the baby.

"Ellen," Vera replied, looking away. She had started another game of *Angry Bugs* and didn't want to get drawn into pointless small talk.

"Would you like me to knit her a hat?" the woman offered. "I've got some nice soft yarn here that would look lovely on her. I could have it done by tomorrow morning."

"No thanks. I'm dropping her off at Renaissance tomorrow. They do a great job of regulating her temperature and keeping her outfitted in the latest fashions."

The flies were coming at her more rapidly than before, but she'd discovered a secret can of bug spray that could knock out a whole swarm if you waited until just the right time to spray it. You had to avoid hitting the ladybugs, though, or you'd lose 200 points. Ladybugs were good — not angry, so you didn't want to kill them. Same thing with the caterpillars, which would eventually turn into butterflies if you could protect them from wasps while they were little. That earned you a bonus of 2,000 points. But you had to watch out for the black widows — they'd get you every time.

She paused the game when the *Two Minute Spate* began its evening report on her MyndScreen. An Evildoer regime in the Middle East had used chemical weapons on a mid-sized city, killing tens of thousands of civilians and injuring fourteen Globalian soldiers who had taken too long to get their gas masks on. This had allowed the evildoers to capture a key strategic city that could cause the entire country to crumble.

They should send in the drones, it's got to be drones. You can't kill a drone with chemical weapons!

Worse yet, there were new accounts that a clandestine Fear Monger enclave had switched allegiances and was now assisting the Evildoer regime. This was troubling because Globalia had armed the Mongers with assault weapons, anti-aircraft guns and shoulder-fired anti-drone missiles.

Fine then, automated tanks and artillery. There's got to be a way. Global security and stability are at stake!

The baby stirred in its crib and seemed like it was about to spit up. The woman on the sofa glanced at Vera with a look of calm concern and a gentle smile. Vera began to feel a little anxious and overwhelmed. All the videos she'd watched hadn't really prepared her for moments like this. But, she didn't want the intrusive stranger to offer any aggressively friendly help.

The *Two Minute Spate* cut to a live shot of a huge explosion. A submarine had just launched a cruise missile, which had eradicated all the evildoer troops in the strategic Middle Eastern city. "Look at that beautiful image!" said the announcer as a red and black plume of smoke and flame mushroomed in the sky. "That's all for today folks, but rest easy knowing that the evildoers are on the ropes."

"Watch *Big Sister*, the best reality Miiii-ster! Brought to you by Timeless Warning — Amusement in Peace" came the jingle. The *Two Minute Spate* was over and a brand-new spin-off reality show was about to premier. Its jingle was catchy:

Hey there mister,
Watch some 'Big Sister' in an episode,
The way she moves ain't real you know,
Your MyndScreen stays,
On the front lobe of my left side brain,
I knew I couldn't forget ya,
And so I went and let ya,
Blow my mind.
You really blew my mind.

Vera let out a breath of relief and washed down her last bite of hash brownie with the soda. The oxymorphine she'd taken in the morning had begun to wear off, but the hashish was finally kicking in and providing some relief.

Although she hadn't previously been that into *Big Mother Gets Real*, this new spin-off seemed pretty cool. Contestants were in a South American jungle and needed to figure out a way to catch fish using nothing but a beach umbrella, a machete, and dental floss — all while arranging painted coconuts into a pattern that resembled the logo of Cokaid when seen from an aerial drone cam above. One key contestant had double-crossed his team-mates, and Vera was dying to find out if they'd chop him up for bait to catch the fish. She knew it wasn't real, but then again, what is? She had to admit that it was fascinating, suspenseful, and ultimately just fun to watch — even if she was pretty sure what was going to happen in the end.

The baby had spit up and was flapping its arms in the air and kicking its blanket off in an attempt to roll over on its side. Vera thought she'd pick it up in a minute and see if she could figure out how to burp it.

But first, she really needed to see what happened in the coconut challenge. She could tell that they were doing it wrong, but this Brazilian woman, Lola, was trying to get the team back on track by telling them all to concentrate only on the coconuts and ignore the topless hula dancers who were cheering them on from the sidelines.

Vera was really starting to enjoy this show.

She loved *Big Sister*.

Really.

ACKNOWLEDGEMENTS

This book is dedicated to my mother, Rachel Cressman, who encouraged me to take the plunge into fiction writing. Special thanks to my content editor Mary Rakow and copy editor (and amazing wife) Deniz Tuncer as well as cover designer Margaret Rainey. Julia Anker, Jodi Cressman, Doris Dent, Chris Finnie, Devin LaVelle, Levi Raskin, Lavinea Sharp, Lori Ward, and Shelley Whelpton provided extremely helpful comments on an early draft of the manuscript. Thanks also to Ayshe and Mary Tuncer for backing this book on Kickstarter.

Thanks, finally, to you, dear reader, for making it through this challenging book. The premise of Reality™ 2048 is that independent, critical thought requires effort and that women and men cannot live on spoon-fed entertainment alone. I appreciate your effort and look forward to your reactions in reader reviews on Goodreads, Amazon, and elsewhere.

ABOUT THE AUTHOR

Derek Cressman has written two non-fiction books, *The Recall's Broken Promise – How Big Money Still Runs California Politics* (2007), and *When Money Talks – The High Price of "Free" Speech and the Selling of Democracy* (2016), which received an honorable mention in the 2016 Foreword INDIES Book of the Year Awards for political science. He edits and writes for The People's Rule, an online journal that serves as a yardstick for measuring democracy in the United States.

Derek spent 25 years working for nonprofit, nonpartisan organizations to protect voting rights and reduce the role of big money in politics. In 2014, he ran for California Secretary of State.

When he's not writing or spending too much time in the Chattersphere, Derek farms olives in northern California, teaches middle school debate, and enjoys mountaineering, woodworking, and travel. He graduated with honors from Williams College in 1990 earning a degree in political science.

Read more at www.DerekCressman.com